Sardines
and
Applesauce

Sardines
and
Applesauce

JOHN REDDIE

iUniverse, Inc.
Bloomington

Sardines and Applesauce

iUniverse books may be ordered through booksellers or by contacting:

iUniverse
1663 Liberty Drive
Bloomington, IN 47403
www.iuniverse.com
1-800-Authors (1-800-288-4677)

ISBN: 978-1-4620-2410-0 (sc)
ISBN: 978-1-4620-2411-7 (ebk)

Printed in the United States of America

iUniverse rev. date: 06/06/2011

For my late wife Anne, the love and the light of my life.

CHAPTER ONE

N ew England is known for its changing weather. The four seasons are full of surprises because one can have an abnormally warm day in the winter as well as a really cool day in the summer. This is the case on this particular Sunday in March of 1964 in Fairdale, Massachusetts. It is the last weekend in March and the weather is more like summer than the tail end of winter. By eleven thirty in the morning, people are around town in shorts and tee shirts. It is a glorious day. Residents can hardly believe that only three weeks earlier, they had experienced a raging snowstorm that dumped a substantial covering of snow and ice on the area. Melting piles that remain can be seen everywhere on this warm, sunny Sunday.

Fairdale is located in central Massachusetts. It is a large town area wise and the Pine River flows along the western border and continues on down into Connecticut. Much of the land along the Pine River has become valuable in recent years and new homes have been constructed. Residents who own property in this area have been sought after by builders and land prices are increasing. The river is also noted for it's fishing, swimming and boating during the summer and fall months.

Willow Street in Fairdale runs up to the center where it then becomes Main Street. Main Street runs through Fairdale center and then to the next town which is Oldensburg. On Willow Street about a mile before Fairdale center, there is a large, white

Episcopal church and across the street is Willow Street Auto Service. The garage is set back from the road with a half circle driveway that runs up to the gasoline pumps, the three service bay doors and then back out to the road. In front of the driveway is a small grass covered lot where several used cars sit.

One car has written on it's windshield "'57 Mercury—New Brakes and Tires." Another reads "'1960 Chevrolet—stan. Shift6 cylinder—great gas mileage."

If one is standing and facing the front of the garage, to the left is a long, high wooden fence with a gate that is connected to the side of the building. Behind the fence is a huge auto salvage yard, also owned and operated by Willow Street Auto Service. Just before the gate is a side overhead door for an additional service bay. On the fence there is a sign that reads—" USED AUTO PARTS AND TIRES." If the gate is open, as it is during the week, discarded automobiles with various parts missing can be seen. A green wrecker truck is parked just to the left of the gate with the garage name painted on both doors as well as the words—24 HOUR TOWING.

The garage office is located on the right side of the building. Above the office on the roof stands a large wooden sign that reads—WILLOW STREET AUTO SERVICE—HARLAND J. WILKER OWNER. Beside the garage to the far right about two hundred feet away is a single level gray house which is where the Wilker's live. Harland Wilker started working at the garage when he was a teenager and bought the business in 1934 when the owner passed away. Harland is better known to everyone as Ike. He is sixty three and besides his family, his two greatest loves are working on automobiles and fishing. He still works in the garage everyday but he doesn't have the stamina he once had. Two fused vertebra in his back and a broken heel that never mended properly have taken their toll. Many weekends he leaves and goes fishing with his wife Edna. Ike has a small house trailer that he hooks up to his '57 Chevrolet station wagon. The trailer is equipped with a stove and ice chest and a small bathroom. It is just the right size for the two of them. Sometimes they will travel up along the Pine River where the fishing is plentiful or other times they will head up to New Hampshire or Maine. Ike's hair is very gray but has remained full. He is just six feet in height and probably ten to fifteen pounds over what he should be. He likes to smoke his pipe but only when he is relaxing and especially when he is fishing. He is not one to keep the pipe in his mouth constantly. His dentures would not be happy with this. When he is fishing, he fills his pipe bowl with Half and Half tobacco and enjoys life.

On Sundays, the garage is open until twelve-thirty. Church lets out just before noon and folks will stop by for gasoline and maybe a Sunday paper and cigarettes. No repair work is done on Sunday as a rule. It is eleven fifteen in the morning and three men are seated on chairs just outside the garage office enjoying the day. One man is in his late forties and very bald. He is about five feet ten and heavily built with a red face. What hair he has is cut close to his head. He is Benny Benson. His actual first name is Arnold but he is happy being called Benny. During the week, he runs the salvage yard for Ike. He is a master at removing parts from the cars in the yard because he gets the desired parts out without damaging anything else. He also knows the value of second hand auto parts and makes money for the business.

The second man is actually a seventeen year old. His name is Danny Call and he stops by the garage often because he is car crazy like many teens his age. He is tall and lanky and has his hair combed and cut just right. He is a junior at Fairdale High School and a pretty good student when he can take his mind off of cars and girls. He is talking constantly to the third man, Paul Wilker. Paul is Ike's nephew and he lives with Ike and Edna. He works at the garage doing lubrication and oil changes. He also does brake work and tunes up cars. He has been learning the auto repair business from Ike, Benny, and Larry Nicholson who is a mechanic and works at the garage during the week too. Paul is twenty four years old and has kind of a running joke with people. He was born on December 31st 1939 at five fifteen in the afternoon. Because he was alive for six hours and forty five minutes before1940, he likes to tell people that he grew up in the thirties. Paul loves cars from the thirties and forties. His pride and joy is his 1948 Plymouth convertible that he has had since he was sixteen. It is his only car.

Paul is five feet ten inches tall and weighs one hundred and seventy five pounds. He is an average looking man with a really nice personality. His hair is light brown and parted on his right side. He has it cut close on the sides and back and leaves the top longer and combed neatly. His face is clean shaven. He comes across sometimes as being rather meek but this is not the case. He will speak up if the situation arises. Paul's mother died ten ago when he was fourteen and his father is still living but confined to a sanitarium. On Sunday mornings, Paul opens the station at 7:30 and takes care of business until 12:30.

A tired looking Nash sedan pulled up to the curb and stopped. The driver got out and walked over to the '57 Mercury that is for sale and peered in the driver's side window. He walked slowly around the car inspecting it. He glanced to where the three men are seated and then turned and headed back to his car.

Benny stood up from his chair and stretched.

"I thought we had a live one there Paul . . . but I guess not" he said as the Nash drove away.

"I guess he'll think about it and if he likes it, then he will probably come back" Paul said.

"Well boys" Benny said, I'm off to the tavern for some pool and a few cold ones. See you in the AM" he said turning and heading for his pickup truck.

"Don't show up here loaded and hung over tomorrow" Paul said to him smiling.

Benny waved as he walked without turning around. Paul and Benny are always insulting each other and it is all in good fun.

Danny has been talking to Paul about his car which is a 1946 Plymouth business coupe. Mechanically, it is the same as Paul's '48 Plymouth.

"My brakes are screwed up" Danny said to Paul. "The master cylinder is leaking and I have to put brake fluid in it every day now."

"Leave it here. Don't drive it like that" Paul said looking at Danny with one eye squinted because of the bright sun.

"How much to replace the master Paul? My money is tight" he said.

"It shouldn't be too bad" Paul said. "This is important. Ike will let you give him so much a week and he probably has one of the cylinders in his parts room that he rebuilt. That will be a little cheaper and it will be as good as a new one too."

Back it the earlier days, there were no parts stores locally so Ike used to take parts from the cars in the salvage yard and rebuild them. He would take starters, generators, carburetors, brake cylinders, fuel pumps and after they were cleaned and rebuilt, he would keep them in his parts room. He would also recondition radiators. Now there is a NAPA store in Oldensburg and Coleman's Auto Parts right in Fairdale as well as a new Western Auto. Ike can call one of these stores and have parts delivered to him, usually within the hour.

A blue '59 Dodge sedan pulled up to the gas pumps and stopped. Inside are two nicely groomed young ladies. Paul got up from his chair and went to the driver's door window.

"Fill it please" the girl driving said smiling.

"Would you like the oil checked?" Paul asked.

"Oh no" the girl said. "It was just changed yesterday."

"I'll get the windshield" Danny said.

"Yeah and you'll get an eyeful too" Paul mumbled to himself.

Paul filled the tank and the Dodge drove off up the road out and of sight. Danny stood by watching it.

"Wow." Danny said. "They were two honeys huh Paul."

"You couldn't handle one of them" Paul said smiling and shaking his head.

"That's what you think" he said walking up close to Paul.

"Please" Paul said shaking his head again.

Both men returned to their seats. Paul glanced at the clock inside the office. He wants to close up and take his Plymouth out for a ride with the top down on this super day.

"I want to fix up my Plymouth like you have done Paul. It has that sweet, mellow sound and you don't have duals on it."

"I put a Pacemaker muffler on it. It's a glass pack. Yours will sound the same with one" Paul said.

"Well where can I get one?"

"NAPA has 'em. They're not too expensive either."

Both of them are looking at Paul's Plymouth. It looks nice parked beside the station with the top down and the whitewall tires nice and clean. The car has the original Sumac Red paint on it. The paint is dull and several spots have the primer showing through but with the tires and chrome trim rings around the hubcaps, it is looking pretty sharp. Paul is planning to get it painted when the summer arrives.

A green '61 Oldsmobile four door sedan pulled into the station past the pumps and stopped. It is Mr. and Mrs. Call, Danny's parents. The passenger door opened and Mrs. Call leaned out and looked back toward Danny and Paul.

"Dan, come right home. Aunt Arlene and Uncle Lloyd are coming for lunch and they want to see you. Hi Paul" she said waving.

"Shit" Danny said quietly so his mother couldn't hear him. "Just what I feel like doing, sitting around with them all afternoon."

"I gotta come with you guys. My brakes are bad" Danny said slowly walking towards his parent's car.

"Stop by tomorrow after school Danny. We should have you back in business by then" Paul said, giving Danny a pat on the back as he began to walk towards his parent's car. "And I'll try to have Ike put on one of his rebuilt cylinders on for you. Cheaper."

The Call's car drove away and Paul began thinking about how he had acquired his Plymouth eight years back. It was a Sunday morning and Paul was sixteen. Ike and Edna had gone off the night before and would return home by early evening. Paul opened the station for the morning and on the counter was a bill with car keys and a note clipped to them. It was from Benny and it said:*Paul, collect $30 from this guy when he shows up. I had to tow it in last night. Motor is shot. I had to speedy dry the road cause it leaked oil and antifreeze all over; a big mess. Thanks Benny.*

Paul looked at the bill and saw that it was Butch Henderson's '48 Plymouth convertible. Butch was two years older than Paul and had graduated from Fairdale High School the month before. Paul did not like Butch much because he was a bully. He and several of his buddies used to delight in picking on certain kids in school. Butch is a big kid too and uses his size to intimidate people. Paul remembered one time when he was a freshman he went into the boy's room and Butch and two other students came in when Paul was standing at the urinal. As soon as they were inside, one boy lit a cigarette and they passed it back and forth. Butch went by and pulled Paul backwards causing him to pee on the floor.

'Wipe it up!" Butch said to Paul.

'Wipe it up or I'll slap you all over the shithouse!" he yelled as the other two laughed.

He moved up close to Paul and was about to grab him when Mr. Abbott, one of the Geography teachers, entered. The boy who was holding the cigarette quickly threw it into one of the toilets.

"What is the yelling about!" he said looking back and forth at each boy.

"Oh we were just joking around" Butch said smugly.

"I smell cigarette smoke in here! Who's been smoking?"

"Wilker was when we walked in" Butch said.

"That's a lie" Paul said. "I don't smoke."

"Well get back to your classes, all of you" said Mr. Abbott." You're not to be in here goofing off and if I catch anyone smoking here or anywhere else on school property, they will be suspended!"

Paul put the bill on the counter and went out to the side of the garage where Butch's Plymouth sat in front of the salvage yard fence. He opened the driver's door and pulled the hood release. He lifted the hood and couldn't believe the mess. There was a gaping hole in the side of the engine block. Apparently, one of the connecting rods had let go from the crankshaft and punched through the side of the crankcase.

"GOD!" Paul thought. "Butch must have really ran the shit out of this thing; nice little car too."

A car pulled up to the pumps for gas. While Paul was putting in the fuel he looked up the street and saw Butch coming up to the station on his younger brother's bicycle. He looked terrible. His face was the color of dried concrete. He rode up to Paul and stopped the bike beside him. He was wearing a white tee shirt, blue dungarees and loafers with no socks. Rolled up in the left sleeve of his tee shirt was a package of Camels. Butch is six feet one inch tall and weighs around two hundred pounds. He has a round face and has his hair crew cut and spiked up slightly in the front. He also has a gap between his two upper front teeth and he has a beer belly starting too.

"Hey Butch" Paul said.

"Hey" he said softly.

"My old man sent me down to pay the bill on the car. He said it got towed here."

"It's over there. Boy the engine is really wrecked huh" Paul said.

"Yeah?" Butch asked. "I don't remember nothin about last night. My head is killin me. I'm still shitfaced" Butch croaked.

"So how much is the bill?" he asked.

Things were a little different now for Butch. He was no longer the school tough guy. He was in Paul's court now and he was kind of at his mercy. Paul looked down at the ground and then over toward the car before answering.

"The bill is thirty bucks" Paul said. "Benny had to speedy dry the road to soak up the oil and stuff".

"Thirty bucks! Shit!" Butch groaned turning his head from left to right. "I'm leaving to go in the Army Tuesday and I was gonna go out tonight and party and maybe get laid . . . . ya know, before I go for basic training. I only got fifty bucks and this is gonna leave me twenty. Then I owe my sister fifteen and I gotta give it to her today cause she's knocked up and her husband just got laid off from work. My old man found out I borrowed it and he's tearass. Then five's all I'll have. I think I'm gonna puke" Butch said looking even worse than when he arrived.

'What are you going to do with the car now that you're leaving?" Paul asked. "I might be interested in it if you want to get rid of it."

"You wanna buy it . . . . with the engine jocked?" Butch asked.

"Come here and look at this" Paul said walking off towards the Plymouth.

Paul lifted the hood and pointed to the side of the engine where it was broken out.

"It needs another motor. Holy shit" Butch said leaning in under the hood next to Paul. He smelled like alcohol and stale tobacco.

"I remember racing at the quarter mile last night and the engine blowing now. The cops were there and my car was fulla kids. Everybody was shitfaced."

The quarter mile that Butch referred to is a lonely stretch of road on the outskirts of Fairdale where teenagers took their cars to race each other. There had been several serious accidents there over the years and the local police were always chasing the kids out of there.

"Tell ya what" Paul said. "Forget the thirty bucks. You keep that and I'll throw in another twenty. That way you can pay your sister and still have money to party."

"What about the motor?" Butch asked.

"I can pick one up and I've been looking for a car to fix up anyway. This would be good."

"You got it Wilker" Butch said. "It's a deal. It's got a brand new top on it."

"Are you sure your kid brother wouldn't want it to fix it up now that I think of it?" Paul asked.

"Who, Jackie?" Butch said. "That asshole couldn't open the hood."

Paul laughed out loud and Butch even displayed a slight grin.

The two started walking toward the office when a '53 Chevrolet station wagon stopped just outside the first bay door and Mr. Henderson, Butch's father, got out. He looked just like Butch only heavier. His hair was cut the same way but his hair line was receding slightly.

"Did you pay your bill?" Mr. Henderson said glaring at Butch.

"Paul Wilker here wants to buy it" Butch said quietly.

"What?" Mr. Henderson said. "Paul, you want to buy this car after he ruined it? The cop last night told me that if he hadn't blown the engine he would have cracked it up and killed people. That's how fast and crazy he was driving and how loaded he was!"

"I've been looking for a car like this Mr. Henderson. My aunt in New York has a '41 Plymouth convertible that is similar to this car. I'm sure I can pick up an engine for it."

Mr. Henderson walked over to the Plymouth to look at the ruined engine. Butch's younger fourteen year old sister Vicky and a girlfriend who had slept over with her were in the station wagon back seat.

"What happened Butch?Wreck your car?" Vicky said rubbing it in sarcastically and smiling.

"Shut up!" Butch snapped.

"Hi Paul" Vicky said in a flirty tone.

"Hi" Paul said back to her.

"Nice going dummy" Butch's father said heading for the station wagon. "It's a good thing you're goin in the service. Finish up here and get back to the house."

Butch's father drove out onto the road and up towards Fairdale center. Paul and Butch went into the office to fill out the bill of sale for Paul's new car. Afterwards Butch got on the bicycle to go home.

"Hey Wilker, thanks huh" Butch said lighting up a cigarette.

Paul looked around and saw that two cars had pulled up for gas. As he was taking care of the customers, Benny pulled up as he did most Sunday mornings and got out of his pickup truck.

"Benny, I bought that convertible that you towed in" Paul said to him grinning.

"Why?" Benny asked looking a bit shocked.

"It will be a good car to fix up and I got it cheap.

After the cars at the pumps drove away, Paul and Benny went over and checked out his new car. The convertible top was down and Paul was concerned about raising it.

"That top is vacuum operated" Benny said. "You gotta have the engine running to raise it."

Paul was looking the body over and noticed that it was in decent shape. A few scratches and a small dent in the right rear fender was about all they could find. The paint was dull and the original primer was showing through in places. That was not important now though. Paul needed an engine.

"Benny, where can I get a decent engine for this?"

"I think you're screwed" Benny said shaking his head and looking down at the ground. "Yup, screwed. A good engine will not be easy to find."

Paul looked at Benny with a really disappointed look.

"Why is that?" Paul said.

Benny looked up slowly and a wide grin appeared on his face. His lips parted slightly exposing the gap where one of his front lower teeth was missing.

"What the hell are you smiling at?" Paul asked looking slightly confused.

"Man I love pullin' your leg. You bite every time" Benny said laughing. "I got a motor up back there that will lay right in there and it's a factory rebuilt."

"What motor is that?" Paul asked still wondering if Benny was still being a wise guy.

"Don't you remember that Plymouth woody beach wagon that we hauled in from the Pine River Resort last summer? Ya know, the one that got wrecked?"

Paul did remember the wagon that Benny was referring to. It was a '47 Plymouth station wagon. It had been used at the Pine River Resort to pickup supplies and transport guests to and from the train station and other duties as well. When the engine became worn, the Resort people decided to fix it rather than buy another car. The engine was replaced at Harrison Chrysler and Plymouth in Oldensburg. The past summer, one of the college students who was working there for the summer had not parked the car properly and it rolled backwards down the long hill driveway and into the road where it was broadsided by a passing dump truck and totaled. It was hit right at the passenger side rear door and practically bent in two. The front part of the car was intact and escaped damage.

"It's way up back by the storage sheds" Benny said pointing towards the salvage yard.

"If I were you, I'd put the engine and transmission in your car. The way that nut kid ran the shit out of the convertible, he probably wrecked the clutch too. I'm sure that they put in a new clutch disk and pressure plate when the motor was changed" Benny said lighting a cigarillo.

'You figure that motor is a good one?" Paul asked.

"Yes, I've had it runnin. That's a factory rebuilt right from Chrysler. It's like a new motor. I know it ain't got ten thousand miles on it. You lucked out" Benny said, grinning slightly at Paul. "Don't worry about the top being down. We'll get this inside later" Benny said pointing towards the garage.

A Buick sedan drove in and pulled up to the pumps bringing Paul back to reality. He glanced at the clock inside the office which reads twelve fifteen. Paul is thinking to himself that after this car he will start closing up for the day. As the Buick drives away after Paul filled it with fuel, he put the rack with cans of oil and transmission fluid inside. He took the gasoline pump readings and went inside and shut the power to them off. He went over to air pump and disconnected the hose and took it inside the office. He lowered the one overhead door that he had opened earlier and went into the office to total up the mornings sales. He took the cash and checks and locked them in the back office safe.

It is just after twelve thirty and Paul is done for the day as far as the garage is concerned. He can now take his Plymouth convertible out with the top down like he's been waiting all winter to do. The radio playing in the office has stated that the weather for the next two days is supposed to be cooler but nice, sunny and clear.

Paul slid in behind the steering of his Plymouth and closed the door. He switched on the ignition and pressed the starter button. The Plymouth started right up and rumbled through the glasspack muffler. Paul shifted into first gear and let up on the clutch pedal and began to move when a green '61 Pontiac Catalina convertible drove up to the front of the station. Steam is blowing out through the grille and underneath. Paul stopped his car and got out and approached the overheating Pontiac. The driver's door opened and a girl in her early twenties got out leaving the door open and moving away from the car. She is really pretty and stunning. She has naturally blond, dirty blond hair which she has pulled back into a pony tail. She is wearing a very short white tennis skirt which is exposing most of her extremely shapely legs. She has on a white short sleeved tee shirt with a sweater tied around her neck. She has on white sneakers and white socks.

"Now that's what I call a hot car" Paul said looking directly at her.

"I was on route 10 and it started steaming like this" she said walking up close to Paul. He noticed that her eyes are an emerald green color. He can not recall ever seeing anyone with eyes this color before. She is tanned and looks really attractive.

"You look like you are closed. Can you help me . . . . please?" she said looking a little desperate.

"I'm on my way home. I live in Saxon."

Saxon is a town about forty minutes away. Paul has been through there before several times but never paid much attention to it. Paul thought to himself "Gee, I sure would have remembered if I had seen her there before. She is a dream girl."

"Let it cool off for a few minutes and I'll take a look at it for you."

"Oh you're a doll. Thank you so much" she said, smiling at Paul.

Paul opened the office door and then locked and closed it behind him. He walked through the office and over to the side bay that faced the salvage yard entrance. He figures he will pull her car into this bay where it is not visible from the street. He does not want people pulling in. He wants to fix her car and get away from the station for the afternoon. He opened the overhead door and walked out to the front of the garage and up to the girl and the car.

"I like convertibles too" said Paul pointing to his Plymouth.

"Nice. It's an oldie and a goodie" she said walking over and looking inside his car.

Paul checked out her backside and concluded that she is pretty much flawless. Her legs are shaped perfectly.

The Pontiac has stopped steaming for the most part and Paul lifted the hood and looked into the engine compartment. He looked around for a moment and spotted that her fan belt has snapped and is lying down on the bottom radiator hose.

"Your fan belt broke. That's why it's heated up" Paul said.

"It was making a squealing noise too. Is that the belt down there?" she said leaning over the fender on the opposite side from Paul and pointing to the frayed belt..

"That's it. Where are your keys?" Paul asked. "I want to bring it inside out of the way."

"In the switch in the car" she said.

Paul lowered the hood and drove the Pontiac inside and turned off the engine immediately. "Hopefully we have a new belt for you" Paul said.

He went into the office and looked up the correct belt number belt for this engine.

"Is this your business?" the girl asked.

"It's my uncle's. I work here for him. It's a very good business" Paul said walking from the office with a belt in his hand.

He went over to one of the tool boxes and grabbed several wrenches. On his way over to the car, he picked up a fender cover. He raised the hood and draped the cover over the fender. The girl assumed her position on the opposite fender to observe what Paul was doing.

"I'm Norma Clay. What is your name?" she asked smiling at Paul again.

"Oh. Paul Wilker . . . . at your service" he replied smiling back at her.

Paul is uneasy around girls. He has dated a few times but never anything serious. He is an only child, no siblings. At this point in his life, he is beginning to feel that women are not really attracted to him. As he is attempting to install the new belt, he discovers another problem, a more serious problem.

"Oh Oh" he said. "Your alternator is seized, it won't turn. That was the squealing you heard probably."

"Do you have another one?" Norma asked looking serious.

"I don't have a new one but I may have a used alternator from the salvage yard. Let me make a quick phone call."

"You are really sweet" Norma said looking a little sympathetic.

"A used one will get you home and probably last quite a while."

Paul called the tavern where Benny said he is headed for. Benny came to the telephone but is sure that he does not have one.

"What the hell are you still doing there?" Benny asked.

"A car came in just as I was leaving boiling over and everything. The alternator is seized."

"Tell em they will have to leave it".

"I'll tell her" Paul said.

"Her" Benny said. "I get it now. I hope she's cute."

"Oh she is. She's beyond cute" Paul said chuckling slightly. "Thanks Benny."

Paul came out of the office and walked over to Norma who is sitting in her car. She watched as he came closer.

"I'm sorry but we don't have a used alternator either. If you want to leave the car overnight we can get you a new one and put it on in the morning."

"If that is the case, may I use your phone to call home and try to get somebody to pick me up?"

"Well . . . . I was gonna take my car for a ride this afternoon. It's so nice out and I haven't had the top down since October."

Norma looked at him rather strangely, wondering what he was getting at.

"I mean . . . . I could take a nice trip to Saxon as well as anywhere else. That is where you're going, Saxon right?"

"I am but isn't that way out of your way?"

"Not at all" Paul said. "It would be a really nice ride and besides I wasn't going anywhere in particular anyway. It's up to you."

"You're so kind. I'd love to go in your car with you."

Paul closed the garage up and walked over to his car. The passenger outside door handle did not work very well so Paul had to open the door from the inside. Norma had taken a gym bag and a tennis racket from the trunk of her car while Paul was getting the belt in the garage office. When she was seated in the Plymouth, she opened that bag and took out a pair of sunglasses. Paul glanced over at her as she put them on.

"Now you look like a movie star" he said.

Norma smiled at him exposing her perfect, straight white teeth.

Paul drove the Plymouth out onto Willow Street and turned right heading out of town. When he came to the Foster Street intersection, he turned left onto Foster and headed to route 10.

Norma and Paul walked out into the back yard of her house and down to the tennis court. There are chairs set up near the court and two women are seated there and two men are playing tennis vigorously. A small girl wearing a pretty blue dress is running around playing near the two women. One of the women seated is Rita, Norma's mother. The other is Meredith, Norma's older sister and mother of the little girl. Rita is forty nine and pretty. She has the look of a woman who has maybe partied and drank a little more than she should have over the years but is still attractive. She is wearing gray shorts and a peach colored blouse. Her hair is a silver blond shade and comes down to base of her neck. Meredith is five years older than Norma and not as pretty as her sister. Her hair is the same color as Norma's but the two look completely different. She has a kind and caring look about her and is constantly looking over at her young daughter. She is wearing white shorts and a sleeveless light blue top.

"Hey ladies. This is my new friend Paul. He rescued this damsel in distress" Norma said beaming at Paul. "My car is at his garage in Fairdale . . . . Broken."

"I'm very happy to meet both of you" Paul said extending his hand to both of them.

Rita took a puff on her cigarette and placed it in the ashtray. "Oh I think I like you" she said standing up and looking Paul straight in his eyes.

"So polite and delivering my daughter safe and sound. Thank you."

"We'll have her back on the road tomorrow. Good as new" Paul said grinning at each of them shyly.

"Dad, Brent, come here and meet Paul" Norma shouted to the two men playing tennis.

The men leaned their rackets against the net and walked over to where Norma and the people are. Their faces are wet with perspiration. Edwin Clay is Norma's father. He is tall and slim with wavy brown hair and some gray showing. He is a nice looking man with a square jaw and deep blue eyes. He is fifty one but can pass for a younger man. The other man is Brent Royce, Meredith's husband. He too is a handsome man with slim build and dark hair but his hair is thinner on the top than Edwin's. Brent is twenty nine and would look right at home in an ad for men's clothing. The two men are dressed in tennis shorts and tee shirts, both white as are their sneakers.

"Paul, this is my dad and my brother in law, Brent" Norma said. "My car conked out over in Fairdale and Paul here ran me all the way home. He has a car repair place and he is going to fix it tomorrow. He is really kind and nice."

"Glad to meet you Paul" Edwin said reaching out to shake hands.

"Nice to meet you sir" Paul answered.

Paul reached out to Brent with his right hand. Brent put out his hand and gave Paul a very quick limp handshake. He looked away towards Norma as they were shaking hands.

"What happened to your car, what is broken?" he asked Norma.

"Something in the motor seized and the belt broke off or something. Paul, what is it?" Norma asked looking confused.

"Her alternator seized up and caused the belt to break off. I was hoping that we had a used one that could get her home but we didn't have one.

"Alternator seized up? That doesn't make any sense" Brent said looking at Edwin.

"You are very kind to help Norma out like this Paul" Meredith said to him. "When cars break down on a Sunday, it can be difficult to get someone to help you let alone drive you all of the way home."

"Well, it's like I told your father, I was going to go for a cruise this afternoon anyway so it worked out fine for everyone."

"Still, it is most kind of you."

Norma returned and pulled another chair over closer to Paul and Meredith. She has changed into a pair of blue jeans. She still has on her white tee shirt but has replaced her tennis shoes with a pair of black flats. She is not wearing socks. She has taken her hair out of the pony tail and it now is parted in the middle and comes down to her shoulders. She looks even more ravishing than before.

"Paul, how would you like to have supper here? We're having fried chicken. C'mon and stay" Norma said.

"Well sure . . . . if it's no trouble" Paul said smiling.

Norma and Meredith both said "Good" at the same time.

The fried chicken that was served was delicious. Brent, Meredith and little Alice left shortly after the meal. Paul talked to Edwin, Rita and Norma in their living room until seven thirty. He figures he should be getting home because Ike and Edna will more than likely be home by the time he arrives so he thankedNorma's parents for the great supper. Paul is stuffed.

Norma walked out to Paul's car with him. They stood and talked for several minutes before he got in.

"Boy it sure has cooled down since earlier hasn't it." Paul said. "I am putting up the top before I go for sure."

"I was thinking Paul, why don't you bring my car here tomorrow night and I'll drive you home. I'd really enjoy seeing you again . . . . that is of course if you'd like to see me."

"Ah yeah . . . . sure. I would definitely like to do that" Paul said.

He started to get that funny feeling in his stomach that people get when they are attracted to another person of the opposite sex.

"I stop work at five and I can be here a little before six if that's good."

"That sounds really good. I'll have something for you to eat when you get here" Norma said picking a dead leaf off of Paul's car." "Thank you so much for all you did for me today."

Paul looked at her as the twilight is approaching and thinking how nice she looks with her hair down and her well fitting jeans and tee shirt.

"Well, I'll see you tomorrow" Paul said starting his car. "Oh Norma, let me have your telephone number in case we have a problem with your car . . . . I mean we shouldn't but just in case."

Paul leaned across the seat and took a pen out of his glove box. He moved the contents around but could not find a piece of blank paper.

"No paper" he said.

"Give me your hand" Norma said smiling at him again and looking rather sexy.

Paul extended his hand out and she wrote her number on his palm. She backed away from the car and waved to Paul as he backed his car around in front of her garage. When he got to the bottom of her driveway, he stopped and raised his convertible top and rolled up both door windows. It has gotten cooler since the sun is setting but after all, it is still March. Who knows, he thought, we could still have snow before spring.

Chapter Two

Route 10 is not that crowded because it is Sunday and early evening. Paul entered the on ramp and moved onto the highway. He pushed the Plymouth up to sixty five. It sailed along smoothly and the engine sounded sweet from the straight though muffler. After about a mile he dropped it back to fifty where both he and his Plymouth seem happy.

Paul turned his radio on and the Sunday night hits station is playing "Another Saturday Night" by Sam Cooke. Paul's mind is on all of the things that have happened in just one short afternoon. He has met Norma and ended up eating fired chicken, delicious fried chicken, with her. "She seems genuinely interested in me" Paul said to himself. "This girl is absolutely gorgeous in every way and she seems interested in *me*."

Paul was never popular with girls in school and he had only been out several times on dates since school. Nothing ever really connected. Paul has always tried to treat a girl with respect and kindness but it always seems to him at least, that girls seem more attracted to guys that are boisterous and slightly wild.

He began thinking back to his High School senior prom that he was unable to attend. He had asked Sally Keene and she accepted. Sally and Paul had gone all through school together and had always been friendly toward one another, not as girlfriend and boyfriend but friends. Sally had red hair and hundreds of freckles.

He took a long wooden cotton tipped swap and took a culture of Paul's throat. He also took Paul's temperature and left the examining room for several minutes. When he returned, he told Paul to come over to his desk and have a seat. The doctor began to write a prescription on his pad.

'I'm sorry to tell you this Paul but you're not going to feel like dancing tonight or tomorrow night either for that matter. You have an old fashioned strep throat. It's very contagious and you wouldn't want this girl to catch this would you?"

"Oh boy. No. no of course not" Paul said. "I just feel bad for her."

"Who's the girl you were taking?"

"Sally Keene. I went all through school with her. She's very nice."

"Sally, oh she will understand. She is a fine young lady" Dr. Bristol said smiling. "Things like this happen you know" Dr. Bristol said with a kind, sympathetic smile.

"Do you know Sally?"

"I brought her into this world and I am still her doctor . . . . her mother and father's too" said the doctor.

"Alright now, you get the prescription filled that I am giving you and take it as directed. I want you to go to bed and rest, then come back and see me in four days. Call me if you get worse, higher fever, stuff like that" Dr. Bristol said standing up from his desk.

Paul left the office and drove back to his house. He would have to call Sally and break the news to her but he was not looking forward to it. As he was pulling into his house he saw Bobby Myres pumping gas at the station. Bobby came in during the morning to take care of the gas customers. He was a nice young man and two years older than Paul. Bobby was an orphan and lived with Mrs. Taylor at her foster home on the opposite side of Fairdale.

Paul got out of his car and walked over to the front of the station by the pumps where Bobby was.

"Bobby. I've got a huge favor to ask you. Please help me out here."

Paul explained the situation and told Bobby that he had a rented tuxedo and that it should fit him seeing how they were both close to the same size. Paul had ordered a corsage to match Sally's dress and Bobby could pick it up at the florist in the afternoon. Bobby accepted the offer and agreed to escort Sally to the dance. Dr. Bristol was right. Sally was more than understanding and was sincerely concerned for Paul's well being. Actually, things worked out very well because Sally and Bobby ended up getting married several years later. Now when she comes to the station for gas and Paul waits on her, she often speaks of how things turned out back then. Paul thought, "If Sally was a card in a deck, she surely would be an ace."

A huge tractor trailer truck pulled up and passed Paul bringing him back to present times again. The drone of the trucks tires changed back and forth as they passed over the unevenness of the highway. It has cooled down considerably now that the sun has left and Paul turned on the heater. Paul keeps thinking how Norma seems to really warm up to him. He keeps remembering her beautiful smile and her friendly manner. He has not ever had a lot of success attracting girls. There were several in high school that he liked and would not had minded dating but he was always afraid to ask.

"Hey, I got laid . . . . once" he said aloud to himself ; "and with one of the hottest girls in school too, Charlene Howard" he said aloud again.

35

Paul started drifting back again in his mind to that night eight years ago when it happened. It was a Saturday night about nine thirty and the garage was closed. As usual Ike and Edna had gone up country for the remainder of the weekend and Paul had just received his driver's license. Paul was in the garage working on his Plymouth convertible. The broken engine had been removed and the salvage yard engine and transmission installed in its place. The car was running like a top but he had a few more repairs to complete before he registered it.

On this particular night in the early part of May, a car pulled up in front of the garage bay doors with just the front parking lights lit. It was a '52 Ford two door sedan. Paul had all of the outside lights off but inside the bay was lit up. Paul looked out to see what was going on and saw Charlene Howard walking up to the outside door and peering into the bay. When she reached the door and spotted Paul inside, she tapped on the window. Paul walked over and unlocked the small door that was within the overhead door and opened it.

"That asshole Rick smashed out my headlights" she said slurring slightly. She was referring to her boyfriend, Rick Bailer. Rick was one of Butch Henderson's bully buddies in school and not a favorite of Paul's either. Paul noticed right off that Charlene was a little drunk. She was wearing red and gray plaid shorts and a gray short sleeved top. She had shoulder length chestnut brown hair parted in the middle. She was about five feet three inches tall and weighed just under one hundred and twenty five pounds. Her complexion was dark and her eyes were a deep brown color. She was quite pretty and had a robust look about her with perfect olive toned skin. Charlene was big boned, strong, and definitely had her girl shape. She was barefoot.

"Why would he do that" Paul said moving aside as she walked into the bay.

"Because him and his buddies were going out of town to screw around with broads and he didn't want me following him. He can go to hell! I have had it with him! Paul, can you get me a couple lights. I can't see to drive" she asked in a pleading tone.

Paul was looking at her remembering the previous summer when she was a lifeguard at the Pine River Resort and how fantastic she looked in her tight, red one piece bathing suit. She looked like she was about to burst out of it. He remembered how his friend Phil Gray would whisper to him when they were swimming "Here comes Charlene, get the Vaseline."

Paul thought to himself that Rick must be nuts to want to screw around on her. They had been going steady for a long time. Rick was six feet two and weighed about two hundred and ten pounds. He was a nice looking kid and could probably have his pick of most of the girls in school.

"Sure, I can fix you up with some headlight bulbs."

"I don't have a cent. I spent it for booze because Rick said we were going to party tonight. You want a beer, Paul?" Charlene asked as she walked back out to her car.

"No, no thanks, not right now" he said.

He walked out with her as she opened the trunk of the Ford. She had a cooler with beer inside and a paper bag beside it containing three half pint bottles of blackberry brandy.

"If you want, I'll pull your car into the side bay out of sight. I don't want any cars pulling in for service now, ok?" Paul asked.

Charlene reached in the car and pulled out a can opener and punched two holes in the top of her beer can. Paul slid in the front seat and started the car.

"Go inside and hit that up button beside the overhead door will ya?" he said to her.

"Are you sure you want to do this Charlene, I mean . . . . Rick?"

Charlene interrupted Paul." I told you I'm done with his shit. He can go screwing every night if he wants to."

Without any hesitation, Charlene peeled all of her clothes off.

"Now, are you gonna get a rubber or what?" she said as she faced him and pushed her hair back with both hands. "I'm waiting" she said and strutted over to the sofa. Standing there naked she looked like she belonged in a girlie magazine.

Paul's heart was going like a jackhammer. He was nervous that Rick would find out but when he returned to the office, Charlene took complete control of the situation. She obviously was not a novice when it came to screwing as she called it. She knew exactly what to do to get things moving. Among other treats, she introduced Paul to French kissing. Afterwards, she fished out her cigarettes from her shorts pocket and lit one up.

"Paul, go get the can opener from my car will ya?"

Paul pulled on his pants and tee shirt and went out to the Ford. He went back to the office and Charlene was still naked and sitting on the couch. Paul handed her the opener and suddenly realized that a car had pulled up to the front bay door.

"Shit" he said. "Some body's here. Get dressed ok?"

Paul peeked out and saw that it was Jeff Dooley, one of the local policemen. Jeff was out of the patrol car and looking inside the garage. Paul went over and opened the small garage door where Jeff was.

"Hey Paul" Jeff said. "I saw some extra lights on so I wanted to be sure that everything was good."

Paul's face was still perspiring.

"You must be working too hard. You're sweating bullets."

"Oh, just working on my car, ya know" Paul said.

Jeff asked if Ike and Edna had gone fishing and was talking a little about Ike's fishing trips. Jeff was a really nice and decent man. Paul was a little anxious to have him leave because he didn't want him to see Charlene there. He figured that the less people knew, the better. Jeff started talking about the time Ike gave him some really good fresh trout. Before he could get too far, he got a call on the police radio. He went the police car and answered the call.

"Gotta go Paul. Accident" Jeff said hurriedly getting into the car. He pulled out onto Willow Street with his blue lights flashing and sped away from town.

Paul went back into the station and returned to the back office. Charlene was dressed and apparently had gone to her car and popped open one of the blackberry brandy half pint bottles. Paul noticed that it was a little more than half empty and Charlene was unsteady on her feet. She walked unsteadily up to Paul and put her hand on his arm.

"Thanks for fixing the lights" she said looking in his eyes with an incoherent gaze. "I gotta go home now. My sister and her boyfriend are there and they're doin what we were doin. I gotta go."

Paul knew that he could not let her drive in the condition that she was in. This would be a recipe for disaster. He got her to give him the car keys and get into the passenger seat. Paul took his J.C. Higgins bicycle and put it in the Ford's trunk. Charlene only lived about couple of miles away so Paul could peddle back home with no problem. After he backed the car out of the bay and closed and locked the overhead door, he got in the car and drove out onto Willow Street.

"What are your parents going to say when we get to your house?" Paul asked her.

"They went away for the weekend. Just my sister and her boyfriend are home" Charlene said resting her head against the passenger door window and her right hand on her forehead.

Paul noticed that she had almost finished the half pint of blackberry brandy and with the beer she had consumed earlier, she was very drunk now. When Paul pulled into the Howard's driveway and stopped the car, Charlene had passed out. Paul got out of the car and went to front door of Charlene's home. He rang the doorbell and heard a dog beginning to bark. The barking got louder as the dog got closer to the door.

After about a minute passed, the door opened and Charlene's older sister Linda appeared with her boyfriend standing behind her. She recognized Paul from the garage because she had stopped occasionally for gas.

"Hi Paul" she said.

Paul explained to them that Charlene had had problems with her lights and had been drinking. He told them that she was in no shape to be driving and that he couldn't get her out of the car. Linda's boyfriend went over and carried Charlene into the house where she promptly got sick.

"Thanks Paul for bringing her home. I wouldn't want her head in the morning" Linda said grinning a little. "Want a ride home?"

"No thanks. I've got my bike" Paul said pulling his bicycle out the Ford's trunk.

As he rode along in the dark on his bicycle, he thought about how nice Charlene felt. He skin really smooth and her body firm and toned. He thought about her most of the next day too.

Right after that night, Charlene and Rick broke up. Nothing more happened between she and Paul and he figured that she was probably so buzzed that she didn't remember the sex that they had. It was just as well because he did not want Rick to find out about it. He didn't want to have to deal with him. Paul thought to himself that he had done Rick's girlfriend and he used one of his rubbers to boot.

The night of their senior prom, both Charlene and Rick attended with different dates. Paul had heard that Charlene had her hair up and looked sensational in her strapless prom dress. As the evening progressed though, Rick and Charlene began dancing together and shortly afterwards they disappeared and were not seen until the following afternoon. One month after school graduation, they were married. Just about nine months later, Charlene gave birth to a daughter and thirteen months after that, she had twin sons.

Rick traded his '55 Ford Sunliner convertible in for a Ford station wagon. He went to work for his father who owned and operated Bailer Building Company. Charlene stopped by the garage once in a while for gas with her kids. She looked a little worn and slightly heavier but three children in diapers can do that to a mother. She could still get dolled up and look quite nice Paul thought. He is sure by now that that night back in the rear office was not something that she remembered; at least she never mentioned it. Paul is glad for that.

It is just eight thirty in the evening as Paul pulled up beside the garage and parked the Plymouth for the night. It has cooled down considerably since earlier in the day. He is still keyed up from everything that has happened today. His mind keeps thinking about Norma and how friendly she has been to him. He thought about how she has invited him to have supper with her when he returns her car the following night. He figures that she is being grateful for him helping her. She must have some steady guy . . . she's got to. After all, a girl with her looks and shape must be waving guys away everyday.

Ike and Edna are in the kitchen. They had returned from fishing an hour earlier. Paul explained to Ike about the problem with Norma's car and how he will deliver it to her home in Saxon tomorrow after work.

"Wow, that's what I call service, good service. Is this girl special?" Ike said winking at Edna.

"Yeah, she's pretty nice" Paul answered. "Actually, quite nice."

Edna fixed Paul a ham and cheese sandwich on dark rye bread with some potato chips. Paul got up and got a bottle of beer out of the refrigerator and talked to Ike and Edna for a short while. After they went off to bed, Paul sat and looked at television until eleven o'clock. When he got into bed, he was still not tired and lay there thinking about the day, especially Norma. If things work out that she does want to see him more often, that will be just fine with him. It will be a change because the few previous girls that he has dated have not gone that well. It seems that after the second or third date, they lose interest. It was one o'clock before he finally fell asleep.

CHAPTER THREE

Monday morning is bright and sunny but a bit cooler than the day before. Ike has gone over to the garage and opened up while Paul is finishing his breakfast. Edna made them dropped eggs with wheat toast and bacon. Paul had a glass of tomato juice and some coffee.

He walked over to the garage and entered the office where Ike, Larry Nicholson, and Benny are. The men are discussing what they have done during the weekend. Several cars pulled up for fuel and Paul took care of them. One of the cars drove over beside the garage and parked. Two retired men got out and went into the office. One man is Stan Adams and the other is Fred Cooley. They usually stop in first thing in the morning and visit Ike and the boys for a short while.

"Hey Ike. What was that old coupe that you made into a service car? Remember, it had a plank for a front bumper and you did road calls with it? What the hell kind was it?" Fred asked.

"A '33 Huppmobile" Ike said laughing a little. "That old bastard could push anything."

On the wall of the office there is a large bulletin board with faded business cards and newspaper clippings that have turned brown from age. One reads how the income tax was only to be a temporary tax and then just for people who earned ten thousand dollars or more a year. Another small, wrinkled clipping features a poem:

MY PENNY

PENNY WAS A SETTER DOG THAT I HAD LONG AGO

I HAD HER FOR EIGHTEEN YEARS BEFORE SHE HAD TO GO

AND IF I FOUND A MAGIC LAMP THAT WOULD GIVE ME A WISH IF ANY

I'D WISH FOR A BEAUTIFUL SUNNY DAY AND SPEND IT WITH MY PENNY

POET UNKNOWN

Larry Nicholson has gone into the shop and opened his tool box. He is a tall man, thirty nine years old with dark brown wavy hair. He is broad shouldered with a protruding stomach. His face is clean shaven and his eyes are hazel. Larry is married and has a son and a daughter, both in their teens. He has a kind face and has a warm, friendly smile. He was a great help to Paul when he first got his '48 Plymouth and several times stayed after hours to help Paul install the engine and transmission. Paul thinks a lot of Larry and is always joking with him and vice-versa.

"What's wrong with the Pontiac convertible?" Larry said poking his head back into the office.

"Paul's working on that. It belongs to his new honey" Ike said pointing at Paul and laughing.

"Well now. How about this" Larry said laughing as well.

Paul and Larry exchanged a few insults to one another before Paul began removing Norma's damaged alternator. At the same time, Ike called the NAPA store to have a new one dropped off at the garage.

Norma got up at eight o'clock and went downstairs to the kitchen. Wanda, their maid, fixed scrambled eggs, toast with tomato juice and coffee. Norma greeted her and took a plate for herself.

"Come out on the porch. It's beautiful, a little chilly, but beautiful" Rita called to Norma.

The porch is long and wide and perched on a stone foundation. It overlooks the spacious back yard where the heated swimming pool and tennis courts are located. Beyond the backyard is a pine grove covered with a bed of brown pine needles which is a nice, peaceful spot to walk through. It is the kind of backyard that any one would love to have. The house and property originally belonged to Rita's parents which she inherited when her father passed away in 1950. Some outdoor furniture has been brought out due to the unseasonably nice weather. Both women are wearing slacks and sweaters. Rita is sipping her coffee and smoking.

"Paul seems like a very nice guy, and so polite" Rita said.

"He sure is. He was actually closed and leaving when I drove in there with my car steaming. He's going to eat supper here tonight when he brings my car back."

"Good" Rita said. "That's good."

"When is your photo shoot for the clothing company catalog?" Rita asked pushing her cigarette out in the ash tray.

"Tomorrow morning. I'll need my car then."

"Where is Paul's garage again?" Rita asked. "Fairdale?"

"Fairdale, yes" Norma said as she finished her coffee.

"Nice boy" Rita said again and staring out into the back yard.

Paul backed Norma's Pontiac out of the bay and pulled it up past the bay doors. It is just after five o'clock and he is ready to leave on his trip to Saxon. Business had slowed down in the middle of the afternoon and things had gone fine for him as far as fixing her car. Paul went into the rear office where Ike and Larry are. He asked Ike to let Edna know that he will not be eating supper at home and Ike informed him that he is sure that she has already figured that out. The two started teasing Paul about being a real ladies man and started calling him Romeo. He waved his hand at the two of them and left.

He drove along Willow Street and noticed a rattling sound coming from the dashboard area. He opened the ashtray and saw two cuff links and a matching tie clip inside that are making the noise. They appear to be sterling silver with small chess knights on them. This particular part of Willow Street is a bit rough with potholes and poor pavement from the past winter snowplowing. Paul closed the ashtray and started to think again that Norma must be involved with a guy.

Paul approached the entrance ramp for route 10 and pulled the car down onto the highway. He stepped on the accelerator and moved into the travel lane. Traffic is fairly light so he does not have any cars in front of him. He glanced down at the speedometer and the car is going eighty five.

"Holy shit!" Paul said aloud.

He immediately backed off and got down to fifty five. A ticket, wouldn't that be nice he thought. "This old 389 motor in here really gets up and goes" he said aloud again.

He turned into Norma's driveway and drove up back to the spot where he had parked his car yesterday. He turned off the engine and removed the key from the ignition switch.

"You fixed it, you're a doll" Paul heard.

He turned towards the house and saw Norma standing on the back steps. She is wearing a tight fitting gray wool long sleeved dress and black high heeled shoes. The hem of her dress ends just above her knees. Her hair is pulled into a twist at the back of her head. She looks stunning.

"Aw man, here I am in work clothes and you look like fashion plate" Paul said staring into her green eyes.

"You look fine. C'mon inside. Supper is almost ready. We are having Wanda's homemade meatloaf" Norma said reaching out for Paul's hand.

Edwin has not arrived home yet but Rita is in the living room when Paul and Norma enter. Rita is drinking a cocktail and smoking a cigarette.

"Paul, how nice to see you again" she said. "Would you like something to drink?"

"I'm fine" Paul said as he sat down on the sofa.

"Mom, he has my car and it's fixed. I'm so happy."

"My husband will be here shortly but if he isn't, we'll start eating without him" Rita said glancing at the mantle clock.

Norma sat down right next to Paul on the sofa and smiled at him. Paul felt that funny felling in the pit of his stomach again and his face is flushed slightly. He still feels a bit uneasy because he just can't figure out why Norma is not involved with someone.

"She certainly can have almost any guy she wants" Paul thought to himself. "But maybe she is involved and just showing me gratitude. After all, I've only known her for a day. Yes, that's probably it. She's showing gratitude" he kept thinking.

"Are you sure you don't want something to drink, a bottle of beer maybe?" Rita asked as she fixed herself another cocktail.

"All set thanks" Paul said. "I'm ok."

Edwin appeared suddenly in the room and seated himself in a large easy chair. He is wearing a white dress shirt and brown tweed slacks. His coat and necktie have been removed.

"Nice to see you again Paul. How did you make out with the car?"

"The car is all better. We put on a new alternator and replaced the belts" Paul said looking directly at Edwin.

Rita looked at Paul and smiled. Paul can see that Norma has inherited her looks from Rita only more so. Rita also seems a little buzzed from her cocktails.

After the delicious supper and apple pie dessert, Norma asked Paul if he was ready to have her drive him back to Fairdale. Paul thanked them for the food and they in turn thanked him for fixing the car. Paul and Norma talked fluently on the trip back to Fairdale. She told him about her clothes modeling and how she is getting more photo shoots than ever now. She models dresses, coats, swimwear, and sleepwear for large department store catalogs. Almost all of the catalogs are printed by Edwin's publishing company which is now really flourishing. She told Paul that Edwin has purchased a building in Allendale and plans on outfitting this building with two more printing presses. Things are really looking great.

Norma turned into the station and drove up to the office door stopping just beyond it. The station is closed and it is just eight thirty. The night is clear and crisp with a practically full moon. She put the shift lever in park and turned off the ignition switch. They talked for a few minutes about the full moon and the clear evening.

"Paul, I'd like to see you again soon, that is, if you would like to see me. You're a nice guy and really easy to talk to. I like that."

The moonlight is shining into the car and Paul can see her face. Her eyes seem to be glistening. She has turned slightly to her right so she can face Paul and the back of her head is resting against the driver's door window.

"Hey, that sounds great. I'd like to see you again too but I can't believe that you don't have a steady boyfriend" Paul said.

"You can believe it. Let's see, this is Monday . . . . how about Thursday after work?" Norma asked him quietly.

"I'll come by your house on Thursday then" Paul said.

"It's a date."

Paul opened the door and started to get out of the car and to his surprise, Norma got out and walked around to the passenger side of the car where Paul is. She walked up to him and placed her hand on his elbow. She leaned forward and gave Paul a quick kiss on his lips.

"Until Thursday then" she said with a wide smile. "Thank you again for everything. You're the best."

As she drove out of the station onto Willow Street, Paul does not feel like going in the house yet. He is too pumped up so he decided to take his car out for a ride. He needs to think about what has happened to him in the past several days. He drove into Oldensburg and out into the country where it is desolate. He is a little stunned with the fact that Norma wants to see him again. He has never really had a girl truly interested in him before and now this dream girl wants to see him again. He can't quite fathom it yet.

Paul's thoughts about Norma are well founded. He has no idea what is going on with her in reality. An attractive young woman with an outgoing personality she is but a young woman that is seeking a true loving relationship with Paul she is not. Her reason for wanting to see him is purely selfish on her behalf. She has been trying to devise a plan to benefit her needs for a while and she now feels that Paul is just what she needs. He is perfect. He is naive and not a ladies man. Her plan actually will involve marrying Paul to get what she is after. A seized alternator and a broken fan belt have played out quite well for her. He seems gullible and she senses his strong interest in her.

If the truth be known, Norma has two interests, that is all, only two. One is her brother in law Brent. She is madly in love with him and has been since she was sixteen. It was just after her sixteenth birthday that she and Brent first had sexual intercourse together. Brent and Meredith had been married for eight months at the time. Brent and Norma have had sex together ever since whenever they can. Norma is obsessed with having sex with him. Brent is six years older than Norma and so is Meredith.

Her other interest is her parents business. Rita, who actually owns everything legally, has told Norma that when she marries and settles down she will sign the publishing business over to her and Meredith. Rita has more than enough riches now, not to mention the very valuable property she owns up along the Pine River that her father left to her along with the publishing business which he started.

In 1916, Rita's father bought one hundred and twenty acres of land along the river. Back in those days, the only road that ran along there was dirt with holes and ruts and was barely traveled. Because of this, he was able to purchase the land for practically nothing. Today however, the road is much better and homes are being constructed there all of the time. Rita's land is all prime building acreage and she is constantly receiving offers on it, generous offers.

Norma's plan is to get married and once she gets control of the business; she will create a situation where divorce will be the solution. Brent also will divorce Meredith and then they can be together and have a very successful business too. They can live the good life. They have been very careful not to get caught because that will really destroy their plans. Very often times when they can get away together, they go to the Pine River house which is nicely secluded with no neighbors near by. They always use Norma's car because that way if someone does show up, Brent can hide out in the basement but that has not yet happened.

After Rita's father bought the Pine River property, he built a small cottage which over the years has been added onto and is now a nice house with an upstairs and a two car garage underneath. Upstairs, there is a full dormer on the two rear bedrooms with windows that look out to the river. The view is spectacular, especially in the fall when the leaves on the trees display their rich colors. The house sets on a small hill with the driveway branching off to the left accessing three parking places. If one stays to the right, the driveway leads around to the side of the house and down into the double garage under the house. Behind the house in the back yard, there is a wooden dock that goes out into the river. On many a hot summer afternoon, family members have jumped into the river from the dock to swim and cool off. Once when it was dark and late, Norma and Brent went skinny dipping taking a big chance that no one would catch them.

The reason that Rita has control of everything is because she discovered awhile back that Edwin was unfaithful. Edwin had and still has a penchant for young girls, not teenagers but girls in their twenties. He can afford to take girls out and show them a good time and he is still a nice looking man for his age. He has always been oversexed. When he and Rita married, their marriage was ideal but Rita did not realize that he was having relations with other women besides her.

She discovered it by accident at the Pine River house one Friday evening some years back. Edwin told her that he was going to

New York to attend a publishers meeting and that the meeting would be late into the night, perhaps until nine o'clock. He said it would be easier for him to stay at the Pine River house that night rather than come all the way back to Saxon. He did have a meeting but it would be over by six o'clock at the latest.

Rita decided to surprise her husband that night. She arranged to have Wanda stay overnight with the girls and she would drive up to the Pine River house and have a nice romantic evening with him. Upon arriving, she put her car in the garage so he would not know she had come up, and closed the door. She went into the house and took a nice bubble bath, slipped into a sheer, white flowing nightgown with high heeled slippers. She was all powdered and perfumed for her husband and she had picked up a bottle of champagne on the way up.

As she was putting the finishing touches on her hair and makeup in the downstairs bathroom, she heard voices outside of the house. One was a girl giggling and then Edwin's voice as they got closer. Rita quickly ducked down a few of the basement stairs and waited. She heard the front door open and Edwin and a girl entered the living room.

"I must use the bathroom my sweet" he said and headed for the bathroom.

"Do you want me to strip now?" the girl said still giggling slightly.

"You bet" Edwin said.

A minute later Edwin came out of the bathroom with just his under shorts on and embraced his naked partner.

"Are you sure your wife doesn't know you're up here?" the girl asked as he was trying to kiss her mouth.

"I told you. Don't worry about a thing. C'mon . . . . upstairs."

Rita was absolutely crushed. She was on the verge of tears but suddenly anger took over. She came into the living room and scooped up all of the girl's clothes and heaved them down the basement stairs. She removed her slippers and quietly went up the stairs to where Edwin and his girlfriend had gone. She went to the guest room door which was partially open and entered. The two were on the bed performing sex and were unaware of Rita's presence.

"Surprise Eddie!" Rita said loudly.

They both bolted upright on the bed. Edwin's face flushed.

"Rita . . . . I didn't . . . . Jesus" Edwin stammered.

Rita glared at the girl.

"Get out of my house whore!" she bellowed like a maniac. "Get the hell out of my house.!"

Rita lunged at the girl who quickly leaped up and headed toward the door.

"Rita, please" Edwin said putting his hand on her shoulder.

Rita twisted away from his hand.

"Don't touch me you asshole!" she shouted "Keep away from me!"

Rita went downstairs where the girl was standing in the living room.

"Where are my clothes?" she said to Rita in a loud voice.

"Whore, get out of my house . . . . now!"

Rita walked to the front door and yanked it open. She went to grab the girl who was now sobbing. At this point, Rita had the temperament of a wolverine. The girl went around Rita's grasp and out onto the front step of the house.

"I . . . I can't go out like this. I can't go . . ."

"Just go down to the road and stick out your thumb honey, believe me the first guy that comes by will pick you up. And you won't even have to take the time to take your clothes off" Rita hollered slamming the door.

Rita noticed that the girl's shoes were still on the living room floor. She bent over and grabbed them and went to the front door. The girl was still standing at the base of the steps. Rita threw the shoes at her with one of them bouncing her hip. The girl began sobbing harder now.

"Here's something for you to wear, whore" Rita shouted.

She slammed the door and noticed that Edwin had put on his bathrobe.

"You can't send her away like that" Edwin said barely audible and sheepishly.

"Well why don't you go and give her a ride, and then why don't you go to hell" Rita shouted with her voice shaking.

"Just go to hell why don't you!"

As it turned out, the girl walked to Edwin's car and noticed his overcoat in the backseat. She opened the door and put that on and then walked slowly and unevenly down the gravel driveway to the road.

Rita walked over to the lounge chair and flopped down. Her butt was right on the front edge and she slouched with her legs out straight. She put her hands over her face and bowed her head. Edwin went over and knelt down before her. He looked down at the floor as he spoke.

"How can I show how sorry I am. How can I?" he said looking slowly up.

To his surprise, Rita was glaring at him with a look that scared him for several seconds.

"I just bought you. You can stay or you can leave, I don't care. That bitch knew that you are married but I don't care because I just bought you" she said in a low, guttural tone.

All of this happened not very long after Rita's father passed away. His wife, Rita's mother, died in 1944. Rita's only sibling, a brother, died from meningitis in 1938 at age nineteen. Rita was left her father's entire estate, the properties as well as the business and his large savings. The estate is in her name only and she had planned to put Edwin as half owner of the business and the property. This did not happen after this incident. She decided to stay with Edwin for their daughter's sake and the fact that he has operated the business quite well. Edwin manages the company so Rita does not have to be involved in it. It is to his advantage to make it prosper for his own financial gain and he knows that if the company doesn't do well, she will surely give him the gate.

Rita is deeply hurt because she had loved Edwin deeply and suspected nothing. She was heartbroken but also angry because he had deceived her. She never told anyone except a private detective that she has hired several times afterwards to check on Edwin. Each time he reported his findings to her, Edwin was with other women. She has even engaged in a few steamy sexual encounters with her detective. Rita found it difficult to act as though nothing had happened when they were around other people. She eventually has had sex with Edwin again but much less frequently than previously and with little enjoyment on her part. Edwin runs the publishing company and it has made tremendous money over the years. In a sense though, he is actually working for Rita. He is not about to leave because his lifestyle will plummet if he were to do so. As Rita had told him that night, she bought him.

CHAPTER FOUR

Six weeks have passed since Paul and Norma began seeing each other. Paul has really fallen for Norma and she is giving him the impression that she feels the same about him. She does not intend on having sex with Paul because she really only wants that with Brent. Whenever they reach the heat of passion, she always stops and tells Paul that she will not have sex until she is married. He respects her beliefs but finds it difficult to restrain himself sometimes.

Norma has told both Rita and Edwin the she wants to marry Paul in the future. Rita is delighted because she can see that Paul is a trustworthy young man and would treat Norma very well. Norma has asked Edwin about putting Paul to work at the publishing company and letting him move up as he learns the ropes. Paul is in love with Norma and is anxious to marry her.

Paul has decided to leave the garage and work at the publishing company and has discussed this with Ike and Edna. Ike told Paul that what ever he decides is alright with him. He feels that in a year or so he will retire and Larry Nicholson will take over the business. Ike will still own it and receive rent from Larry but Larry will be in charge of everything. Paul thinks that this is a fine idea because he likes Larry very much and appreciates his help with his Plymouth when he was getting it roadworthy.

Paul has moved to Saxon and is renting a small apartment on the opposite end of town from where Norma and her family are. His apartment is on the first floor which is divided into two small apartments. It is a large house with two upstairs units also, one which is occupied by Mrs. Bradford, the owner of the house. Paul has his own parking spot, a small kitchen, and best of all, his own bathroom. He will be close to work and close to Norma too.

It is the first week of May and Paul and Norma have been seeing each other every night. On Sunday, Paul and Norma were having lunch at her home. Edwin called Paul into his den after the meal to discuss his new job that he will be starting the next day.

"Paul, when you get to the plant in the morning, go into the office and see Jenny Morris. She is Brent's secretary and receptionist and she will get Brent to show you around. We're going to have you work with Herb Lester or Lester as he likes to be called. He is the union steward and you will be his assistant. The guy who was his assistant died out in the parking lot not too long ago so I want Lester to have another assistant. If he should be out sick, than you will be the steward until you move up."

"Gee, I don't know anything about union business" Paul said nervously.

"Not to worry. Lester has been working for us for many years and he will show you what you can do and besides, we don't have any work related problems at the plant."

"What I want to do, Paul, is after a short while, put you on the second shift. It is a little slower paced and you will be trained to be a press man, that is, you'll be able to set up and operate publishing jobs. We are going to open another publishing plant over in Allendale and if you work out well, I'll have you manage it. That would make you and Norma happy wouldn't it?" Edwin said with a broad wide grin on his face.

"Gosh, are you serious? I mean I . . . ."

Edwin interrupted him. "You see Brent in the morning. He'll get you set up" as he got up and started to leave the room.

Paul realizes that this will mean a major increase in his financial status. When the time comes for him and Norma to marry, they will be more than comfortable. Right after Edwin left the den, Norma and Rita came in and went to Paul's side. Norma gave him a nice kiss on his mouth and Rita patted his shoulder.

'I am so happy about all of this" Norma said to Paul with a pretty smile. "You're going to be a big shot."

"Well, I don't know about that" he said looking back and forth at both of them.

"I do" Rita said squeezing Paul's hand and winking at him. She had a dreamy look about her.

Paul left the den to use the bathroom leaving Norma and Rita together.

"Gal, you did alright for yourself. If I wasn't married to your father and a few years younger . . ."

"Oh mother, you're too much" Norma said snickering with her hand over mouth and nose.

Paul and Norma went outside on the back porch. He gave her a big hug and looked her directly in her eyes.

"I love you and I am so grateful for what you have done for me."

"What have I done for you?" Norma asked him.

"Oh you know, getting your father to give me this opportunity to learn the publishing business."

Paul and Norma decided to take a ride out into the country in his car. It is warm and sunny so the convertible top went down. Norma suggested that they drive up to the Pine River house because Paul has not yet been there. Paul can see immediately upon arriving at the Pine River house why the family really loves being here. It is really secluded and landscaped nicely and the view looking down onto the river from the back of the house is gorgeous.

Norma showed him around both outside and inside. As they embraced in the living room and were passionately kissing, Norma pulled away from him slowly.

"Paul, I can't trust myself. I don't want to go too far until we are married" she said apologetically.

Her acting was superb. She has Paul convinced that she wants to remain a virgin until she weds, something she has not been since she was sixteen. Brent and she have taken care of that.

Before leaving, they went down to the dock and watched the river flowing past. Norma pointed to the surrounding land that the family own. The land is prime for building and becoming more valuable each year. On the ride back to Saxon, they passed a sign that reads GREENGROVE6 MILES with an arrow pointing to a road leading off to the right.

"That's where my dad is. He is a patient and the Longworth Sanitarium there in Greengrove."

"Has he been there long?" Norma asked.

"Ten years. Unfortunately, he won't be leaving."

"God, those places give me the creeps with all those bars and everything" Norma said. "I could never go to one of those places."

"Norma, those places are really important and necessary. People have serious mental problems and need caring. I mean . . . my dad."

"I'm sorry Paul but can we talk about something else. I'm really sorry about your father but I really don't like to think about those places" Norma said interrupting him.

Paul glanced over and looked her. She is facing straight ahead and he looked at her perfect profile. Life has been good to Norma. No sanitarium patients or wanting for anything in her family. Life has been good. Paul feels depressed but realizes that never having to deal with a situation like this, Norma can feel this way. It is depressing to see his father when he visits him. To see this man who was once an accomplished draftsman and great husband and father now a confused and mentally unstable person is extremely difficult for Paul to realize.

They returned to Norma's house at five thirty and Norma told Paul that he should go to his apartment and get ready for his new job in the morning. Paul agreed and told her that he would come by to see after he got through work. Norma slid across the seat and kissed Paul with her mouth slightly open which drives him wild.

"Good luck darling, you'll do just fine" she said quietly.

"Love you" Paul said to her as she walked by his car and towards her back door.

Paul drove out to Temple Street and headed back to his apartment. He figured he will telephone her later in the evening. When he got to his apartment, he made himself a cheeseburger and reheated some leftover French fried potatoes. He is quite hungry. He took a cold bottle of beer from his small refrigerator and ate slowly in his living room. His apartment is small and comfortable.

When Norma went in her house, Edwin was sitting at the kitchen table eating his supper that Wanda has prepared for him. Norma sat down across from her father and is served a helping of what Edwin is eating by Wanda.

"Where's mom?" Norma asked.

"She went out to dinner with Meredith. They're going to a movie afterwards."

Norma ate quickly and went to her bedroom and closed the door. She immediately called Brent and his home. Brent answered on the third ring.

"Brent, are you alone?" Norma asked.

"I'm babysitting Alice."

"Would you like me to come over?"

"Yea, hurry. I put her to bed and she's almost asleep."

They take advantage of any free time that they can get alone together. Meredith and Rita will be out until at least ten o'clock so they will have some good sex. Meredith has taken Rita so she will drop her off first before returning home.

Brent and Meredith live two towns away in Dolesboro. They have a nice split level home with an attached two car garage. The neighborhood is one of the nicest in town. There are several professional people that reside in the area. The front yard has three large oak trees and a pine grove on both sides of the house that provide privacy. As soon as Norma arrived at Brent's house, they had sex and within an hour they had had it again. Afterwards they are lying beside each other and talking.

"I don't like you being with this guy" Brent said to Norma. "I really don't like the idea of you marrying him either."

Norma started kissing Brent's face and ears slowly.

"Look my sweetness, don't you want to have me and the business? You've got to let me do this because it is the only way and besides, I'm not going to be married to Paul for that long."

"How long?" Brent said in a little calmer tone than before.

"Mother is just waiting until I am settled and married and then she will sign the business over to me and Meredith. She likes Paul so there is no problem there. She and my dad are going to retire from the business."

"You don't think Wilker suspects what we're up to here?"

"Are you kidding? He's really dense. He must have grown up in a fairy land."

They both chuckled and Brent put his hand gently on Norma's face and kissed her.

"Hey, I better get out of here before Meredith gets home" Norma said standing up and starting to get dressed.

They kissed each other goodnight and Norma left and headed home but she chose a different route than Meredith will be taking. She does not want her to think that she has been to her house when she is out. She must be extra careful.

CHAPTER FIVE

Paul pulled into the parking lot of the publishing company where he is to start work this Monday morning. The building is constructed of concrete blocks and a single level. On the far end there are two large overhead doors with a loading dock in front of them. Trucks back in to unload the huge rolls of paper and drums of ink while other trucks pick up the flyers and catalogs that are done and on wooden skids. A large wooden sign painted white with blue lettering reads ROLLINS PRINTING & PUBLISHING COMPANY. Charles Rollins was Rita's father and creator of the publishing company. He began by printing business cards and letterheads and over the years he expanded it into the empire that is now.

Paul saw the office sign and parked his car. He got out and walked towards the office. Several other cars pulled in and parked. Men got out and walked to the shop entrance. Paul pushed open the office door and walked up to the large counter. A young girl is seated at an office desk talking on the telephone. She looked at Paul and held up her index finger. A half a minute went by and she hung her telephone receiver up.

"You must be the new man that Mr. Clay told me about. Paul Wilker is it?"

"Yes I am and you must be Jenny Morris" Paul said with a friendly smile.

"That's me" Jenny said pointing toward the name plaque on her desk and showing an equally friendly smile in return.

Jenny is about five feet four inches tall, not overweight but looks as if she put on ten pounds she will show it. She is wearing gray framed glasses and only lipstick. Her hair is brown and pulled back tight against her head. Her face is smooth and has a kind and caring look about it. Paul likes her right away as she does not seem at all pretentious.

She went to the file cabinet and pulled out several papers. She walked over to the counter and placed the papers in front of Paul. He reached his right hand out to her.

"It's very nice to meet you Jenny" Paul said shaking her hand and looking straight in her eyes.

"It's nice to meet you too Paul. If you could just fill out these papers and give them back to me, I'll put them into the system. They are basically for payroll and personal information."

After Paul completed the forms that Jenny had given him, he returned them to her and told her that Edwin had told him to contact Brent so he could introduce him to Herb Lester. Jenny pushed the button on her intercom and called Brent's office.

"Hello Brent. I have Paul Wilker here and he said that you wanted to take him out to meet Herb Lester."

Brent's voice came on. "Come in my office for a minute Jenny" he answered.

Jenny stood up from her desk and started for Brent's office. A minute later she returned with Brent.

"Hello Paul" Brent said as Paul stood up from his chair.

"Good morning" Paul answered him.

"I'm going to have Jenny take you out on the floor to see Lester" Brent said.

"That's fine" Paul said looking over at Jenny who was standing beside Brent.

As Brent was talking, Paul noticed that his tie clip is silver and has a small chess knight on it like the one that was in the ash tray of Norma's Pontiac. Paul glanced quickly to see if he is wearing matching cuff links. *He is.*

This could have been a real slip up for Brent and Norma except that Paul does not suspect anything wrong with this. Brent may have borrowed her car; after all they are brother and sister in law.

"Where do you live Paul?" Jenny asked as they walked out into the publishing area.

"I have a small apartment in Saxon . . . . on Davis street. How about you?" Paul asked.

"I have a small apartment in Greengrove" Jenny said smiling at Paul again.

Greengrove. Paul sure knows where that is.

The publishing area is very spacious with two large printing presses. Only one press is presently running and Paul is amazed at how many flyers are coming out of it at one time. They walked over to where Herb Lester was. He is in his late forties and about Paul's height. He is slightly overweight and his face is a red color. He has his hair cut short, a crew cut. He is wearing a gray chino work uniform with ROLLINS PUBLISHING COMPANY over one breast pocket and LESTER over the other.

Jenny introduced Paul to Lester and asked if she needs to do anything else.

"No, we're all set" he said to Jenny.

"OK then. Welcome aboard Paul" she said and proceeded back towards the office. She is thinking to herself that Paul seems like a nice polite guy, unlike some of the people here.

Lester took Paul over to the press that is not printing at the time and showed him how it worked. Several men are loading the ink trays while two others are loading a gigantic roll of paper at the rear of the press with a mobile gantry crane.

"What they do is develop what they want to print onto a thin metal plate and then the plate is fastened to this roller on the press. Water and ink are mixed but the ink only sticks to the printed areas and not the blank part. It's called offset printing. We print tons and tons of stuff and there are a lot more contracts coming in this month" Lester said to Paul.

"Over there is where the plates are made. They call it paste up cause that's kinda how they do it" Lester said pointing to a large workroom at the side of the publishing area.

"Your gonna be workin with me for now. If someone's out we cover his job for the day or however long he's out for. We've had a guy out for a couple days so when this press starts printing, I'll have you jog."

"What's jog?" Paul asked.

"When the flyers come down off the press on the conveyor, you stand at the table where they land and pick up a bunch and bounce the bundle up and down until they are in a neat pile. Then you hand the bundle to the guy next to you who weighs it. He weighs them to get the bundle count. Then he stacks them on the skid."

An elderly man walked over to where Paul and Lester are standing. His hair is white and combed straight back on his head.

His face is thin and long and his neck is wrinkled with loose skin. He reached in his side pants pocket and pulled out a package of Old Gold Straight cigarettes. He pulled one out and lit it and returned the pack to his pocket.

"Lester, you want me to work on this job when it's set up?" he said with the cigarette bobbing up and down in his mouth.

"Yup. This new guy will be jogging with you. He's Paul .... what's the last name again?"

"Wilker, Paul Wilker" Paul said reaching out to shake the older man's hand.

"Nice to meet you Paul. I'm George Baxter. We heard that a new man was coming in."

"Paul, see these bundles here, grab that two wheeler and take them down to the other end will you" Lester said pointing to where the other press that was running was.

Paul grabbed the two wheeler and picked up the stack of bundles. The bundles contain flyers from a small job that was done the previous night.

"Where do you want these to go?" Paul asked Lester.

"See those two guys standing down there by the other press?" Put them there. The guy wearing the baseball cap is Fletcher. He'll have the routing papers for them."

Paul wheeled the bundles down to where the men were standing. Fletcher is at least six feet tall and slim built. He is wearing the company's uniform. He is clean shaven except for sideburns. He looks to be in his late twenties. The other is named Denny and he is fifty years old. His hair is full and gray in color. He is slightly shorter than Fletcher and has an obvious pot belly.

"Hi" Paul said to the two men. "Lester told me to bring these bundles to you."

Paul set the stack down just outside of Fletcher's office door and pulled the two wheeler out from under it.

'Yeah, don't leave it there!" Fletcher said in a raised voice. "Don't leave it there!"

"Where do you want it then?" Paul asked beginning to get uneasy.

"Never leave anything that size outside my office! Put it inside the office!"

The man called Denny stood grinning at Paul. He looked rather peculiar. Paul pushed the two wheeler in under the stack and moved it inside the office. When he came back out he told Fletcher that Lester said that he has the routing papers. Denny has moved in back of Paul and he can see Denny's reflection in the glass in Fletcher's office window. He is making the jerk-off sign with that silly grin on his face. Paul turned around quickly and Denny put his hand quickly down at his side.

"What are you doing that for?" he said to Denny. "What's the problem?"

Denny stood there shrugging his shoulders and still grinning. Paul turned and walked back up to where Lester and George are.

"What's with those two guys?" What's that older guy, a mute?" Paul asked pointing towards Fletcher's office.

"Ah ya gotta get used to them" Lester said.

While the printing job was being set up, Lester began telling Paul what he will be doing again. He said that they will handle any labor problems that the union members encountered. They will also fill in a position if someone is out.

"The guy that had your job before was Frank Beal. He was a good union man and worked here for quite a while."

"What happened to him?" Paul asked.

"One morning he got out of his car and dropped dead in the parking lot. He was only fifty one."

"That's too bad. I guess you just don't know what's coming."

Lester went over to the table where the flyers land when they come off of the conveyor. He took a pile of papers and began to show Paul how to jog the papers into a neat pile. He explained how he will then pass the pile to George who will weigh them to get the correct count and then stack the bundles onto the pallet that they will be shipped out on.

"When we start running this job, there will be another guy to help you jog" Lester said. "George can handle the pallet. He can keep up no matter what."

A man wearing a white work shirt and gray chino work pants came over to where Paul and Lester. He is Mike Cole, the day foreman as it says on his shirt.

"I'm Mike Cole and you're Paul, right?" he said.

"Nice to meet you" Paul said reaching out his hand.

Mike gave him a quick handshake and told him to work with Lester and George. Lester left and went down to the other press, leaving Paul and George together. George asked Paul where he is from and what he has been doing before he came to work at the publishing company. Paul is quite surprised when George told him that he is seventy eight. He looks older but seems in great shape for his age. He told Paul that he was the tax collector for many years in Wellton before retiring. His wife passed away some years back and his daughter lives with him.

"Those two guys down the other end seemed kind of strange" Paul said.

"They don't think it's right that you got the job you did with Lester. They figure that you got it because of your connection with Clay and his daughter. But between me and you, if they had offered either one of them that job, they would have refused it" George said quietly, even though nobody was near by.

"You're kidding, that's what was going on?" Paul asked.

"You'll find a few weird people here Paul. Some of them are pissed because I don't retire and open up a slot for a younger person but they'll get over it and if they don't, so what" George said grinning.

Paul feels comfortable talking to George and he thinks that he and Jenny are the most normal people he has met so far.

"You know Wilbur Hutchinson?" George asked Paul.

"Doesn't sound familiar, why?"

"He used to work here and he also had a big auto junkyard over in Southbrook, well, his father did. I thought that you might know him where you say you work with cars ya know."

"Hutchinson. You know that does sound familiar but I don't . . . . I'll have to ask my uncle" Paul said with a wondering look on his face. "There aren't many car people around here that he doesn't know."

Lester came back up to where Paul and George are and told them that the press will be starting up shortly. He told George to go back and help the two pressmen thread the paper into the press.

"We don't have many union problems here but if one should happen, we are here to handle it" Lester said. "Twenty dollars a month comes out of your pay each month for dues. You can have it taken in one check or five bucks a week however you want to do it. Let Jenny in the office know how you want to do it."

"OK" Paul said. Boy that's bugging me now."

"What's that?" Lester said.

"Well, George asked me about Wilbur Hutchinson and the name sounds familiar but I can't place it."

"You know him? He was a trouble making asshole. He took on Frank Beal, they guy who died. Frank was twice his size and would have broke him in half."

"Really?"

Yeah. See Frank couldn't fight him here. Any fighting here and Clay will fire your ass. He's big on that."

"How come he left?" Paul asked.

"Aw I don't know. I heard he had some hippie girl living with him and he knocked her up. After that, she overdosed on drugs I think and died. He lives like a hermit I heard. He's a nut case."

Paul decided to call Ike after work and ask him if he knows this Hutchinson.

That night after work, Paul called Ike and during the conversation, he mentioned Wilbur Hutchinson.

"You must be talking about Junior Hutchinson" Ike said. "I used to do business with his father, Wilbur senior. He went kind of nuts when he got old and didn't want to sell anything. He's got a big yard over in Southbrook with a lot of old stuff. Why do you ask?"

"I heard that Junior used to work where I am working" Paul said.

"Oh that I don't know. When the old man died, I heard the business slowed down. I will tell you this about Junior. He's a good guy to stay away from, especially when he's been drinking."

"Is that right" Paul said laughing a little.

"I heard that he's not afraid of anything. I remember old Wilbur telling me that Junior got into a brawl with two guys and one of them stabbed him with a screwdriver. He still flattened both of them and when the cops took him in, he still had the screwdriver stuck in him."

"Your kidding" Paul said.

"Well, how's it going out there Paul?" Ike asked. "Are you learning the printing business yet?"

"Yes a little at a time but I miss you guys too ya know."

"How's Norma. She seems like a nice girl and real pretty too."

"She's fine" Paul said. 'Everything is fine."

Paul doesn't want tell Ike about the weird atmosphere that exists at the publishing company and some of attitudes there. He really likes George Baxter and Lester seems ok as do some of the other workers. During his first week, he has worked mostly with George.

One of his daily duties is to take the job sheets from the second and third shifts into Jenny. She is always cheerful and it is a high point in his day to talk to her.

Jenny thinks that Paul is very nice and looks forward to seeing him each morning. Jenny is not involved with any men and dates rarely. She was seeing a man briefly who lived in the apartment house next to where she lives but he was rather possessive so she stopped. She knows that Paul is really involved with Norma but she often thinks that it would be nice to date him. She thinks that he would treat a girl right. Although she doesn't want to, she is beginning to have feelings towards him, romantic feelings.

On Friday afternoon at work, Paul is constantly thinking about Junior Hutchinson. He is contemplating going over to his salvage yard on Saturday. He would like to see what he has for old cars for one and he also is curious to see what he can tell him about the publishing company. When he left work that night, he definitely had decided to drive to Southbrook the next day to Junior's yard. He has been looking for a front and rear set of bumper bars for his convertible and Ike is pretty sure that Junior will have a set.

Paul really doesn't want to take Norma with him as he plans to ask Junior about the plant. He was relieved when Norma told him that she has several things she can do and that she will see him on Saturday night. What Paul doesn't know is that she is planning to spend time with Brent in the afternoon. So far they have been together and had sex numerous times and no one suspects anything. Brent has lied to Meredith so many times that he lost count. She loves him so much and trusts him in the same way that Rita had trusted Edwin.

CHAPTER SIX

Saturday is beautiful and sunny and about eighty degrees. It is a perfect day to tour a salvage yard. Paul got up at eight o'clock, showered and had a shave. He ate breakfast at his apartment which consisted of corn flakes, toast with grape jam and a glass of tomato juice. He figures that he will stop on the way and pick up a cup of coffee. He just can't seem to make a good cup at his apartment. Just as he finished eating, Norma called him and told him that she will see him that night.

"Want to go to a movie?" she asked softly.

"Sounds good. Love you" Paul said.

"Oh, you too. Bye bye" Norma said.

Paul started his Plymouth and headed out of Saxon towards Southbrook which is about fifteen miles north. He stopped and got a cup of coffee and broke down and treated himself to a chocolate doughnut too. He got his order to go and drank it in his car in the parking lot. The coffee and doughnut hit the spot even though he has just had breakfast.

Southbrook is not that far from Saxon but is nowhere near as developed. Up until about 1955, this town was sparsely populated and most of the townspeople were farmers. After that, a few housing developments appeared and then in 1961, more were constructed. Paul is unfamiliar with the area and is not sure where Junior's yard is located. Ike has given him some directions but he still is not really sure. When he reaches Southbrook center, he figures that he will stop and ask someone where the yard is.

In the center there is small building with a post office and barber shop. There is a small restaurant with a bar room connected. On the opposite side of the main street, there is a large, old fashioned hardware store and beside that is another building occupied by a doctor, a lawyer and a dentist. This is pretty much Southbrook center.

Just outside of town is a filling station and Paul pulled in and stopped by the gasoline pumps. A minute passed before a heavy set man in his late fifties came slowly out of the garage. Paul got out of the car and stood by the driver's side rear fender where the tank fill is located.

"Help ya?" he asked Paul

"Yes, fill it please."

"Can you tell me where Hutchinson's salvage yard is?" Paul asked the man as he pushed the gas nozzle into the fill pipe.

"Hutchinson's? You go down this street about three miles and turn left onto River Road. He's about two miles down on the right. There's a sign there."

"Thanks" Paul said. "I hope he's there now that I think of it."

"Hutchinson? He's always there. He don't go anywhere" the big man said.

He withdrew the nozzle from Paul's car and replaced the cap.

"How's the oil?" he asked Paul.

"Oh the oil is good, thanks."

"Ok. That's two eighty" the man said.

Paul paid him and got back in the car. As he started to drive away, the man said "River Road." Paul waved and drove out onto the street. He noticed that just outside of Southbrook center, there are dense woods on both sides of the road with no dwellings. When he got to River Roadit is the same thing. Paul noticed that there are telephone poles with power lines so this is a good sign at least.

After traveling just over two miles, Paul spotted the sign that the attendant had mentioned. It is a large, badly faded wooden sign that simply reads: HUTCHINSON'S AUTO SALVAGE and below that: USED PARTS. Beside the sign, there is a dirt road that appears to be oiled down periodically to keep down dust. Paul turned onto the dirt road and began to follow it. Many huge pine trees line both sides and suddenly Paul begins to see the remains of some cars. A 1937 Lincoln Zephyr two door sedan is nestled amongst a group of Fords and Chevrolets along with a prewar Nash coupe. The Lincoln is missing its trunk lid and left rear wheel. The front wheel is still on the car with a flat, dry rotted tire. The hood is raised and the driver's door is open exposing the front seat which is badly tattered with its white stuffing popped out. There are pieces of the headliner hanging down like icicles and most of the window glass has turned white. Some of the original blue paint is visible but most of the car, as are most of the others, is covered with surface rust and brown pine needles.

Further on, the wooded area becomes more packed with junk automobiles, mostly thirties and forties cars. Several pickup trucks are included also. The road widens and a small house with a very large wooden barn beside it has come into view. Paul pulled off to the side of the driveway and got out of his car. Beside the house and in back there are junk cars pretty much as far as you can see. There are less trees than in front of the house so the cars are packed in tightly together. It is a dream come true for Paul.

In front of the barn door, there is a man bent over the passenger side front fender of a 1935 Plymouth two door sedan with the rear mounted spare tire. The Plymouth is a faded coffee brown color with black fenders. As he gets closer to the car, a brown and white female boxer dog comes barking out from the barn. Paul notices that her nipples are protruded due to the fact that she has recently given birth to three pups. Paul stopped and opened the car door. He let the dog smell him. He can see that the she is friendly and just doing her job. The man straightened up and walked over to Paul wiping grease off of his hands with a rag.

"Hi" Paul said.

"I got four of them" the man said stooping down and patting the dog that has pushed herself up against his leg.

"Four?" Paul asked.

"Four Plymouths like you have. No convertibles, just two and four door sedans. What do you need?"

"I have been looking for a set of front and rear bumper bars. My uncle thought that you might have some. He is Ike Wilker. Are you Junior?"

"I am. How is Ike?" Shit, I haven't seen him in years. He used to deal with my old man when he was alive."

Paul pointed to the '35 Plymouth that Junior was working on. "Boy, this old gem is still in pretty good shape."

"The old man had this in the barn for years and never did nothin with it. I got it runnin and when I redo the brakes, I'm gonna run it on the road. It ain't got fifty thousand on it and look, it's still got the spare tire cover on it with the locking hubcap."

"Actually, I came here for two reasons. Besides the bumper bars, I wanted to ask you about the Rollins Publishing Company. I just started working there and I was told that you worked there once too. I found some of the people who work there to be . . . . well, a little difficult."

"Aw Jesus, what do ya want to spoil a nice day like this talking about that God Damn place" Junior said sounding a little angry.

"Hey, I'm sorry. I didn't mean to upset you. I've just never run into a situation like this before. I have worked for Ike until last week when I started there. Some of the people there, most of them, seem ok, but some can be trying."

"What the hell did you go to work there for?" Junior asked. "That place is a suck job."

"Well, ... I'm kinda getting engaged to Norma, you know, Norma Clay. She got her dad to hire me and they put me in the job that Frank Beal had before he died."

"Want a bottle of beer? C'mon. We'll go in the house and sit for a spell" Junior said and began walking towards the house.

Norma and Brent met at a Woolworth's store on the way up to the Pine River house. Brent left his car in the busy parking lot where it will be unnoticeable. When Norma arrived, he got into the passenger side and they drove away towards their hideaway as they have done many times. When they arrived, Norma drove her car around back and pulled up to the garage door. As soon as she shut off the engine, they began heavily making out.

"Let's go inside now" Norma said breathing deeply. "I can't wait any longer."

They went in through the basement and had sex on the living room floor. "That was fantastic", Norma gasped. "You're fantastic."

"Am I as good as Wilker?" Brent asked smirking a bit. "How do you keep him from raping you?"

"I told you before, I just tell him that I won't because I can't be untrue to my parents. I've been brought up this way. A girl doesn't have sex until she's married" Norma said gently running her finger over Brent's lips.

"He buys that does he?"

"Of course. He's so thick but . . . because of him, we can make our dream come true."

Often times when they do this, Brent goes home and has sex with Meredith the same night. Meredith suspects nothing. She, unlike her sister, is a faithful and decent woman who cares deeply for her family. She is like Paul in the sense that she had not dated that much before she met Brent. Brent is so good looking and he charmed her off her feet. Her family financial status was a key factor in his interest in her. When Brent first met Meredith, Norma was away at school. When he first met Norma, he was bowled over by her looks. At fifteen, she could have easily passed for a girl in her early twenties because of her appearance and the way in which she dressed. Brent and Norma are a good match and don't mind using people. They left the Pine River house at one thirty and once again, have had another successful rendezvous without getting caught.

Junior and Paul entered the salvage yard office which is a part of his house. There is an old wooden desk and office chair and the top of the desk is covered with papers. An old style telephone is visible among the papers. A large wooden bookcase full of automobile and truck interchange manuals is beside the desk. On the top of the bookcase, there are several carburetors and a generator. The pieces are marked with a yellow crayon identifying what vehicle they belong to. By the window there are several padded folding chairs and Paul sat down on one of them. The boxer came over and stood beside him and looked very content as Paul patted her head.

Paul can see Junior's kitchen from where he is sitting. Junior took two bottles of Schlitz beer from his refrigerator and popped off the caps. He is about five feet ten inches tall and has a stocky build. He is in his early forties and his face is slightly red in color. His hair is brown and wavy with some gray streaks showing and can use a trim. His hands are large and strong and he has several of his bottom front teeth missing. His face is covered with a two day growth of stubble.

"So you think the printing company is, how did you say it, difficult?" Junior asked handing Paul a bottle of beer.

"Well, there are two guys there, Fletcher and Denny, that don't seem too fond of me and I haven't done anything. I only deal with them when I have to" Paul said. "That Denny doesn't say anything. He just stands there with a dumb grin on his face and everything I bring to Fletcher, he finds fault with it."

"Those two guys are pissers" Junior said.

"I work mostly up on the other press with George Baxter and this newer guy named Owen" Paul said.

"George Baxter. Nice old guy, the best guy in the plant. Ya know, that old bastard is almost eighty I think" Junior said and taking a swig from his bottle of beer. "Ya know Paul, some people are just tougher than others; I don't mean that they can beat everybody up. Their body parts and their guts just last longer ya know. George is like that."

"I fully agree with you. He told me that Fletcher and Denny are pissed because I got Frank Beal's job."

"In other words, you were hired as Lester's assistant and alternate union steward, right?"

"Exactly" Paul said.

"OK, first off, that union is a company union and a big joke. The only thing that the dues that all you guys pay each month does is fund the big cookout that Clay has at his house" Junior said raising his voice slightly.

"Oh yes. I think that is coming up in a couple of weeks."

"What did Lester say about me?" Junior asked.

"Well, he said that you got into a row with Frank Beal and that you were lucky that he was at work and couldn't fight with you."

Junior let out a huge laugh. He got up and went into the other room. Paul is not about to reveal everything that Lester said about Junior but to Paul, Junior seems like a decent guy so far. The dog suddenly had a sneezing spell and looked guilty for doing so. Paul reached out and patted her head.

"Are you ok?" he said to the dog.

"Her name is Minnie" Junior said as he came into the room from the kitchen.

He is carrying a photograph with him and handed it to Paul. It is a picture of a young girl, showing her head and shoulders, with long brown hair, a pretty, friendly smile and large, lovely eyes.

"Her name was Bonnie. She lived here with me and died in the other room there" Junior said pointing towards the hallway but not looking there.

Paul does not know if she was his girlfriend or daughter but whatever the case, she was certainly much younger than Junior. He doesn't want to ask because he can sense the sadness that Junior is showing.

"What happened?" Paul asked.

Junior got up and went to the kitchen and returned momentarily with two more opened bottles of Schlitz.

"She was a hippie girl that showed up here with two other girls and three boys. They were on their way to California and asked me if I had any work that they could do. They also wanted to stay in one of the old school busses that I have up back in the junkyard. Well, I gave them a job loading old tires and junk batteries into a couple of truck box trailers that I haul out of here when they get full. My old man had just died and I was still working at the printing company."

"Why did they want to go to California?" asked Paul.

The telephone rang and Junior answered it.

"Hutchinson's" he said. "Fifty five Chevy, yup I got two of em. Come on over and take a look. What's that? Oh yeah, they both have complete fronts on them. All right then."

He hung the telephone up and turned to Paul. He took another sip of beer.

"These kid's growing up today are different than before. They don't like being told what to do by grown ups, especially their parents. A lot of them are heading to California to those communities where kids live and do what ever they want. You watch Paul. Things are really changing."

"How come she didn't get to California?" Paul asked Junior looking a little confused.

"Well, she was with one of the boys, ya know, she was his girlfriend. I didn't like this guy right off. He seemed slick, kinda sneaky and two faced; the kind of a guy that would be really friendly to ya and then steal you blind."

"Well, anyways, they stayed up back there for several weeks and like I said, I was working everyday so I didn't see them much. One night I was in the house here and it was raining, I mean pouring like a cow pissin on a flat rock."

Paul laughed out loud at Junior's description of the rain storm. Junior laughed too a little because Paul did.

"Well, I hear someone outside knocking on the door. Minnie lets out her bark and we went to see who it was. It was Bonnie and she looked like a cat that someone had tossed into a raging river. She was soaked to the skin. I brought her inside and asked her what happened. That jerk that she was with made her pregnant and took off with the other kids. They snuck off and left her. She was shaking and crying hysterical like. I had her take a hot bath and cooked her a steak dinner. Her father is from the old school like most parents are and he threw her out of the house. Her mother went along with the father but was a little closer with her. Bonnie said that she couldn't go home and didn't know what to do."

Two young men pulled up outside with a 1955 Chevrolet two door sedan. The front of the car is pushed in. To repair it, they will need a bumper, hood, grille and both front fenders. Junior looked out the window and then went to the door.

"In here" he yelled to the two young men. "What the hell did you do, bang your car up?"

"Yea, I need a nose for it" the shorter of the two replied.

"Go ahead up back. You'll find them "55's up back. Look em over. They both have good complete noses on em."

"Thanks" they said.

"What were you doin, racin and drinkin? C'mon, smile if you were shitfaced" Junior said laughing at the two.

The two boys chuckled and went outside. Junior stood at the door and told them again where the cars are located and then came back to his chair and continued where he had left off.

"I called Bonnie's house and talked to her father but he wanted nothin' to do with her. He said that when any of his kids thought they didn't have to live by his rules, they were out and that was that. Good riddance he says. I guess she was kind of rebellious when she was livin at home but she was in with that group see."

"Jesus, I feel bad and I never even knew her" Paul said shaking his head. "Did she stay here with you? Well she must have because she died here."

"Paul, she was so grateful that I took her in that she started doing stuff here for me. Shit, she'd clean the house and make food for me . . . . She'd answer the phone and all that."

"Well you were good to do that for her, I mean you helped her out when here own family wouldn't" Paul said.

Junior looked away and then quickly looked back at Paul.

"We were gonna get married. She was seventeen and I was forty one. I really fell for this girl and she wanted to marry me too. Whether she really loved me or was just gonna do it for the kido I didn't know and I didn't care. I think though that it would've worked good. You see, my old man got sick and didn't have insurance, didn't believe in it. That's why I took the job at the printing place; to pay his medical bills ya know. He had seventy eight acres of land here but wouldn't sell any of it. There's land here that runs way past the junkyard all the way down to the Pine River. I sold thirty five acres by the river after he died and I've got enough money now to last me for a long, long time and I still got more valuable land left up back."

"Junior, why did she die?" Paul asked

"Somethin burst inside her. The doctor said it was the strain of being pregnant or something like that. I had gone off to pick up a couple of junks and I was gone a good part of the day. I got home and found her in the bed dead. I still can't believe it happened" Junior said leaning back in his desk chair.

"Her mother came back and I helped her make the arrangements to have Bonnie sent back to her hometown. The mother turned out to be nice but that father . . . . I can't believe him, I mean not even coming here with his wife."

"He didn't go to her funeral?" Paul asked looking shocked.

"Oh, he was there. I went there but I told her mother not to tell anyone who I was", Junior answered.

"Her service was in her hometown in New York. I'll go back there later this year on her birthday and put down some nice flowers on her grave."

The telephone rang and Junior answered it. He spoke for a minute and hung up.

"So Lester told you about me and Beal did he?" Junior asked.

"He said that you and him had words" Paul said.

"Frank Beal. Big guy, always pissed off. In the three years that I worked there, I don't think he said ten words to me. He was in with Fletcher and Lester. I never heard him say anything nice about anybody. He was always tellin George Baxter to retire before he croaks. "They're gonna carry your dead ass outta here," he'd say. Well, one day at lunch a lot of the guys were sitting at the big lunch table. I came around the corner and heard Lester say that I was living with some young bimbo as he called her. Beal says "What does he do, take off her diapers before he screws her? Everybody starts laughing see. I went up behind him and grabbed the back of his collar and yanked it back. A couple of buttons popped off his shirt. Hey Beal, shut your fat mouth I says. He jumped up and came up to me and says that if he runs into me on the street, he'll break my neck. I told Lester if he called her a bimbo or anything else, I'd put his lights out."

"Did Beal come after you?" Paul asked.

"Na, he was all talk like the rest of them around there. If he came at me, I would'a ripped his throat out. One morning, not too long after that, he got out of his car in the parking lot and dropped dead. Heart attack they said. All those guys said what a great union man he was. He never did anything for anyone there except himself."

'Wow, he sounds like a guy that wasn't easy to get along with" Paul said finishing his beer.

"I'll tell you this Paul, the guy there that will really screw you over is Lester. He is a major asshole."

"Lester?" Paul said surprised.

"He is a sneaky, backstabbing prick. I don't know what he's got on Clay but he don't do nuthin and he gets more money than any of those guys there and that's the truth."

"Really" Paul said surprised again.

"I'll give ya an example of what a snake this guy is. We had a guy there when I started named Melvin Pine. He was a good, decent guy. He was honest and hard working, salt of the earth, ya know? I used to kid him that they named the Pine River after him. He used to stay over and work a couple hours on the second shift for nuthin so he could learn how to set up the presses. After a while, they made him a pressman and he was runnin off jobs on the second shift before he went back on days. I used to jog like your doin with his group when they put him back on the day shift and he was great to work for."

Junior got up and went out to get more beer. Paul was feeling a little buzzed and figured that this would be his last. Just as he came back into the office, the door opened and the two young men that owned the damaged '55 Chevy came in. Junior put the bottles of beer on his desk and directed his attention to the two.

"How much for the nose on that blue one?" the driver of the Chevrolet asked.

"A hundred and a quarter if you take it off."

"You aren't open tomorrow cause it's Sunday are you?" the driver asked Junior.

"I ain't supposed to be but I'll open up if you want to take it off. Get your asses over here early though. I don't want you working up there at night."

The two young men thanked Junior and left. They seem pleased with the deal that they have made.

Junior returned to his chair and took a sip of beer.

"Where was I?" he asked Paul.

"You were telling about Melvin Pine."

"Oh yeah. He had a nice wife and a cute little daughter. Well he finds this house that needed some work to make it better to live in. Mel was handy and wasn't afraid to try stuff and the guy who owned it had a new house built on Cape Cod so he's really trying to sell it. Mel could have bought it for a song but when he goes to get a loan, the bank says that he ain't makin quite enough money to be a good risk. Now as luck would have it, Vic Mann, the night shift foreman was retiring. One thing about Clay, he pays his foreman good money, much more than the pressmen.

So Mel figures that he'd be a good choice for this slot and he would've been."

"Oh yeah, especially where he used to stay on his own time so he could learn the procedures" Paul said.

"That's right. So he goes and tells Lester, him being the union representative and all, and Lester tells him that that's a good idea and he was going to put a good word in for him with Clay. Mel told him about the house and the deal he can get on it too."

"What happened?" Paul asked.

'I'm tellin ya. Lester strings Mel along when all the time he knows that his shithead nephew Marcus is goin to get the job, even though he only worked there for a little over a month and didn't know squat about anything."

"Oh, I didn't know that he was Lester's nephew. When Marcus comes back to work, probably next week, I'm supposed to go on the second shift to learn how to do publishing jobs so I can become a pressman" Paul said.

"How come Marcus ain't working?" Junior asked.

"He's out. He injured his back."

Junior had just taken a mouthful of beer and when he heard that, he bowed his head down and let the beer go back into the bottle so he wouldn't choke. He began shrieking laughing. Minnie jumped up from the floor and went over to Junior with her little stub of a tail wagging. She seemed to want to involved in the humor.

"Well, he musta fell of the sofa cause he sure didn't get hurt from working" Junior said still laughing.

"Anyway, Mel was supposed to find out on the Friday afternoon whether or not he was going to get the job. He had it as far as he was concerned because of the line of shit that Lester had been feeding him. He planned to leave an hour early and go to the bank to arrange his loan and all. After lunch, he was supposed to report to Clay's office to find out but when he gets there, they tell him that Clay has left for the weekend. Now he goes to find Lester and guess what, he's gone too. Mel sees Frank Beal and asks him if he knows anything. So Beal, who had no tact at all tells him "Marcus is getting the job, not you" and walks off."

"That's terrible "Paul said.

"These are the kind of slimes that are working there Paul. It could be a nice place to work but it ain't. So Mel leaves and goes to Clay's house to talk to him. The story I heard is that he caught Clay in his driveway so he didn't have a chance to blow him off. After they talked for a few minutes, Mel got really upset so Clay fires him just like that. Now he's really porked. He can't get the house cause he has no job. And here's the payoff. Ya know who bought the house? Marcus. He went down that afternoon and put down the money for it. Nice huh?. It was all planned beforehand."

"That's unbelievable" Paul said. "Hey, can I use your bathroom. I gotta take a leak."

"Go in here" Junior said standing up and walking into the kitchen with Paul following him.

"Right in there" Junior said pointing to the bathroom door.

He took two more beer bottles from the refrigerator and went back to the office and waited for Paul to return from the bathroom. As Paul came through the kitchen, he saw Minnie lying on an army blanket in the corner and suckling her three adorable puppies.

"Junior, those pups are great."

"Want one?" Junior asked.

"Oh no thanks. My landlady would shoot me I'm afraid."

"Here's another thing that goes on there" Junior said handing Paul an opened beer bottle.

"Clay loans a lot of those guys money. There's a few that are divorced or aren't married and have kids they're supporting. He has them sign a paper stating that they agree to take a certain small sum of money from their pay each week and if they quit for some reason, the loan is due in full at that time. This way here he's got em."

"Why don't they go to a bank" Paul said.

"They got no credit or collateral. I'll bet you that a lot of the people there driving late model cars got loans from Clay and most of them never pay the loan in full. They borrow more before they pay up. The guys that work there do good work. They get the jobs out on time and they can keep the presses runnin right but they don't get paid anywhere near what a real union printing shop would pay."

"Why don't they try to get more money?" Paul asked.

"Because nobodies got the nut to. That's why the union there is such a joke. That's what asshole Lester should be doing is trying to get more pay for those guys but he's got a good thing going for himself and he ain't gonna mess it up for anybody."

Chapter Seven

After Norma left Brent at Woolworth's parking lot to pick up his car, she drove to her house and decided to take a swim in the family pool. Meredith is there with Alice and they are in the shallow end. Rita is sitting in one of the lounge chairs sipping a cocktail and smoking a cigarette. Norma put on her pearl white one piece swimsuit which looks quite nice against her tanned skin. It is low cut and allows a generous view of her cleavage. It has been custom made for her and fits perfectly. She pulled on a flowered bathing cap and dove into the deep end of the pool. When she came up she swam over to where Meredith is and started to play with little Alice.

"So when are you and Paul going to tie the knot?" Meredith said to Norma and turned and winked at Rita.

"Don't know yet" Norma said as she lifted Alice up out of the water and then dunked her back in again. Alice laughed and squealed and splashed the water with her hands.

"Better not wait too long. Nice boys like him don't come along everyday" Rita said.

"Oh mother, I know, I know" Norma said and turned and swam away towards the other end of the pool.

"Alice. Here's daddy" Meredith said as she waved to Brent as he walked up to the edge of the pool.

"Did you get everything done that you wanted to" Meredith asked.

"Everything" Brent said.

Norma grinned and thought to herself that he sure did get everything done that he wanted to. She climbed out of the pool and started to dry herself off.

"Are you seeing Paul tonight dear?" Rita asked.

"I think we are going to a movie" Norma said pulling off her bathing cap and fluffing her hair with her hand.

"Oh what are you going to see?" Meredith asked.

"The Carpetbaggers. I haven't seen it and it's supposed to very good" Norma said.

As Norma started to walk off towards the house, Brent gave several quick glances at her. He was thinking of how only hours earlier, they had been all over each other. He went into the pool house, changed into a pair of trunks, and joined Meredith and Alice in the pool.

Paul finished the bottle of beer that Junior had brought him and stood up. He went in and used the bathroom and was feeling a little woozy. He really didn't want that last bottle but Junior had told him so much about the plant that he didn't refuse.

"Before I go, can I just walk up back in your yard and look at the cars that you have? I love the old thirties and forties ones you know."

Paul wanted to do that but also he wanted to clear his head a little from the beer.

"Oh sure. C'mon with me" Junior said heading out into the yard.

The road is dirt with rocks scattered about and large oil stains are visible. Both sides of the road are lined with all different makes of automobiles from the past. Along with the Ford, General Motors and Chrysler models there are others too like Studebakers, Hudsons, Packards andNashes. Paul noticed several Grahrams, a Huppmobile and even a Franklin four door convertible. The cars are surface rusted and most have been up here a long time.

"Wow, you've got some really nice old gems here" Paul said to Junior. "Really nice."

"Further back is the real old shit" Junior said pointing. "There's cars there from the early twenties. I got model T Fords and model A's too. I even got an Oakland and a Moon. Ya see Paul, my old man was a weird bastard, I mean I loved the guy dearly but he was weird. After a while, he didn't want to sell nothing. He'd just keep bringing more autos in here and sometimes in the afternoon, he'd just come up here and wander around and look at the cars. When I took over, I was gonna junk a lot of the stuff but now I got people wanting some of these old parts. They're fixin old cars back up now and some stuff I ship by truck to other states."

"Oh man, I love it here. "You've got treasures here" Paul said putting his hand on a rusty '36 Cadillac coupe. The hood was missing and Paul looked at the engine which appears to be pretty much complete.

"Geez, I didn't really that these old engines were this big. This one is huge."

"Come with me" Junior said. "I'll get you those bars you wanted."

Paul followed him up a little further to a large, old wooden shed with a rusty corrugated steel roof. Paul had forgotten about the bars he had asked Junior about when he first arrived. Junior took a ring of keys from his pocket and slid them around until he found the correct key for the padlock on the door. As Paul looked up above the door he noticed a bee's nest the size of a basketball with hornets zooming in and out of it.

"Careful" Paul said pointing up at the nest.

"Holy shit! I'll have to come up in the early morning and spray that bastard or better, why don't you take it and put it in Lester's locker" Junior said laughing and once again exposing where his lower front teeth were missing.

Junior quickly unlocked the shed door and both men entered. The building is stuffed with various car body parts. Bumpers and rims are neatly stacked on top of each other, probably a dozen trunk lids and much more. Everything has been marked as to what it belongs to. Junior went to one of the shelves and looked over several bars. "Here's a front and I know I have a rear one here . . . . yup, here it is. What are they worth to ya?"

Junior looked at the bars. The front was really nice and the rear bar can probably be polished up to look as nice.

"Is ten dollars fair?" Paul asked.

"Deal it is" he said "although I should charge you more seein as how your gonna be a big superintendent and all" Junior said slapping Paul lightly on his shoulder.

Junior likes Paul and feels that he is too nice a guy to be working for Clay's company but he has decided not to say anything. When they got back to the house, Paul thanked Junior for taking the time to fill him in on facts regarding the publishing company. As Paul drove away he began thinking about what had gone on and was shocked at what Junior had told him about Lester and his nephew Marcus. It is unbelievable what has happened to that guy, Melvin Pine.

Back at the salvage yard, Junior has pulled the '35 Plymouth that he was working on back into the barn and went into his house. He went to the kitchen and took out another bottle of beer. He poured himself a shot of whiskey and took it and his beer into the other room. He sat and sipped his beer while he held the picture of Bonnie. He looked at it with a slight smile on his face and teary eyes as Minnie curled up at his feet.

CHAPTER EIGHT

The weekend has gone by quickly for Paul. He has spent the better part of Saturday at Junior's and then that evening he went to the open air theater with Norma. He went to the Clay's house for lunch on Sunday then he and Norma visited Meredith and Brent at their home. Monday morning came quickly and when he got to the plant, he picked up the completed worksheets and took then into the office for Jenny. Paul likes this part of his job because Jenny is always pleasant and talkative.

"Hi Paul, how was your weekend?" she asked.

"Too short" Paul said and they both laughed.

"Well starting next weekend, *I* am on vacation for a week and *I* am going to enjoy every second of it" Jenny said.

"Ah, that's nice. What are you going to do with yourself?" Paul asked.

"I'm going to visit my aunt. I used to live with her before I started working here."

"Where is she?" Paul asked as he handed her the sheets.

"She's in Perkinsville".

"Oh I've been there before once, a long time ago" Paul said.

Jenny's phone rang and Paul waved to her and went back out onto the floor. The back press is set up and is ready to start up. There is a large store flyer job to be run off so Paul is to work with George Baxter and a new man named Owen. The previous week he had worked with George all but one day. The other day he was down where Fletcher and Denny are. Paul is much more comfortable with George and Owen.

Norma had mentioned to Paul that the weekend after next, her father will have the big company cookout at his home. The whole plant is invited and it goes from noon to nine at night but usually later. There are burgers and sausages along with steaks and hot dogs. Beer and wine, liquor and soft drinks are there too. According to Norma, almost every employee shows up at some point. It does not set well apparently if one doesn't attend.

Paul noticed a man working on the control switch on the press that he has not seen there before. He asked George quietly who the man is.

"He's Alvin Brown. He does a lot of the maintenance work here. He can do anything but he's a boozer. Too bad cause he is a genius when it comes to fixin stuff. He comes in regular but then all of a sudden, he's out for four or five days. A few times, he had to go and dry out."

"They never fired him?" Paul asked with a wondering look on his face.

"No, no. They could never get anybody to do the stuff that he does here for the kind of money that they're payin him" George said almost whispering. "I've seen him here when they had to call him in and he'd be shaking so bad he couldn't hardly hold a cup of coffee. They'd be tryin to sober him up so he could fix something on the press."

Alvin walked over to where George and Paul are standing. He wiped his hands with a shop cloth.

"How's it lookin?" George asked him.

"Should be all right now. I put another speed control switch in."

"This here's Paul Wilker. New fella" George said to Alvin.

Paul reached out his hand and Alvin shook it limply. Alvin is a short man, about five feet seven and slim built. He has curly hair cut short and has a serious, almost worried look on his face. He appears to be in his early fifties and wears brown framed glasses. He is clean shaven and his eyes are blue in color.

Fletcher walked up to where the men are.

"Hey Al, take a look at my press will ya? I think one of the rollers is off center" he said.

"George, when are you gonna retire, when you're a hundred?" Fletcher said with a smirk.

"Maybe" George said to Fletcher. "But you'll have to work harder when I do."

Fletcher ignored Paul and walked away with Alvin Brown. Gus Tanner is the pressman so he controls the speed that the flyers are being printed at. He also checks to be sure that the flyers are being printed correctly and the paper rolls too. He will check the different ink troughs and add ink as needed. When the press is operating correctly, it will put out a lot of flyers per minute so this is where Paul and Owen come in. They will jog the flyers into neat piles and hand them to George who will weigh them to get the correct number per bundle. He then stacks them on a pallet. When the pallet is full, it is banded and taken to Fletcher and Denny to be set up for delivery.

One thing that Paul has noticed is that when several people are out, he will always fill in for one of them but Lester never will fill in the other absent spot. Paul wondered about that and remembers what Junior had told him about the goings on there. He is beginning to look forward to going to Allendale and the new plant. Brent told him yesterday when Norma and he were visiting him and Meredith that Marcus is returning to work this week and that Paul will be going on the night shift next week to learn to be a pressman.

He also told Paul that next Monday morning, he wants him to drive out to Allendale and checkout the new plant. Before very long the two new presses will be coming there on tractor trailer trucks. Inside of the building there is a ten ton gantry crane that runs the length of the building. There is a long cable that comes down and has the controls so it can be operated from the floor. The new presses are to be unloaded inside of the building and then the manufacturer will send their installation crew in to set them up. They will be identical to the presses that are used at the Saxon plant.

Paul worked the rest of the day with George and Owen and they bundled and stacked a lot of flyers. When Paul got to his apartment, Norma was waiting there for him. She gave Paul a very passionate kiss when they got inside.

"Missed you" she said looking at him with her penetrating green eyes. "Let's go out to dinner."

"Only if I can have a dozen more kisses" Paul said pulling her close to him.

"Later, I'm starved" she said pulling her head back from him. "Change and let's go. I need food, I haven't eaten a thing all day."

Paul went into his bedroom and changed into a pair of slacks and a short sleeve dress shirt.

"How'd your photo shoot go today?" he asked Norma.

"Great. Long but great" she said.

When Norma had first arrived, she had her hair up in the back but while Paul was changing she had let it down and brushed it out. It came down to her shoulders and flipped up slightly. She looks lovely as usual. When they arrived at the restaurant, Norma ordered a steak dinner and Paul had the New England pot roast. When the meal ended, they were both stuffed.

They went back to Paul's apartment and Paul made coffee. They sat and talked and did some hugging and kissing.

"Not too much longer" Norma said softly. "We'll announce our engagement by the end of the summer for sure".

"Ok by me" Paul said.

"You'll be out in Allendale then and once we get married, Mom and dad will turn the whole business over to Meredith and I. Oh, things will be great won't they?" Norma said longingly.

After Norma left, Paul took a hot shower and climbed into his bed. He is thinking about everything that is happening and feels a little uneasy. He doesn't know why but he thinks to himself that things will be fine. He lapsed into deep sleep and slept until the alarm clock buzzed him awake.

Paul dozed off again and when he woke up, he immediately got up and got dressed. It is a little later than he likes so he decided to pick up a cup of coffee and a doughnut on the way. When he arrived at the plant, he was still early so he drank his coffee and ate the doughnut in his car before going in. No sooner did he get into the press area when he heard his name being called.

"Hey Wilker, come here" he heard.

Paul looked down by the far press and saw that it is Fletcher calling him. Fletcher called again and waved his arm for Paul to go down to him. Paul figures that this can not be good. Fletcher only speaks to him when he has a complaint or something work related and never a "Good Morning." Paul stopped and said hello to George Baxter and Owen. Again Fletcher called for Paul; this time louder. Denny and several men who work in Fletcher's gang are there with him.

"Good morning" Paul said as he approached Fletcher. "What is so important that you are speaking to me this early?"

"What are you going to do for us?" Fletcher asked looking Paul straight in the eye. "Seein how you're the steward, what are you going to do for us?"

Paul looked at each of the men and when he looked at Denny, he shrugged his shoulders and has that annoying smirk on his face.

"What am I going to do?" Lester's your steward. I'm the assistant" Paul said looking confused.

"Lester's gonna be out for a while. Broke his leg yesterday in two places and needs a operation" Fletcher said pointing to his own leg.

"Really. That's not good at all. How did that happen?" Paul asked.

"I don't know but we want to know what you're gonna do for us cause you're the steward now" Fletcher said in a demanding tone.

"What do you want me to do?"

You're the steward now". You should know what to do" said Art, one of the guys in Fletcher's crew.

Fletcher turned back and grinned at Art and then looked back at Paul straight faced again.

"I am a representative for your union body here. You tell me what you want and I will propose your requests to the management" Paul said looking back and forth at the men.

Yeah, then what?" Fletcher asked.

"Then they either agree to the proposal, or part of it, or submit a counter offer, or they reject it" Paul said.

At this point he realizes that Fletcher and his cronies are putting pressure on him so he decides to call their bluff.

"So what do you guys want. More money, more vacation time, sick leave, seniority rights, pension, what? And if they don't give you anything, would you walk?" Paul asked dying to hear their response.

"Walk". You mean strike?" Fletcher said

"That's right."

The buzzer sounded indicating that it was time to begin working.

"Yeah, we want all that stuff" Fletcher said.

"OK. I'll prepare a proposal and present it to Brent and we'll see what happens."

Paul turned and walked up towards the press where George and Owen are. He felt pleased with himself for his performance with Fletcher and the others. He has every intention of following through with this. He remembered Junior's statement about the guys there being all talk. We shall see, Paul thought to himself.

Back where Fletcher and his crew are, the men are still talking and have not started to work yet.

"You think he's gonna do that what he said?" Art asked Fletcher.

"Na. What does he care. He gonna be runnin the new plant and marry into the family. Ya think he gives two shits about us" Fletcher said as he started to check the ink trays.

As Paul joined Owen and George, George asked him what they wanted him for.

"I guess Lester broke his leg and will be out for a while so they want me to submit a proposal to the management for more money and vacation time" Paul answered.

George laughed exposing his tobacco stained teeth. Paul picked up the job sheets from the night shift and went into the office. Jenny looked up at Paul from her desk and smiled widely.

"Paul, I was just coming out to get you. Brent wants to see you in his office."

Paul thought to himself that Brent could not possibly know about the proposal already.

"Really?" Paul asked.

"Uh huh" Jenny said smiling at him again. You're just a really important guy here it looks like."

Paul likes Jenny and feels very comfortable talking to her.

"Thanks Jenny. I'll see you later" Paul said exiting and walking towards Brent's office.

When he entered, Brent is talking on the telephone to Norma.

"Gotta go" he said as soon he saw Paul.

Brent opened the top drawer of his desk and took out a manila tag with two keys attached to it.

"Paul, these are the keys to the building in Allendale. I want you to drive out there this morning and check it out. Later this month, two new presses are to be shipped there and I want you to unload them and uncrate them at that time. When that is done, the manufacturer will send a crew out to set them up for us."

"Where exactly is the plant located in Allendale, how do I go?" Paul asked.

Brent took a paper from his desk with the driving directions to the plant and handed it to him.

"Look the place over good because eventually you'll be there once we have it set up. Make sure you lock it up when you leave."

"OK. I'll see you when I get back" Paul said.

Paul started his car and pulled into the street and headed toward Saxon center where he will take route seven and head towards Allendale. Route seven is a nice highway to travel. The traffic is light for the most part and this morning is bright and sunny. The temperature is already up to eighty four. Paul glanced at his direction sheet and saw that he is to turn off at the Calvert exit and get onto Summer Street which leads through Calvert center and on to Allendale. Just before Calvert center, Paul can see a large factory with a sign that reads REPUBLIC CHEMICAL COMPANY. As he gets nearer, there is a large crowd of people in front of the entrance and a picket line.

People are holding large signs with protest slogans against the company. A tractor trailer truck has slowed down but is not going to enter because of the strike. Paul drove past the company entrance and pulled his car into the first available parking spot on the opposite side of the street. As soon as there was a break in the traffic, he crossed and approached the picket line. As he got close, a middle aged man wearing dungarees with a brown tee shirt and dark blue baseball cap stepped in front of him. He is wearing a pin on his hat that reads "SUPPORT YOUR UNION."

"We have a labor dispute going on here sir and we would appreciate it if you would honor our picket line" he said politely.

"Oh, I have no intention of crossing your line. I'd just like to ask your steward a few questions if it's ok" Paul said smiling slightly at the man.

The man turned away from Paul and called to another man who was talking with a group of men and women.

"Ray, this fella wants to see you."

Ray looked over and waved and then turned back to the people that he was talking to. He said a few words to them and then walked up to Paul. Ray is a barrel chested man in his late forties. He is just under six feet tall and red faced. He is clean shaven to the point where he looks as if he doesn't grow facial hair. His hair is light brown and neatly cut and combed. He is wearing a dark blue uniform with the company name over one breast pocket and his first name over the other. Just below his collar is a round gray pin that reads "STEWERD" in black letters.

"Hi. I'm Paul Wilker" Paul said reaching his right hand out.

"Ray Webber, What can I do for you" he said shaking Paul's hand firmly.

"Well, where I work, the steward is injured and out of work so I'm the assistant steward and will be filling in for him. I thought you could possibly answer a few questions for me about unions. You see, I don't have much knowledge about this."

Two canteen trucks pulled up and the striking workers gathered around them.

"Coffee?" Ray asked Paul.

"Yeah, sounds good."

Paul and Ray went over and got in line by the first truck. They bought coffee and doughnuts and moved away to a less crowded area. Paul told Ray about the union and how he is planning to submit a proposal to the management for more money, more vacation and more sick leave. Ray is interested in the union but speaks frankly with Paul.

"A company union like that never works and you say the dues or most of them go for the company cookout each year? That don't sound very good" Ray said grinning slightly.

"I don't think the company is gonna go for the proposal either. These companies want you to work your ass off and when it comes time for more money, they balk like hell. From what you're saying, you will be fighting for these things alone."

Paul told Ray how he thinks these guys are leaning on him because they don't like him. He also told him that he is going to call their bluff and submit a proposal.

"These guys do good work and they work hard. In all honesty, they should get more pay and extended benefits but none of them seem to have the nut to push for it" Paul said.

Paul and Ray talked a little more and Ray reached in one of his breast pockets and took out a small pad of paper and a ball point pen. He wrote his name and telephone number down and handed it to Paul.

"Gimme a call anytime you need advice and I wish you luck."

'Good luck to you too with this strike and thanks very much" Paul said.

"Like I said, call me if you need help with anything but I really think you're wasting your time." Ray said backing away and heading toward the group that he was talking to before.

Paul stood and looked at the picketers for a minute and then slowly walked back across the street to his car. He put Ray's note in his wallet and got into his car.

CHAPTER NINE

Allendale, like Southbrook, has been a very small town until recently. Only in the late fifties did it begin to build up. Before the second World War, there were mostly small farms and lots of vacant wooded land. A small textile mill employed some of the residents from Allendale and its surrounding towns but the mill closed down in 1954.

Right after the war started, the government found Allendale to be an ideal town for an army training camp and several supply depots. The main reasons for their interests was that Allendale is located right next to a state highway and also that the railroad runs through it. They built two supply depots and ran a railroad track spur right beside them. Boxcars were parked beside the rear loading platform and loaded or unloaded.

After the war, the training camps and supply depots were no longer used. The railroad spur is now rusted from years of not being used. One of the buildings is the one that the publishing company bought. It is a one story wooden frame building with a large loading dock and three large overhead doors. Inside there is a ten ton gantry crane supported by steel I—beam framework, and runs the length of the building. The crane is controlled from the floor with an electrical box that is suspended from a long cable. The plant can function without it but since it is there, it will be used to place the large rolls of newsprint onto the presses. It will be used to unload the new presses from the trucks and placed in their designated spots. The building is outfitted with metal framed windows on both sides. An office will be constructed on one end and the washrooms will be updated.

The building next to this is divided into two businesses. There is a small hardware store in one part and an automobile repair shop in the other. Beyond that building there is a lumber yard and across the street, a diner.

Paul parked his car in front of the building and opened the door with the key that Brent had given him. The building has been completely cleaned out and is ready to be painted and wired for the new set up. As soon as the new presses arrive and are unpacked, the building will then be set up. He looked at the paper that Brent had given him and went over the proposed floor layout. As far as Paul can detect, it appears to be well planned. The outside loading platform will be most useful for unloading the thousand pound rolls of newsprint and loading of the published material. Paul feels that this will work out quite well. He is beginning to look forward to managing this plant.

That evening, after spending a short time with Norma at her house, Paul went to his apartment and drew up a proposal with the workers requests to present to Brent the following morning. He listed pay increases, seniority rights, more sick leave and more vacation time based on length of service. He has not proposed any drastic requests but fair ones he feels. He will present it to the union body in the morning.

Lester is laying in his hospital bed with his leg in a cast. He has been given pain medication and is feeling somewhat better that he was earlier. His wife has been in to see him and left about seven thirty. He had been operated on very early in the morning to repair the broken places in his leg. At just after eight o'clock, his bedside telephone rang. He picked up the receiver and answered the call. It is Fletcher on the other line.

"Hello" Lester said in a sleepy voice.

"Hey. Are you gonna live?" Fletcher asked laughing slightly.

"I'll live. What's going on?"

"Well this Wilker is gonna tell Brent Royce that we all want raises and other shit. He asked us if we'd strike if we didn't get it."

"What the hell is he doin that for? Why is he gonna do that?" Lester said loudly into the telephone.

Fletcher told Lester that he and Art and Denny and several other men had tried to put Paul on the spot and how they figured that he would get flustered and back down.

"Jesus, that was a real dumb ass thing to do; real dumb ass."

"He sounded serious the way . . . ."

"Shut up! I'm thinking" Lester interrupted.

Lester paused for a few more seconds. He is no longer as groggy as when Fletcher first called him. His leg is painful but he is concentrating more on this business.

"Get the guys together first thing in the morning and when he comes in, play along and act like you're all in favor of it. He'll look real stupid later but so what. He's going to Allendale before long."

"Well, he ain't done it yet so maybe he won't but he sounded like he is gonna" Fletcher said.

"Clay would throw you guys out into the road and call in your loans too if you guys went on strike, don't forget that!" Lester said sharply.

"Could he do that?" Fletcher asked meekly.

"Christ sakes, just do what I told you .... And don't give this nut any more ideas! Call me tomorrow night and let me know what's goin on!"

"Ok" Fletcher said.

Lester hung up the phone without saying good bye. He reached to the table beside his bed and picked up the newspaper that is there and began to read it. He will call Edwin later that evening and let him know what was happening. He has everything under control. He knows that Edwin will not agree to anything that is proposed and that Paul will look like a jackass when everyone votes against it later.

The following morning, Fletcher arrived at the plant one hour early as he always did. He told Art and several of the other men that worked in his crew what the plan is. By the time that Paul walked in, the word was out. They did not tell George Baxter because it is evident that he likes Paul but George isn't stupid and will figure it out before long.. Lester has worked at the publishing company for many years. Fletcher has too but not as long as Lester has. Fletcher controls his crew and the other workers follow along.

When Paul came into the press area, he walked over to where all of the men are gathered. He is carrying a brown manila envelope which contains the proposal that he has prepared.

"This is a good time to bargain for these items. There are a lot of jobs coming up with overtime available. Here, pass it around. I will get copies made later" Paul said handing the proposal to Fletcher.

"So what are we supposed to do now?" Art said to Paul in a sarcastic tone.

"Read it over and tell me if this is what you guys want. Hey, you guys wanted to know what I am going to do for you. This is what

I'm doing and it's up to you to decide what you want me to do" Paul said right back to him.

"We all want it. Go show it to Brent Royce" Fletcher said handing the papers back to Paul.

"Are you sure . . . . every one's sure?" Paul asked.

All of the men in the pressroom areas are now gathered around Paul and showing their agreement. The buzzer sounded and the men slowly begin to go to their respected work areas. The employees who worked in the office in paste up and design are not hourly. They are salary so they are not in the union.

Paul took the job sheets and went in to give them to Jenny. She looked up at him when he entered and stopped typing.

"You must be counting the hours now" Paul said.

"Counting the hours?" she asked and then realized that Paul means her upcoming week's vacation.

"I can't wait. But I know that once I'm out the week will fly by. They always do" she said laughing slightly.

"We've gotta figure out how to get the work weeks to fly by the same way" Paul said.

"Is Brent here yet?"

"He is. He is in his office" Jenny said

"Thanks. I'll talk to you later" Paul said to her as he headed towards Brent's office.

Paul went in to Brent's office. He is looking over some papers and looked up and then back at the papers.

"Seeing as how Lester is out, I've decided to have you work with Gus Tanner next week and remain on days rather that do the second shift with Marcus. Gus will train you to be a pressman so when you get to Allendale, you'll be able to manage it."

"OK. I have drawn up a proposal and am presenting it to you on behalf of the union members."

Little did Paul know that Brent is already aware of the proposal. Edwin had telephoned him at home last night and filled him in on what is going on. He told Brent how Lester is handling the situation. The only reason that Edwin is going along with any of this is due to Rita. She really likes Paul and wants nothing more than to see he and Norma married. Edwin is walking on eggs with Rita nowadays and he knows where he stands.

Brent looked over the proposal and pretended to be surprised a little. Paul has entered wage increase figures and the other requests for seniority rights and vacation time also.

"I'll have to discuss this with Clay and see. There are a lot of demands here."

"You have good qualified people here they get the jobs out on time and done well. The cost of everything is rising steadily" Paul said softly.

"I'll get back to you" Brent said and resumed his paperwork that he was doing when Paul had entered.

Paul headed for the pressroom and was just at the door when Jenny called him.

"Paul, I have Lester on line two for you. Take in my office if you like."

She held the door open for Paul as he approached her office.

"Hello Lester. How are you doing?"

"I'm sore. What's goin on there? I hear you're trying to get a contract approved."

"Well the men agreed to it so I submitted it" Paul said.

Jenny held out a piece of Doublemint chewing gum to Paul. Paul accepted it and nodded his head to thank her.

"Well you keep me posted on what happens" Lester said.

"All right" Paul said and hung up the phone. Lester has really played dumb just as Brent has done. As Paul walked out into the pressroom and headed down to where George Baxter and Owen are, he realizes that someone has notified Lester what is going on.

"Probably Fletcher" Paul said quietly to himself.

The rest of the week went smoothly. Paul informed Fletcher and the other men in the union that he has submitted the proposal and will give Brent and Edwin time to go over it and come back with a counter offer. The men are going along with Paul as Lester has instructed them to do. On Thursday, Jenny came out on the floor and told Paul that Brent wants him to go out to Alllendale the next morning because the electricians are going to come there and turn on the power. They will also figure out what they will need to wire the presses.

"Paul, I'm leaving at noon tomorrow to start my vacation so I probably won't see you for a week" she said as she handed him the keys to the Allendale building.

Paul is banding up a skid of printed flyers and stopped and walked up close to Jenny.

"Ah Jenny girl, I'll miss your smiling face every morning I will, but you have a great time and don't think about this place" Paul said smiling widely at her and placing his hand on her shoulder.

Jenny's heart sped up a little and she blushed like a school girl. She waved quickly as she walked back to her office. She thought to herself "I won't think of the company much but I'll think of you Paul, plenty."

She feels strongly about Paul but she does not want to be in love with him. She has those feelings but knows that he and Norma are going to be married. She has made up here mind that when she gets to her aunt's house in Perkinsville, she will get busy and try not to have those thoughts. She has a girlfriend, Sandy, that she went to school with and they talk on the phone at least three or four times a week. She told her about Paul and that she is afraid that she is falling for him. Sandy told her to go out with other guys but Jenny doesn't want to, not yet. Who knows what the future holds she has thought to herself. Sandy does not live too far from Jenny's aunt's house so she plans on seeing her next week.

The next morning, Friday, Paul got up early and drove straight to Allendale. He stopped at a diner along the way and had two dropped eggs on wheat toast, tomato juice, home fries and coffee. The two electricians arrived about forty five minutes after Paul got to the plant. They installed some new overhead lights, some new wall outlets, and turned the power on. They made sure that overhead crane was working properly. They were finished just before three o'clock and shortly afterwards Paul headed back to the Saxon plant.

Paul parked his car and went in through the side door which leads directly into the pressroom. He headed towards Brent's office to report what has been completed at the Allendale plant.

"Hey Wilker" Fletcher yelled from the further end of the pressroom. He waved his arm repeatedly for Paul to come to him.

"Jesus, what the hell does this guy want now?" Paul muttered to himself.

When he reached Fletcher, Art and Denny had come over and are standing beside him.

"Bill Pyle got canned right after lunch. His wife can't work and he gotta have his job back and you gotta get it for him."

'Yeah, you're the big union man now and you gotta help him" Art said to Paul leaning forward slightly.

Fletcher started to say something but Paul interrupted him.

"Wait a minute . . . . stop. Why was he let go. What happened?"

"He backed into a trailer truck that was delivering paper. Flipped the fork lift over and screwed it up" Fletcher said. "He wants you to call him at home."

"Was he injured" Paul asked?"

"No but he wants you to call him" Fletcher repeated.

"Well the first thing I'm doing is find out what Brent has to say and then I will call Lester."

Both Fletcher and Art looked like they were going to say something.

"I will handle this" Paul said and walked away towards Brent's office where he was headed before.

When Paul entered Brent's office he was on the telephone. Brent pointed to the chair next to his desk for Paul to sit down. Several minutes went by and Brent hung up.

"How did you make out at Allendale?" he asked turning around in his chair to face Paul.

"Good. They got everything done that you listed. Things there are pretty much set for when the new presses arrive."

"All right Monday, I want you to work with Gus Tanner on his press. He has three big publishing jobs to do and he'll show you the ropes so you'll know what to do."

"What happened with Bill Pyle? I heard he got let go."

"He sure did. He backed into one of the delivery trucks and overturned the fork lift. We sent him to the hospital and they said that he had been drinking. No good" Brent said shaking his head.

"Why are you asking Paul?"

"I was told that he wants me to call him. He may try to fight it but I won't know till I speak to him."

"He's dreaming" Brent said.

"I'll let you know when I hear more" Paul said heading for the door.

Paul headed out into Jenny's office. Paul noticed that Phyllis Thompson is there instead and then he remembered that Jenny had told him that she was leaving early. Phyllis has worked there before and was replaced by Jenny when she retired. She fills in if Jenny is out.

Paul has never met Phyllis before.

"Hi, I'm Paul Wilker" he said reaching out to shake her hand.

"Hello Paul" Phyllis said as she shook his hand.

Just then Brent came through the office and announced that he was leaving. Paul walked out into the pressroom and headed down to the press where George and Owen are working. Gus Tanner looked back at Paul.

"You gonna be working here now Paul?" he said

Paul nodded his head. Gus turned up the speed now that he had two people jogging.

The second shift help began coming in and as soon as the buzzer sounded, Paul stopped and went to the men's room to wash his hands. He wants to go to his apartment so he can call Lester and inform him what is going on with Bill Pyle. He wants to return Bill's call too. He remembered that Ray Webber had given him his home telephone number. Paul figured he would see what advice Ray can provide to aid him.

As soon as he got home, Paul called Lester at the hospital. He began to tell Lester what had happened but to his surprise, Lester already had been informed about Bill's dismissal from the plant.

"I got a message that Bill wants me to call him at his home" Paul said.

"How should I handle this Lester?"

"Don't handle anything. Pyle's a useless drunk. He was shitfaced and cracked up the forklift. Let em fire his ass" Lester said in a snarling tone.

"Oh I don't think we should do that . . . I mean we at least should look into the whole situation" Paul said.

"My doctor's here. I gotta go" Lester said and quickly and hung up.

Paul has Bill Pyle's telephone number that he had obtained from Phyllis before he left work. He dialed the number and waited for an answer.

"Hullo" a woman's raspy voice said on the other end.

"Mrs. Pyle?" Paul asked.

"Yeah. Who's this?"

"Hi. I'm Paul Wilker and I am the acting union delegate at Rollins Publishing. I'd like to speak to Bill about what happened at work."

"He's gone off. He ain't here. Can you get him back to work cause we're done for if you can't. I'm crippled and can't do much" Mrs. Pyle replied with her voice shaky and sounding as if she was on the verge of tears.

"I'd like to come by your house and talk to both you and Bill. Tomorrow is Saturday. Would that be ok, perhaps in the morning?"

"Yeah. Come at eleven, alright?" Mrs. Pyle asked hoarsely.

'That's fine. Eleven is fine" Paul said. "Where is it that you live?"

"Our house is at the edge of town. Go straight through Saxon on Main Street and when you get to the Maple street intersection, turn left. We're at fifty five" Mrs. Pyle said.

"Ok, I can find it."

"Thank you Mr. Wilker" she said.

"Please" I'mPaul."

Paul hung up the receiver and sat back in his chair for a minute. He pulled out his wallet and looked for Ray Webber's telephone.

Paul dialed Ray's number and sat back in his chair. After several rings, a woman answered.

"Hello" she said pleasantly.

"Hello, I'm calling to speak to Ray Webber if possible."

"Can I ask who is calling?" she asked.

"Yes. I am Paul Wilker. He may not remember me but I spoke with him recently in front of the chemical plant. I just have several questions for him."

"Just a minute Paul" she said.

"Hon, there's a Paul Wilker for you on the phone" she called as she walked away from the phone.

Ray answered the phone and after Paul reminded him about their meeting, Ray remembered him.

"Oh yeah Paul. What's up?"

Paul explained to him the problem with Bill Pyle and is wondering if he can possibly give him some ideas how to conduct the meeting with Brent when the time comes.

Ray could not have been any more help. He gave Paul a good plan of action and they talked for almost a half an hour. He told Paul that his union and the company have not reached an agreement as of yet. When Paul hung up the telephone, he now feels much more positive about the impending situation. He feels fortunate to know Ray.

Paul and Norma went out for supper at a local eating spot. Norma casually brought up the business about him presenting the proposal to Brent and also his choice to defend Bill Pyle. Paul explained to her that because he is filling in for Lester, he has to represent the union body to the best of his ability.

After they ate, they went outside and got into Norma's car. Paul is surprised that once inside, she is all over him. She is repeatedly kissing him with her arms, tightly pulling him against her.

"Just be careful my sweetheart. Don't do anything you'll regret later" she whispered to Paul.

Her mouth is just an inch away from his as she spoke. Her breath feels hot and smells like the after dinner mints that she got at the counter when he paid the check.

After they went back to Norma's house, Paul kissed her goodnight and drove to his apartment. He is very tired and lapses into sleep quickly.

Chapter ten

Bill Pyle is fifty five years old and has worked for the Rollins Publishing Company for twelve years. His main job is loading and unloading trucks with the company fork truck. He also makes deliveries with the company truck if they are within a fifty mile radius. Bill is five feet ten inches tall and is heavily built at two hundred and sixty pounds. He has a full head of gray hair and has it cut short. His face is drawn with sagging cheeks. Bill is a constant complainer and never really seems very pleased with anything. He is a bit on the ignorant side and fits in well with Fletcher and his cronies, but even they become tired with his constant wining at times.

He does however show up for work every day and up until this incident, was considered to be good at what he does. Bill is a drinker and few weekends go by that he isn't "feeling no pain" as they say. Many mornings he has shown up for work hung over but not to the point that he could not perform his duties. Apparently on the day of the accident, Bill had gone out on his lunch hour, cashed his paycheck, and had two bottles of beer and a nip of brandy.

He and his wife have a married son in his late twenties and a married teenaged daughter. His daughter and her husband live with Bill and his wife. Bill's wife is six years younger that he is and was badly injured in an automobile crash some years earlier. Her hips were both broken along with her pelvis. Her knees were also badly injured which has reduced her to using two canes most of the time. She does clothes mending at home to help out with the finances.

Bill was a drinker and a complainer before this happened but all this has not made his nature any better. On his positive side, he has always provided for his family pretty much and has taken care of his wife since her injuries. If his job here is lost, the family will be severely set back.

Paul turned onto Maple Street and notices the he is at the high end with the house numbers in the two hundreds. As he drives along, he notices that the houses are mostly single story with small yards. Some have unattached garages and the homes butt up against other homes behind them that face the opposite direction to next street over. Most of the yards are small and well kept and the neighborhood appears to be inhabited by working class people; a far cry from the other end of Saxon where Norma's family live. Paul slowed down when he reached the houses with the sixty numbers and then he spotted number fifty five. He recognized Bill Pyle's "58 green and white Ford station wagon parked at the end of the driveway.

Bill's house is a single story design similar to most of the others in the neighborhood. It has three small bedrooms, a full cellar and a small one car unattached garage located to the right side of the house as you are facing it. Both the garage and the house have a hip style roof. There is a small fenced in back yard. Most of the homes in this area were built in the twenties and the Pyle's have resided here for twenty two years. There are two very tall maple trees located in the backyard that provide more than adequate shade in the hot summer months.

Paul pulled his car up to the curb and parked it. He noticed that in front of Bill's station wagon there is a '51 Oldsmobile two door sedan. The car is gray with red rims and small hubcaps and has the Oldsmobile rocket 88 insignia on the trunk lid. The hood has been removed and is leaning against the stockade fence beside the driveway. The car's engine has been removed and is sitting on the grass beside the hood. In front of the car is an engine tripod with a chain hoist hanging from it. Directly beneath the tripod is another engine set on wooden blocks. It appears to have been freshly painted and has nice chrome valve covers. A nineteen year old boy is standing by the steps that lead to the side door of the Pyle's house, and seated on the steps is Bill's eighteen year old daughter. The boy is nice looking with a muscular build. His arms are toned and he looks as if he lifts weights. His hair is black and combed over to his right side. He has on blue jeans and a tight fitting black tee shirt. As Paul approached them, the boy looked over at him and spoke.

"Forty seven?" he said pointing out towards Paul's Plymouth.

"Forty eight" Paul answered.

"Looks pretty good" the boy said stepping out slightly so he could get a better look at the car.

"Thanks. Is this a new engine you have here? It looks sharp."

"Na. It's a used motor but I heard it run before I got it. My other motor blew a piston and wrecked the cylinder wall."

Both Paul and the boy walked over close to the engine and examined it.

"I'm looking for Bill Pyle" Paul said. "Is he at home?"

"I'll get him" the girl said.

As she slid forward to stand up, Paul noticed the she is very pregnant and looks as if she may have her baby at any time now. Her face is flushed and she looks to be hot from the weather. She has a pretty face and reddish, brown hair. She is wearing dark blue shorts and a light blue maternity top. As she struggled to stand, Paul asked her if she wanted him to go to the door instead of her getting up.

"No, that's ok. I want to get a Pepsi anyway" she answered grabbing onto the banister.

"Get me one too Babes" the boy said. "Want a soda?" he asked Paul.

"No . . . no thanks."

The girl opened the screen door and disappeared into the house.

"I'll have this car runnin tonight. My buddy's coming over to help me and we'll have this goin tonight, that is unless the wife there pops out the kid" the boy said as reached into the Oldsmobile and grabbed a package of cigarettes.

The girl came back out of the house with two bottles of Pepsi Cola and handed one to her husband. She returned to her spot on the steps and carefully sat back down. Several minutes passed and as she and turned back to the screen door, she saw that Bill was coming out.

'Hi Bill" Paul said walking over to him.

"Hi. So when am I goin back to work? I called Lester in the hospital and he told me you said you were gonna get me back to work."

"Let's go in the house. I want to talk to both you and your wife" Paul said quietly.

They went in through the kitchen and into the living room where Mrs. Pyle is seated in an oversized chair. Beside her are two canes. She is thin and has a drawn look on her face like someone who has been enduring pain for sometime. Her hair is cut short like a man's and her neck is lined. Bill went back into the kitchen and quickly returned with a can of Naragansettbeer and a package of Salem cigarettes.

"Hello, I'm Paul Wilker" he said nodding his head to Mrs. Pyle.

"I'm Ruth Pyle. Thank you for coming here. Bill, get him a beer" she said in a raspy voice.

Bill returned with a can of beer for Paul. Mrs. Pyle asked Bill for a cigarette. He handed it to her and snapped open his Zippo lighter and held it so she could light up. Paul sat down on the sofa and faced Ruth and Bill who is standing next to her.

"It ain't right them getting rid of me like this. It was a accident. The truck driver started backin up as I was goin behind him" Bill said raising his voice.

"The big problem here is that you were said to have been drinking when the doctor examined you" Paul said looking directly at Bill.

"Yeah, I told them I had a few beers at lunch but hell, Al Brown comes in half drunk and nobody's firin him. He misses a hell of a lot more time than I do too. I never miss time."

"That's true Bill but Al Brown isn't the one in question here" Paul said.

"They said that I run the fork lifts and drive the truck and could hurt people. Well hell, he works on the machinery there so he could hurt someone too bein loaded and all" Bill said still in a raised voice.

"That's true too but again, he's not the one in trouble here. Now I have discussed your situation with a man that I know who is an excellent union steward and he has given me some really great advice on how to handle this problem."

"Who, Lester?" Bill asked.

Paul couldn't help chuckling.

"No. This man works for another company and they have a large union."

The pregnant daughter came into the room and asked if there was any more Pepsi Cola.

"There's some more in the cellar but have Nick get it, don't you climb up and down the stairs" Ruth said to here daughter.

The girl left and shortly afterwards her husband came in and went down and brought up some more for her.

"I'm gonna go over to the cookout next weekend and see Clay and tell him he gotta let me have my job back" Bill said walking over to Paul.

"No, no don't do that, do not do that" Paul said firmly. He imagined Bill going over there half bunned and making matters worse.

"Yeah, well I worked there a long time and it ain't right."

"Bill, be quiet and listen to Mr. Wilker" Ruth said, her voice cracking as she raised it.

"Please, call me Paul. Now I have set up a meeting with Brent Royce to try to resolve this. At this time I'd like you to be present Bill, but I'll do the talking. I'm also going to indicate that you are considering hiring a lawyer if this cannot be settled with Brent."

"A lawyer?" Ruth asked.

"If we can't come to some sort of an arrangement but I really think that we can settle this without too much of a problem" Paul answered.

"Jesus, how are we going to pay for a lawyer?" Bill borrowed twelve hundred from Mr. Clay and they said when they let him go, that he has to pay that right up. We can't do that" Ruth said on the verge of tears.

"Don't worry about that yet" Paul said looking sympathetically.

"One thing is very important here Bill. You must tell them that you will no longer have any alcoholic beverages at lunch time and you must not" Paul warned.

"Wait a minute, that's my lunch hour. I can do what I want on my lunch hour!" Bill snapped.

"You have got to realize Bill, if I can get you back, they are going to be watching for you to mess up and if it's even suspected that you have been drinking and operating equipment, that'll be it for you" Paul said standing up.

"Bill, listen to him. He's right" Ruth Pyle said as smoke came from her mouth and nose.

"Now Brent Royce is out on vacation next week but he said that he will meet with us the following week. I'll call you if anything changes. It was nice meeting you Mrs. Pyle."

Ruth stood up very slowly from her chair and with both of her canes, she followed unsteadily behind Paul and Bill out into the kitchen and over to the side door leading outside.

Paul turned back and faced them then started out the door. "I'll call you and let you know the exact time of the meeting as soon as I find out myself."

"Thank you Mr. Wilker . . . . I mean Paul" Ruth said with a strained smile.

Paul carefully stepped down around Bill's daughter who is still seated on the rear steps.

"Bye now. Maybe the next time I see you, you'll be ready to get Mother's Day cards" Paul said to her.

"Yeah, maybe. Bye" she said back to Paul.

Paul walked by the boy who was attaching the lifting chain to the engine that would be put into the Oldsmobile. His friend had arrived and was standing beside the tripod.

"Hey, good luck with the engine huh" Paul said walking close to him.

"Thanks man. Take it slow on the curves" he said moving his head back and smiling.

Paul turned his car around and headed back down Maple Street the way he came. His thoughts are not of Bill Pyle but of Norma. He had had a dream last night in which she was really passionate. She kept whispering to him "Let's do it. Let's do it now . . . . here." Then they began some serious foreplay and he awoke suddenly. He lay in bed hoping that when he got back to sleep, the dream would resume but of course it did not. He thought that it would be so nice if dreams were like movie projectors. If the dream stopped you could go back to sleep, start it back up again, and pick up where you left off.

Paul remembered a dream that he had not long ago. In this sequence, he is walking in an open field surrounded on three sides by a dense pine forest. It is daylight and ahead of where he is walking, there is an old rusty barbed wire fence fastened to weathered wooden posts. When he reaches the fence he stops and looks down at the highway about one hundred feet away.

The cars and trucks passing by in both directions are all pre World War Two models. There are no vehicles newer than that. Across the highway is a service station that is set back from the traffic, and behind that . . . . there is *nothing!* Even though it is bright daylight where he is standing, it is pitch black there. No trees, no rock ledges, no sky . . . . *nothing!* It is like the earth ended there. He has always has wanted to have that dream again so he can attempt to cross the highway and investigate it further but it has never happened yet.

He keeps thinking about his dream with Norma the night before. He figures he will call her when he gets his apartment and hopefully they will go to dinner and then the drive-in theater. He also began thinking about Bill Pyle and how his household is; his crippled wife and his pregnant daughter and son in law living with them. He definitely needs his job back because a person with his background and age will have a problem finding a different job.

As soon as Paul left the Pyle's home, Bill picked up the telephone and called Lester. He told him what Paul has proposed to him to do at the upcoming meeting with Brent. Lester listened intently and then took credit for Paul's ideas.

"That's what we agreed on when we discussed this. Wilker's handling things but I'm still calling the shots. You keep your mouth shut Pyle and don't talk to anybody about this" Lester said.

"Oh yeah . . . yeah . . . Sure . . . sure Lester. I won't say nothing."

Lester is great at taking credit for things that are positive in his behalf and passing the buck when it will not be in his favor. He has always been a smooth operator.

That night, Paul and Norma went out and had a light supper and went over to Oldensburg to the open air theater. "Dead Ringer" with Bette Davis and Karl Malden was the feature film. Neither of them had seen it when it first came out earlier in the year. Paul left his convertible roof up so he and Norma could do some serious hugging and kissing. Norma has on white short shorts and a black sleeveless top. She looks very sexy and desirable. After a while she started talking to Paul about the company cookout at her parent's home the following weekend. She slouched backwards in the seat and rested her knees up against the dashboard and her head against the backrest.

"Oh Paul, the cookouts are so much fun. You'll have a blast."

"I'm kinda uncomfortable at stuff like that; I mean I'll go but I'll be uncomfortable" Paul said.

The real reason that Paul is not relishing the thought of the cookout is that he knows that Fletcher and Denny and some of the other guys from that end of the pressroom that aren't overly fond of him will be there.

"Oh you bet your ass you'll go!" Norma said sharply as she sat back up straight in the seat again.

"That will not fit well at all with my Dad if you don't come to that" Norma said looking directly at Paul.

"I said I'd go."

"You're going to be managing your own plant soon and you must be able to communicate with your employees" Norma said still looking right at him.

"Besides, Lester told Brent that you are unfriendly to some of the guys and that you avoid them."

"What!" Paul said shocked. "There are several people there that don't like me because of the fact that we are engaged and that I got the job that I have because of that" Paul said as he began to get slightly angry. "That's one of the reasons that I submitted that union proposal to Brent. They challenged me and I am calling their bluff."

This infuriated Paul that Lester said that to Brent.

"What guys? Who are you talking about?" Norma asked sternly.

"Fletcher, Denny and Art and a few more. They said that I was rude to them? That is the joke of the day . . . no, make that the joke of the week."

Norma snuggled up tight against Paul. She doesn't want to upset him too much. Things are looking really good for Brent and her.

"No more quarreling sweetheart" she said softly.

She kissed him with her lips parted.

"Just be nice at the cookout" she said beaming at him. "You can do it."

Paul looked at her face which is radiant in the light that is coming off of the movie screen. He thought to himself that he can do this. After all, Norma will be there and George too. He will keep with them as much as possible. "I can do this. I'll be alright" he said to himself.

The following week went by fairly smoothly with two calls from Bill Pyle. Both times Paul had to remind him that nothing can really be done until the next week when Brent returns from his vacation. Bill does not listen very well. He is much better at talking than he is at listening. Paul thought about what Uncle Ike used to say when he had to deal with people like Bill. He would say "GOD gave us two ears and one mouth . . . maybe he was trying to tell us something". Paul misses seeing Jenny in the office too because she is off this week. Phyllis is friendly and nice but she isn't Jenny.

There is a big job that Gus Tanner is setting up for so Paul will work with him and George and Owen the whole week. Paul now knows the set up procedures and is capable of being a pressman. He feels capable of running the Allendale plant and knows that it will be a learning experience at first. He is nervous about undertaking it but he figures he will try his best. Gus is a good teacher and a nice guy.

CHAPTER ELEVEN

Paul woke up Saturday morning and for a few seconds has forgotten that this is the day of the big cookout. Norma has asked him to arrive early and help to set things up. He showered, shaved and got dressed. He had a quick bowl of grape nuts and a glass of orange juice before he left.

When he arrived, he parked his car on the side of the Clay's driveway in case he decides to leave before some of the others. He really isn't looking forward to doing this. As he walked out into the back yard, Norma came over and gave him a quick kiss. She has on a pair of khaki shorts and a white blouse. She is barefoot and her toenails and fingernails are painted a light pink shade.

"Hi sweetie" she said. "Can you give Wanda's sons a hand setting up the tables?" she asked.

"Sure thing" Paul said pleased that he could help out.

Wanda and her husband and her sons are doing all of the cooking. They have hamburgers with cheese, sausages, steak tips, chicken wings and of course potato salad and corn on the cob. There is a bar set up and a local bartender has been hired to serve the guests. Wanda's sons are nice young men and Paul likes them right off the bat. Paul and the boys set the tables up next to the barbeque. They spread out the table cloths and brought out the plates and forks and the knives along with the spoons.

"Hey, there's my special guy" Rita said as she approached Paul. "You're looking fine as usual".

Rita gave Paul a nice firm squeeze and kissed him on his cheek.

"Hi Rita. I always look forward to seeing you" Paul said blushing slightly.

Rita leaned forward and said softly to Paul, "I can't wait to have you for my son in law."

"Eddie, Paul's here" she called to her husband.

"Paul" Edwin said to Paul in a cool tone.

He must be upset because of the business at the plant with the proposal and the Bill Pyle incident. I am only doing what is expected of me Paul thought to himself.

"Paul, over here" George Baxter called out to him.

Paul walked over and joined George who was standing with Owen and Gus Tanner. They are all drinking beer. They talked together for a short while and Paul noticed that not too far away, Fletcher, Denny and Art are congregated along with several other members of the crew. There are pitching horseshoes and judging by the yelling and laughing, they have been drinking a bit already.

"Hey Wilker" Fletcher yelled out beckoning with his arm for Paul to come over to where they are.

When Paul got close to them, Fletcher began asking him about the proposal and Bill Pyle.

"You doin anything?" Art asked in a surly tone.

"Yes. I have been to Bill Pyle's house and I plan to have a meeting with Brent Royce this coming week regarding both the proposal and Bill's case."

"What are ya waitin so long for?" Art asked again in the same tone.

"Well if you recall, Brent was on vacation last week" Paul said trying not to show his uneasiness.

Denny has his usual imbecilic smirk on his face and said nothing.

Paul noticed that the men are looking past him and began smiling. He turned and saw that Norma is coming over to where they are standing.

"Hey Norma. How are ya?" Fletcher asked looking her up and down.

"Hi guys. Paul I've got to see you" she said turning and walking away from the men.

Paul followed her over to a private place.

"I've got to leave. Brent and Meredith had a huge fight and I have to go to her. She is really upset. I'm sorry but I must go" she said concerned.

"Aw Jesus. Alright" Paul said. "Yeah, I understand."

"Remember what I said before about trying to get along better with the other guys Paul. Stop being rude and socialize."

He felt that pang of anger he felt before when she suggested this but he refrained from commenting on it.

"I don't know how long I'll be so let me call you later. Love you" she said and quickly kissed him goodbye.

Of course, Paul nor anyone else know what is happening here, except of course for Brent and Norma. Brent created the argument with Meredith. Afterwards he stalked out of the house and left. This has been planned ahead of time with both he and Norma. They plan to meet at Brent's parent's home that is empty due to the fact that they are vacationing in France and England. Norma and Brent have not been able to get together for three weeks and this will work out perfectly. They can easily spend several hours together, maybe a little more. They'll use Brent's car so if for some unlikely reason Meredith shows up there, Norma will hide out and there is no reason why Brent should not be there. He has in fact, been checking on the house regularly while his parents are abroad.

Paul went back and joined George and began talking to him again. After about ten minutes, they decided to get something to eat. As they were approaching the food table, Paul heard a pleasant voice behind him.

"Hi Paul" he heard.

It is Jenny and she looks really different. She has her hair cut shorter and styled. Along with the lipstick that she usually wears, she also has made up her eyes with makeup and she looks as if she has spent some time in the sun. She is wearing a sleeveless white sun dress with small pink flowers on it. It is fitted to her body down to the waist and then it flares out fully and ends just above her knees. It is slightly low cut and she has a display of small freckles in her cleavage which is more prominent due to her tan. She is barelegged and has on black flat shoes. She is not wearing her glasses and for the first time, Paul notices that her left eye does not look directly at you when her right eye does. It is very slight and Paul feels that this actually adds to her attractiveness.

"Jenny! Gee whiz, a week off sure agrees with you. You look terrific" Paul said standing back and admiring her.

"Hey, I'm the same person" Jenny said blushing and slightly giggling.

"So how was the vacation?" Paul asked.

"Well, it was great except like all vacations, it went by really fast."

"Oh yeah. They sure do don't they" Paul said shaking his head slightly.

Jenny said hello to George and Owen and proceeded to the food table. Paul is not very hungry so he just ate a small portion of potato salad and drank a can of Coca Cola. The temperature is just over ninety degrees and the air is oppressive with humidity. Many of the guests brought swimsuits and plan on using the pool later.

After Paul finished eating, he walked around the back yard and noticed that Jenny is standing off to the side by herself. He walked over to where she is and asked her if she is enjoying herself.

"I am kind of uncomfortable at things like this. I mean I know everybody here but I guess I'm not really a party person. Does that sound silly to you Paul?"

"No it does not because I'm the same way. When I was growing up, my parents didn't have a lot of social events so I guess I really never had a lot of practice".

"So where is Norma?" Jenny asked.

"She left. I guess that Brent and Meredith had a big argument so she went to be with her. This has happened before too. Meredith is a really nice person and I don't know what is going on there. Not my business I guess."

Paul noticed that Fletcher, Denny, Art, and several other men from their group were headed over to where he was. Fletcher had been drinking boiler makers and was noticeably intoxicated. He walked up and put his arm around Jenny.

"Hey lady, yer lookin pretty sharp here. C'mon over and let me get you a beer" he said slurring slightly.

Jenny cocked her head and moved out from under his arm.

"What the matter. Come over and be where the fun is."

"Take it easy Fletcher or you'll have a big head tomorrow" Paul said jokingly."

"Never mind me Wilker. You get Pyle back to work. You get him back."

"How come you never talk like this to Lester" Paul said heatedly.

"Cause he's a good union man that'll fight for ya" Fletcher said pointing at Paul.

"Hey Wilker. If your shit box won't start we'll give ya a push" Art said smirking as they walked off.

He realized that this was booze talking but Paul thought to himself "Gee, a good union man. He sure did good by that Melvin Pine and what was it he said about Bill Pyle; something to the effect that he is a hopeless drunk and should be fired. Oh yeah, a great union man."

Paul looked at Jenny who has a sympathetic look on her face.

"Jenny, I'm leaving. I have to put up with this crap all week and I don't need to on my days off."

"I'm stuck here. My car's in the shop and I came here with Margie from billing. She told me she was going to stay here until late tonight and she'll probably be pretty drunk so it looks like I'll be stuck here." Jenny said looking straight into Paul's eyes.

"You told me you live in Greengrove didn't you?"

"Uh huh. That's where my apartment is."

"I have to go there this afternoon to visit my father. I'd be more than happy to drive you home if you want to leave but I gotta get out of here" Paul said.

"Let's go" Jenny said with a small grin.

They went out and got into Paul's Plymouth and pulled down the driveway and out onto Temple Street. Paul has the top down and the humid air blowing on them is somewhat refreshing.

"Did you want me to raise the top?" he asked Jenny.

"Oh no. I love convertibles. I've never had one but I do love them. This car is neat. Where did you find it?"

Paul told her how he had bought it from Butch and she really seemed interested. He told her about his aunt Polly that lives in Brooklyn In New York and still has a '41 Plymouth convertible.

"I used to go and visit her in the late forties when I was a kid. She would take me and her son, my cousin Ira, to Coney Island and Jones Beach on those hot summer days. We would always have the top down and it was then that I knew I wanted to get a Plymouth convertible. Claire used to come with us sometimes and me and her would sit in the back seat and laugh at Ira and aunt Polly. All they did was argue. Ira would be telling Polly how to drive and she'd tell him to keep quiet. Aunt Polly always had a cigarette in her mouth and the ashes would fall on her dress or the car seat. Oh, I can remember that like it happened yesterday."

"Who is Claire?" Jenny asked.

"She lived next door to them and she and Ira eventually got married. They live upstairs in Polly's house and have a boy and a girl now."

"Wow, she still has that car?" Jenny asked.

"Yeah. I guess my uncle Glenn, her husband, worked in the Brooklyn Navy Yard before World War two. As I understand it, one day, he and a couple of his buddies left work at noon and went to a bar and got feeling good. After an hour or so they decided to go to the movies and I guess they were having a drawing and the top prize was a brand new Plymouth convertible."

"So he won the car? That is so cool" Jenny said laughing.

"He did. A day or so later the theater got in touch with him and he took Polly and Ira down there and surprised them. When the war broke out, Uncle Glenn enlisted in the Navy. When he left, he told Polly to make sure she kept the Plymouth in good shape for him."

"So they've kept it all these years. That's great" Jenny said with her left elbow resting on top of the seat back and facing Paul.

"Unfortunately, Uncle Glenn was killed at sea. His ship was torpedoed and lost. Poor aunt Polly.

"She never got over that and I'm sure she will keep that car for as long as she can" Paul said.

"Oh Paul. That is sad. But I think it is so nice that she kept the car going all of this time."

"Its pretty much dented and faded now but she uses it almost every day. She never was a very good driver though. Back in '56, the engine was pretty worn out so she nursed it up here to my uncle Ike's garage and he pulled out the engine and completely rebuilt it. She stayed with us while Ike did the work."

"Paul, you said that you were going to see your father in Greengrove this afternoon. Does he live there?"

"He's a patient at the Longworth Sanitarium. He's been out there for ten years, ever since my mother died."

"Oh Paul, I'm sorry to hear that. That can't be easy for you" Jenny said.

"I'm taking him some cigarettes and his favorite, sardines and applesauce but it's really hard for me to go there. I do go often but I really find it depressing."

"Paul, it's right up ahead. Why don't you go in now to see your dad. I don't mind waiting and if you'd like, I'll come in with you. Maybe it will be a little easier for you this way. I mean . . . . to have someone with you."

Paul is floored. This is probably the kindest thing that anybody has ever offered to do for him. He glanced over at her in awe.

"Jenny, I couldn't ask you to do that. That is more than kind of you."

"You didn't. Here is the sanitarium up ahead. Pull in and we'll go ahead and see your father" she said pointing towards the sign.

A large white wooden sign which reads "MORTON B. LONGWORTH SANITARIUM" stands at the entrance. A high iron barred fence surrounds the entire property. A small guard building is situated at the point where visitors and personnel enter and exit.

Morton B. Longworth was a physician who specialized in mental disorders in people. He devoted his life helping to improve conditions for people suffering with these illnesses. When he started his medical practice, many people who had family members that were afflicted with mental disorders would keep them in basements or attics. It is said that one man was kept for years in a homemade house trailer with different people bringing him food. He went for most of his life never having medical or dental care.

The sanitarium is located at his former estate which he converted into the sanitarium in 1931. Dr. Longworth died in 1948 at age ninety eight. A bronze plaque with his name and image is fastened to the front of the building next to front entrance.

Paul turned into the driveway and stopped at the guard building. The man in the building knows him because he is usually on duty when he visits.

"Boy what a life you got. Convertible roof down and a pretty young lady with you. Watch out for this guy Miss, he can be trouble."

"Never mind the wisecracks, just drop the chain and let us in" Paul said right back to him.

"I think your dads out in back with his nurse" the guard said in a more serious tone.

"Thanks Ollie. Stay cool" Paul said as he drove forward slowly.

"He seems really nice" Jenny said looking back at the guards building.

"Yes, he's a swell guy. It would be hard to come here and have to deal with someone that is not friendly like he is" Paul answered.

He pulled his car around to the side of the building where the parking lot with shade trees is and shut the engine off. The air outside is very oppressive with humidity and the temperature is still over ninety. Jenny looks hot and Paul noticed that she has little beads of perspiration on her upper lip. She still looks very pretty despite the heat.

"Aw Jenny, I'm sorry. You look very warm. Are you sure you don't want me to take you home first?"

"Positive. Let's go find your dad."

Paul opened his trunk and took out a carton of Winston cigarettes, six cans of sardines, and a large jar of applesauce.

"That's kind of a different combination isn't it" Jenny asked pointing to the food that Paul was carrying.

"Dad has eaten this for as long as I remember. Mom used to leave the room when he did this."

They walked out to the very large back yard behind the sanitarium. The lawn is cut short and the shrubbery has been maintained regularly. There are patients with nurses or aids in different parts. They are seated under the many shade trees. Paul spotted his father sitting with Eileen, one of the nurses at the facility. As they got closer, Eileen pointed to Paul and Jenny.

"Look who's here Peter. You have company."

Peter, Paul's father, stood up quickly and walked briskly but a bit unsteadily up to Jenny and Paul.

He looks a bit older than his fifty nine years. His hair is snow white and his face is lined. He is about Paul's height and very gaunt. He has a confused and scared look on his face.

"Dad. Look what I brought you; your sardines . . . . and applesauce . . . . and some cigarettes."

"Oh Paul, I'm so glad you came. I can't find mother anywhere. Everyone's looking for her and . . . . and she cannot be found."

Peter has tears in his eyes and seems distraught. Eileen came up to them.

"I'll go get you some plates and some cold water" she said with a pleasant, friendly smile.

"This my friend Jenny. Jenny, meet Eileen."

"Hi Eileen" Jenny said with her bright smile.

"Dad, this is my friend Jenny" Paul said to his father.

"Hi Mr. Wilker" Jenny said looking directly into his sad, dark eyes.

"Are you in Paul's class at school?" Peter asked her.

"Dad, she works with me. Remember the last time I was here and I told you about my new job?"

"I'm getting worried because my wife is not around. She does this all of the time. She goes off and I can't find her" Peter said to Jenny.

Eileen returned with plates and some plastic knifes and spoons. She opened one of the cans of sardines with the key that came with it and emptied the contents onto the plate. After that, she added a helping of applesauce to the dish as well. One of the young aids came over with a large pitcher of ice water.

"Alright Peter, come sit and have your treat. Paul, can I see you for a minute?" Eileen asked.

As Paul walked from Peter's hearing distance with Eileen, he looked back and notices that Jenny has pulled a chair over and is seated beside his father.

"Paul, we are going to move your father upstairs onto the third floor. His physical health is good but he will receive more constant attention on that floor. Is that alright with you?" Eileen asked quietly.

"Sure. Whatever is best for him is what I want."

"OK then. If you can just sign this paper which just indicates that you agree to this move, I will submit it to the head nurse."

"Thanks Eileen" Paul said handing the form back to her.

They talked for a minute and then walked over to where Peter and Jenny were. Paul noticed that Jenny has taken a plate and is actually eating sardines and applesauce with his father. Her genuine kindness is overwhelming to Paul. Peter actually looks somewhat happy which is rare.

"Where did you find her Paul?" Eileen whispered close to Paul's ear. "She's a saint."

"Have some, have some more" Peter said to Jenny in a tone like a child would use.

"No, no. These are for you Mr. Wilker" Jenny said softly. "Paul brought them especially for you."

"Eileen, I want a cigarette. Get me a cigarette" Peter asked in a raised voice.

Eileen took one of the packs of cigarettes from the carton that Paul had brought. She opened the package and removed a cigarette. Peter took it from her and with a shaky hand put it into his mouth. Eileen lit it for him and he took large puffs from it.

Paul and Jenny sat for five more minutes with Peter and then Paul stood and announced that he is going to leave. Peter reached out to Jenny's right hand and squeezed it.

"Tell them to find my wife and bring her to me out here. Please tell them" he said almost begging her.

"Ok Mr. Wilker. I really enjoyed meeting you. Enjoy your sardines and applesauce" Jenny said bending slightly forward towards him.

Paul leaned forward and kissed his father on the forehead. "I love you dad. I'll be back to see you real soon. You're the best."

Paul and Jenny walked out to the parking lot and got into the Plymouth. The car is parked in the shade and there is a gentle breeze that has picked up which feels a little better. Jenny took her shoes off and folded her left leg up under her right, resting it on the seat. She positioned her left elbow up on top of the seat backrest and is resting her back against the car door and she is facing Paul.

"Paul, I feel so very bad about all that has happened to you and your father. Do you feel like telling me what happened to him? I understand if you don't."

"Jenny, I can't tell you how much I appreciate what you did today, I mean, you really made a hard situation much easier."

"I am glad to hear that Paul. This must be extremely depressing for you."

Paul turned and faced Jenny and placed his left forearm on top of the steering wheel. He proceeded to tell her the whole story of why his father is like he is now.

CHAPTER TWELVE

Norma and Brent entered the rear entrance of his parent's home. Brent had turned the air conditioner in the bedroom on earlier in the morning so the bedroom has cooled down nicely. They took a nice lukewarm shower together and then once in the bedroom, they went at each other like starved animals that haven't eaten in days and then have suddenly found food. They had intercourse two times almost in a row and then lay exhausted beside each other on the bed.

"So when are you going to marry Wilker?" Brent asked.

"Pretty soon but look at it this way darling, the sooner I marry him then the sooner we can be together. Remember our plan. It's going to work just fine."

"Hey, I don't like the idea of you screwing him" Brent said leaning up on one elbow.

"It won't mean anything to me and as soon as mother signs the business over to Meredith and I, then we will start setting up our divorces. Then we will really be together."

Norma pushed Brent over on his back and started kissing him passionately. This led to a third intercourse episode.

Everything is working out perfectly for them. They will have each other and the business and eventually the real estate. They just have to bide their time. They will have to realize however that they are not where they want to be yet. They have to work their devious plan perfectly to achieve their projected goal. Impatience can not be an option.

It is getting on near four o'clock and Norma is putting on her clothes and then brushed her hair.

"I'd better go over and see Meredith; comfort her after the big fight you two had" Norma said looking over her shoulder and grinning.

Brent came up behind her and embraced her from behind. He kissed the top of her head.

"What excuse did you give Wilker for leaving?" Brent asked.

"That. I told him I was leaving to console my distraught sister."

"Ya know doll, this Wilker is being a pain in the ass with these stupid union things he's doing" Brent said as he tied his shoes.

"Brent, you know nothing is going to happen. The guys are all pretending to go along with him but they won't vote it in and besides he'll be in Allendale really soon."

"I know. I know but he's got this Pyle meeting next week. We don't want that drunk working for us. If he gets hurt or hurts someone, we'll have to pay compensation."

Norma turned and embraced him. "You'll handle it. You know you will" she said looking at him with her sexy green eyes.

They left Brent's parents house and Norma went over to see Meredith while Brent went to the cookout. When he arrived, Edwin came over to him immediately and asked him if he knew where Paul Wilker is. Brent said that he doesn't know and thought that he was there at the cookout.

"He left a while ago. Nobody knows where he's gone. I just called Meredith and I talked to Norma and she doesn't know where he is either" Edwin said.

'He's a strange guy alright" Brent said.

"I'll tell you, if Rita didn't think he was so great, I'd probably can him" Edwin said quietly.

Brent doesn't know that Rita calls the shots and what she says is the way it is. He doesn't care. He has it good and he plans to keep it that way.

"When will Lester be back?" Brent asked.

"I don't know. He just got home from the hospital but he's got things under control."

CHAPTER THIRTEEN

Paul has Jenny's undivided attention as he begins to tell her about his family.

"My parents were the best. They did everything for me growing up. I was their only child and we did everything together. Dad was a draftsman for years with the same company and mom worked for a local insurance company as a secretary. Dad had this friend, well he was more like a brother, that he grew up with. His name was Sid Case and they did everything together. They double dated and they were best man at each others wedding. He was my Godfather and dad is Sid's son Timmy's Godfather."

Jenny listened intently as Paul went on.

"We used to go fishing together all the time, Dad, me, Sid and Timmy. Sid lived to fish and dad could take it or leave it but he just liked being with Sid. Sometimes mom and Sid's wife Janice would come with us too. The only thing wrong was that Sid liked to drink. At first he drank mostly on weekends and by Sunday afternoon, he'd be pretty well loaded. Then he started stopping off for a few after working. He would come home at nine or ten at night drunk. He was never mean and he always went work every day but this was what he did. Dad liked to drink a beer or two or sometimes three but not the way Sid drank."

"That must have been fun, I mean all of you fishing together like that" Jenny said.

"Yes, those are some of my fondest memories."

"So did Sid die?" Jenny asked with a questioning look on her face.

"Yes he did. One afternoon, he quit drinking completely. He called my dad and told him that he was stopping for good for Janice and Timmy's sake. He was going to devote more time to them. He told dad too that he was going to join Alcoholics Anonymous to help him achieve his goal.

He did great for two days and on the third day, he came right home from working and when he went into his house, Janice was there with another man."

Jenny put her hand up to her mouth. "Oh my God, were they in bed together?"

"Oh no, nothing like that but Janice told Sid that she had met this man and was deeply in love with him. She said it happened during the time that he was away drinking and that she wanted to divorce as soon as possible so she could marry this man.

"Well Sid was crushed and broke into tears and begged her not to leave him. She told Sid that she was marrying this man and that Timmy would be with her. He could visit his father but she was going to seek custody."

Off in the distance, faint rumbles of thunder are sounding and the breeze has picked up. Paul started the car and raised the convertible top to be safe. Once he had the top fastened, he turned the engine off again.

"Where was I?" Paul said. "Oh yeah, Janice left with the guy to pick Timmy up at baseball practice and then to her boyfriend's home where she planned to move right in. Sid called Dad and was crying like a child. He was heartbroken and had suspected nothing. Dad went over and stayed with him until midnight. He talked to Sid and it appeared to him that he was feeling better but apparently after Dad left, Sid went out and found where Janice was staying. He banged on the door until both she and the guy opened it. As I heard it, he pleaded with her to give him a chance but she wanted nothing more to do with him. The police were called and Sid was arrested for the remainder of the night.

I guess in the morning he appeared to be rational and calm so where he had not committed any crime, the police released him. He drove to the nearest drug store and purchased a bottle of sleeping pills and then to a package store and got a bottle of whiskey. He drove back to his house, parked his car in the garage, and with the garage doors closed, he started the engine back up and lowered the car windows. He sat in the car and washed down the entire bottle of pills with the whiskey. He really wanted to kill himself and he did."

"Oh Paul. That is so sad" Jenny said softly. "What a shame."

"A couple of hours later, Janice stopped by to pick up some of her belongings and discovered him. I heard that she did eventually marry the other guy but it was a while later."

A bee flew into the car and buzzed around the inside of the windshield. Paul cupped his hand and quickly scooped it out his side window. The thunder is a little more frequent and it sounds closer than before. The air is very sticky and humid.

"Needless to say, both dad and mom were shocked when they heard about Sid. It was really tough for dad to attend his wake and funeral. His doctor had to prescribe tranquilizers to help him with his grief. After the funeral, I went and stayed with my uncle Ike and aunt Edna for a few days while mom and dad went up to Vermont to get away from everything."

"Paul, how tragic this is" Jenny said. "Your poor parents and you too."

"It gets worse. Just after two weeks passed, dad and mom were back working and attempting to cope with all this. It was on a Thursday morning and mom and dad left for their jobs and I was in school. On the way to work, mom was in a fatal car accident. Two fifteen year old boys skipped school and went to one of their houses. The parents were both at work so they went in and started drinking the liquor and quickly became drunk. They went down the street and found a car with the keys in it. They stole it and were speeding and hit mom's car head on and she died instantly. The police estimated their speed at near eighty."

"Oh, Paul, this is horrible. It is too much for anyone to bear. What happened to the two boys?"

"They lived. They were hurt badly but they lived. Well, this put dad over the edge; first Sid and then mom. For me, it seemed to get harder as time went on but for a few days after her funeral, he seemed to be accepting it as best he could. On the third night after her funeral, dad got up and came into my room and was all upset. He came over to my bed and started begging me to help him find her.

"Her car isn't in the driveway and I don't know where she is. Call Ike and see if she's at their house. Please Paul, call Ike" he said with tears on his face. My uncle Ike and aunt Edna came over right away and took him to the hospital. They said that he had had a mild stroke and a severe nervous breakdown. He had to go to the Longworth Sanitarium and he has been there ever since. In the past two years, he has become worse. He will spend the rest of his life there . . . . poor Dad, all he ever wanted out of life was to make his family happy and grow old with my mother" Paul said with a shaky voice on the verge of tears.

"Oh Paul, I am so sorry this all happened. It is too much for anyone to go through" Jenny said and placed her hand on Paul's forearm.

Looking into her pretty face, he can see her sincere concern for him.

"Alright, hey. I can use a drink or two . . . . or three" Paul said as he wiped his eyes. "In fact Jenny, let's go and have something to eat . . . . my treat."

"'Well, I do know a great little place and it's not too far from here but you don't have to pay for me Paul."

"I insist so you tell me how to go and we will have a nice time."

Paul is still in awe about the way Jenny treated his father. He thought about how Norma would not even talk about his father's situation. He has told her about what has happened to his family and she of course is sympathetic but Jenny has been incredible.

Paul started the car and drove out towards the guards building at the exit. The same man is there that was when they had entered. He waved and Paul drove past and out onto the road. He glanced into the rearview mirror and can see that the sky behind them has an ominous look. Ahead of them looks good but a storm is moving up from behind. The humid air is oppressive.

"What is this place where we are going to?" Paul asked Jenny.

"It's called the Pine Acres Inn. It's a nice little restaurant with a bar and they even have outside tables with big umbrellas over them."

"Sounds like my kinda place" Paul said looking over at Jenny and smiling.

"I think you'll like it" she said.

Norma convinced Meredith to accompany her back to the cookout and make up with Brent. When they pulled into the driveway, the place was full of cars and people. Some cars are parked along the side of the roadway in front of the Clay's house. When Meredith and Norma went into the back yard, Brent approached them and he and Meredith went off together. He apologized and made things right with her now because his plan has worked nicely. He had got to spend time with Norma for great sex and that was that.

Norma is looking for Paul and when she heard that he has left, she became angry. She called his apartment but of course, there was no answer. After Brent had made up with Meredith, he sees Norma and can tell that she is upset.

"I told that dope to stay here and mix with the people and what does he do as soon as I leave, he leaves" Norma said in frustrated tone.

"Boy, do you look sexy when you get pissed" Brent said in a soft voice.

"Oh, ya know what? I'll bet you he went to see his father. He said he was going to see him soon" Norma said.

"He's in a nuthouse you said didn't you" Brent asked?"

"Yes and I think some of it rubbed off on him" Norma said wiping the perspiration from her forehead with a paper napkin.

The air is extremely humid and sticky and many of the guests have taken advantage of the Clay's swimming pool. Off in the far distance, periodic sounds of thunder can be heard faintly. It is very common on a day with steamy humidity such as this one to have a thunder storm later in the day. The problem is that often times the rain will make the oppressive air even more so when the storm ends and the sun returns.

Brent looked and sees Lester on crutches who has just arrived with his wife who has driven him here. His broken leg is casted and he is moving slowly and stiffly. The guests walked over to greet him. Fletcher, Denny and Art are among them.

"Hey Lester, how ya doin?" Fletcher slurred.

"It's sore as hell but I'm starting to get around."

Edwin stood close to Mrs. Lester and spoke to her in a low tone. She is a short woman so Edwin stooped forward and he spoke to her.

"He may need more surgery if his leg doesn't heal right. His doctor is checking him regularly to see how it is. He really broke it" she said looking at Edwin.

Norma went into the house and returned with her pearl white bathing suit on. She has a short terry cloth beach robe on and went over to the pool. She put on her bathing cap and removed her sandals and robe and strolled to the edge of the pool. She has the complete attention of all of the males and a good portion of the females. Norma sat down on the edge of the pool and slid into the water. It is really cool and refreshing.

Both Edwin and Brent are talking to Lester away from the guests. They are interested the proposal that Paul has submitted.

"We're not doing that. These guys aren't stupid enough to push for that are they? Edwin asked Lester.

"Don't worry. The guys are just playing along with him but when it comes down to the wire, they're goin to vote against it."

"What about Pyle? We really don't want him back, after all, he wrecked the fork lift" Brent said.

"Have that meeting with him and Wilker and just fire his ass. He's a drunk for Christ's sake" Lester said smirking.

"When's the meeting?"

"Monday" Edwin said.

"Ok then. Can his ass" Lester said coldly.

Paul followed Jenny's directions and turned into the Pine Acres parking lot. It is a cozy little place settled in amongst large pine trees. The inn is well landscaped and maintained on a regular basis. The sky has become really dark and a strong breeze has taken place. Paul noticed that his windshield is dotted with raindrops so he rolled up his windows and he and Jenny headed for the inn's entrance.

Minutes afterwards, the sky opened up and the rain pounded down outside. The inn is not crowded so they are seated right away.

"Order anything you want" Paul said to Jenny. "Anything and everything."

A pleasant young waitress came over to their table and placed menus in front of them. Paul ordered a bottle of beer and Jenny asked for a glass of white wine. The storm is right overhead now and the lightning and thunder is occurring almost simultaneously. The rain is extremely heavy and large puddles are already forming on the roadway. People that entered the inn are wet but it feels pretty good after the highly humid air.

"So Jenny. Tell me about your family. Do you have any sisters and brothers?"

"I have three younger half brothers. My mother and father were divorced when I was five and she remarried and had my three brothers. They were born almost one year apart."

"Do they live near you?" Paul asked.

"Actually, they live in Lakeview next to Allendale and not that far from the new plant. My real father died when I was fifteen. He was a swell dad and I really miss him."

"Oh Jenny, I'm sorry to hear that. What did he do for work?"

"He was a hardware salesman. He was well liked by everyone that he sold to."

The waitress returned and took their order. They both ordered more drinks too. The air conditioning feels very refreshing and being inside sheltered from the storm is comforting too. Jenny is beginning to feel more relaxed and feels like telling Paul about her family. She is beginning to feel the wine.

"I am not fond of my stepfather at all. He is a very dominating person and I now believe that my mother likes a man like that. See Paul, my dad wasn't like that at all. When my mother told him that she wanted to divorce, he was really upset and I don't think he really got over it. Knowing what I know now, I am almost convinced that see was seeing Wayne, my stepfather, while she was still married to my dad."

"Really. You think so?" Paul asked.

"Yes I do. She didn't wait very long to remarry."

"That must have been hard on you growing up. Did your real dad take care of you?" Paul asked looking concerned.

"He really did. My mother told me when I was small that he had no drive or ambition and only paid her support for me because the court made him. She also used to discourage him from visiting me. She told him that when he came to our house that it upset me. I found out later that Wayne told her that he didn't want dad coming to the house except to drop off the support check each month."

"This is unbelievable. How could these people do this to you Jenny? It's shocking" Paul said.

Jenny had not opened up to anyone about her family problems except with her girlfriend Sandy whom she had gone to school with. They have remained close friends to this day. She feels very comfortable telling Paul about her family problems and knows for certain that he will not tell other people.

"I later found out that the reason he only came by once a month to see me when he paid my mother the support money was because she told him that he made me nervous and upset. He later told me that he didn't fight her in court was because he didn't want me to be more uncomfortable and stressed out."

"Gee Jenny, that is really unfair on her part. You did finally see more of your dad though, right?"

"Oh yes I did. When I was thirteen, I was in a school play and I wanted my mother to come and see me. All of the other parents would be there and I really wanted her to come too. Well, my stepfather told her that they were going to my brothers bowling banquet that night so she was going with him and the boys. He told me flat out that that was something more important that some dumb school play. Of course, mother sided with him."

"I'm getting mad just hearing this and I don't even know these people" Paul said with an angered expression on his face.

The waitress brought their food and asked if they would like more drinks. They both accepted and began eating as they were both quite hungry.

"So what happened about your play?" Paul asked.

"Well, it just so happened that this was the day of the month that my dad came with mom's check. I was really upset and went out behind the garage. A few minutes later he came out there and asked me how things were going. How's school and what had I been up to, you know, stuff like he always asked me. I started to tell him and burst out crying. I told him about the play and how nobody would come. He put his arms around me and told me that I would do just fine and that he had no doubt about that. Well let me tell you Paul, I went to the play and when it ended and I ever saw him standing there among the other parents with a little bunch of flowers, I almost fainted. Afterwards, we went out for pizza and from then on I saw him a lot. I also found out that my brothers actually wanted to come and see me instead of going to their banquet. Wayne grounded them for the rest of the weekend for that. I'm sorry but he is a jerk."

"What does this guy Wayne do for work?"

"He is a manager for a sporting goods store. He is a sports fan and very competitive. At dinner time, he was always making my brothers compete against each other."

"How did he do that?" Paul asked her.

"Oh, he'd say that the one who finished first would get a bigger dessert and the one who finished last would get belittled by him. Almost every night, one of them would leave crying and sent to their room."

"Geez, that's really too bad. How do you get along with your brothers?"

"They are the best. Last summer I took them on a camping trip way up in the Pine River Resort woods. We had a blast. We stayed overnight in two tents and the next morning they told me that sometimes bears were around up there. They said they didn't tell me earlier because they knew that I wouldn't go if they had. Then I chased them around and we just laughed and laughed."

"I can't believe that your stepfather acted like that at your supper table. That could not have been pleasant" Paul said looking sincerely concerned.

"Leave my table he'd holler at one of them! One night I couldn't take it and I yelled out, Why don't you leave. You're the one who gets everyone stirred up!"

"Good for you. What did he do?" Paul asked with a slight laugh.

"He reached over and smacked me in the head and sent me to my room. I didn't care though because I wanted to get away from him."

Suddenly outside, an enormous lightning bolt flashed and deafening thunder sounded immediately afterwards.

"Oh man, did you see that?" one of the men who was seated at a booth beside a window said loudly.

Behind the inn there is a beautiful pine grove where patrons can walk and relax when the weather is nice. One of the tall pine trees had been struck and part of it had fallen down into the pine grove. A ball of fire occurred but went out because the tree was drenched from the rain. Paul and Jenny got up from their table and went to the window to look at what happened.

"Jenny, tell me this. How did you turn out so nice after growing up with all that?"

"I guess I just did not want to be like that and my dad was a great influence."

"So when did you leave. How old were you?"

"Seventeen. I left and went to live with my aunt, dad's sister, in Perkinsville. You see Paul, it got worse there as I got older."

"Worse?" Paul asked as they sat back down at their table.

"As I started to . . . . you know, grow up a little, Wayne used to do stuff like grab my butt and say to my brothers, "What do ya think guys, if this gets any bigger the guys aren't going to want her.""

"He did that! Did your mother know this?" Paul said loudly.

"Oh yeah. She'd be there sometimes. She'd say "Oh Jenny. He's just fooling with you. You really need to be more relaxed. It's all in fun". Then he was always staring at me and if I was doing the dishes, he'd stand really close so he was against me."

"You know Jenny, there are laws against this kind of shit. Sorry but this was really wrong" Paul said with his face becoming flushed.

"I didn't know what to do. My dad had recently died of heart failure and I made up my mind to finish high school and get out of there and enroll in secretarial school. The thing that really did it for me was one afternoon right after had I graduated from high school, my mother and brothers had gone out. It was a hot day and I decided to take a shower. Wayne was not home but returned while I was in the bathroom. The lock on our bathroom door didn't work properly so if you jiggled the handle enough the door would pop open. He began knocking on the door and asking what I was doing. I told him that I was finishing up and would be right out. He began to turn the door handle back and forth and of course, the door opened before I could grab my towel. Well, he just stood there leering at me and started coming closer as I wrapped the bath towel around myself. He put his hands on my shoulders and started to pull me to him but just then, my mother and brothers came in the back door. Mom called out and he quickly backed out and closed the door. I heard him say to her "She must be writing her will in there. I gotta go . . . . now" he said standing outside as if he had been waiting to use the bathroom."

"That did it for me because I'm sure if she hadn't come in when she did, he would have raped me" Jenny said with a slight shake in her voice.

The waitress came to their table to make sure that everything was satisfactory. Paul ordered another bottle of beer and Jenny another white wine. They are feeling more relaxed from the drinks.

"Jenny, I can't believe this guy and if I ever run into him, I might just have a little word with him."

Jenny smiled a wide friendly smile at Paul.

"Hey, I didn't mean to get you all worked up" Jenny said reaching out and touching Paul's wrist and smiling. "I just haven't told anyone except my girlfriend Sandy about all this and sometimes it helps to talk about it."

"Jenny, you are a damn nice person and when people get hurt by other people who aren't so nice, I get upset."

"Paul, you are so kind."

"You said your father died when you when you were fifteen?" Paul asked.

"Yes, he had a heart attack. He lost his job and that didn't help matters any, but he had a weak heart for sometime before that. I found out later from aunt Maggie that he had rheumatic fever when he was young and they think that his heart was weak because of that."

"What happened with his job?" Paul said sitting back in the booth.

"Well, he was a salesman and the company changed hands. This new young hotshot guy was put in charge and put dad in an area that was really spread out with all new contacts. He did this because he knew that it would too hard for him and he would leave."

"Boy that stinks" Paul said shaking his head.

"The funny part is that dad had saved a lot of money and when he passed away, he left it to me along with his life insurance. He put in his will that I was to use some of it to further my education so that paid for my secretarial school. I bought a car and pretty much banked the rest of it but my brothers get spoiled by me too."

"It's just too bad that he was so young" Paul said.

"Do you know that Wayne actually tried to make me give the money to him and my mother. He messed up his shoulder and was out of work for a while and said that I owed them, but I found out later that he was being paid right along from his work. I often wonder if that was one of the reasons that he tried that stuff with me in the bathroom; for spite maybe."

"Well Jenny, you sure have done really great for all you've been through" Paul said as he wiped his mouth with his napkin.

"I don't know. Do you think so?"

"Oh yes. You furthered your education and are now you're a first class secretary. When you inherited your father's money, you didn't go out and blow it all like many people do. I'd say that you've done very well. Yes sir. Jenny, tell me something, are there two f's in Jennifer or two n's? I never can remember."

"I believe there is one f and two n's . . . . but my first name isn't Jennifer . . . . it's Genevieve."

"Genevieve. I like that. It's original and one that you don't hear every day" Paul said looking straight into her eyes.

"It was my dad's mother's name but unfortunately, I never knew her because she died three years before I was born."

"That is too bad. I only knew my mother's mother a little. She died when I was four and all of my other grandparents were gone before I was born too."

The waitress came over to their table and asked if they would like some dessert. They both are full and declined so she went to get their check. Paul is feeling a little buzzed from the beers that he has had and Jenny is feeling the effects of her wine too. She drank more wine than she usually does but she feels rather depressed after Paul has told her about his family problems. She feels very relaxed and comfortable now. She really enjoys Paul's company.

Paul paid the waitress and followed Jenny out of the inn and into the parking lot. The storm has passed and the sun has returned. Sometimes in the summer a rain storm can bring in cooler air but this is not the case on this afternoon. The humidity is worse and steam is coming off of the asphalt in the parking lot. The leaves on the trees are glistening in the hot afternoon sun.

"Let's go and look at the tree that the lightning hit" Paul said to Jenny pointing to the pine grove.

As they approach the pine grove, they are amazed at the huge section that has fallen. If it had landed on the inn, it would have crushed part of it for sure. Other people have gathered to see the tree and everyone is talking to each other. The pine grove is nice with the tall trees and the sunlight stabbing through them. After about ten minutes, Paul and Jenny walked slowly over to the car.

"It's so hot but I don't want to put my top down because it is wet and can get moldy."

"Oh, that's ok" Jenny said as she opened the passenger door.

Paul started the engine and pulled slowly out onto the road. Puddles have formed on the sides of the road from the downpour and the bright sunlight is reflected in them.

"So what kind of a car did you buy?" Paul asked her.

"I have a 1960 Ford Falcon. It was a demonstrator and I got it at Perkinsville Ford. It was like a new car."

"Of course. I've seen it at the plant. What is it in the garage for?" Paul asked her.

"They said I need a water pump. It started leaking all over the place but it should be ready on Monday the mechanic told me."

"Those are nice little cars, good on gas too" Paul said.

Paul reached down under the dashboard and pushed on the cowl vent lever to open the vent and get some moving air into the car. The lever is sticking and he gave it a hard push which suddenly opened the vent all the way. A strong blast of air entered the car. Jenny pulled her dress up past her knees and leaned her head back against the seat.

"Oh, this feels so nice" she said closing her eyes and smiling. "It's so hot and sticky out."

"Jenny, tell me where your apartment is. I just remembered that I don't know where you live."

"Oh God Paul, I'm sorry" Jenny said snickering. "Keep going and when we get into Greengrove center, turn right after the Rexall drug store. It's Elm Avenue and that is where I am."

Jenny is feeling nice and a little giddy from the wine. She has really enjoyed this afternoon despite what Paul has told her about his past. She is relaxed and glad that she has told Paul about her family. It is comforting to unload your problems to

171

someone who seems to be seriously interested and concerned as Paul does.

Paul turned onto Elm Avenue. Jenny sat up in the seat and pointed to the house where she lives. It is a nice older house with two floors. On the driveway side there is an outside staircase with a second floor landing and this is where she enters her apartment from. Her landlady is an older widow who lives on the first floor. The neighborhood is quiet and well kept. Paul pulled his car up beside the staircase and put the gearshift into neutral and pulled up the parking brake handle.

"Jenny, I can't thank you enough for coming with me to see my father."

"Well, I can't thank you enough for listening to all of my family troubles so I guess we are both a little better now aren't we" she said smiling her pretty smile at Paul.

"We are for sure" Paul said.

Jenny reached for the door handle and tried to open the door but it will not open. It feels like it is stuck. Paul slid over beside her and lifted the handle up and down and the door finally popped open.

"I'm sorry about that. I must fix that very soon. Something inside the door is messed up I think."

Paul is right beside Jenny and instead of getting out of the car, she placed both of her hands on the sides of his face and kissed his mouth with her lips parted. It is not a quick peck but a nice, passionate kiss.

"I probably shouldn't have done that and I hope you aren't upset at me but . . . . I had a swell time and thank you for a great lunch. I'll see you Monday at work."

Paul looked into her eyes and noticed again that her eye did not quite focus exactly with her other one. This made her look interesting and a little more attractive. Jenny closed the door and walked toward the staircase that led to her apartment. She glanced back at Paul and gave him a quick wave then proceeded to climb the staircase. Paul watched her as she went up the stairs to her apartment door. She looked very nice with her summer dress and her tan. Paul had not noticed at first that Jenny is carrying her shoes instead of wearing them. When he saw her enter her apartment, he put the car in reverse and backed out onto Elm Avenue.

As he drove along, his mind was racing. He could not stop thinking about Jenny's kiss she had given him. It felt different than any of the kisses that Norma and he have shared. He can't understand why this is but he knows how he feels. He feels comfortable with Jenny. He feels uneasy and somewhat confused too though. He figures that he will go to the cookout and face the music. He is pretty sure that Norma is going to be upset with him but he just was not up to spending the afternoon with Fletcher and his followers. He does not regret this afternoon at all; not one bit.

Chapter Fourteen

The cookout had been interrupted by the storm but is now back outdoors again. Some of the people have gone upstairs over the garage and are using the game room. There is a pool table along with a tennis table. Two dart boards were also used and some of the guests played cards during the storm. Some people are still upstairs finishing heated games.

Outside, the smell of charcoal broiled steaks and burgers is filling the air. There is homemade potato salad and chips. The burgers are out of this world because Wanda mixes sharp cheese into them as she prepares them. Anyone that is attempting to diet is sure to go overboard today. Wanda's sons, along with helping her with the cooking, have gone around periodically and collected the empty beer and soda cans and bottles. There are plenty of them. Paul drove up to the driveway but had to park near the end because the top part was full. As he entered the back yard of the Clay home, Rita saw him and came hurriedly over. She has a drink in one hand and a cigarette in the other. She put them down and reached both of her arms out and gave Paul a huge hug and kissed his cheek.

"Where have you been? We missed you."

"I went to see my father. He's out at Longworth you know" Paul said.

"I know. Norma told us. Is he doing all right?"

"He's the same. He really hasn't improved over the years" Paul answered.

Rita patted Paul's wrist and smiled at him. She is feeling her afternoon's drinks but Paul likes her. She seems kind and caring but he can also sense an unhappiness that appears to plague her. He is concerned for her because she drinks more alcohol than she should and she smokes cigarettes constantly.

"Well, the wandering minstrel has returned" Norma said as she walked up and put her arm through Paul's. She has changed out of her bathing suit and is now wearing shorts and a tank top.

I missed you my sweet. How is your dad?"

"He's the same. He is not going to get better without a miracle."

"Oh. I'm sorry. Come in the house with me. I've got to talk to you."

When they got inside of the house, Paul started to give her a kiss but Norma pulled away quickly. She does not seem really upset but slightly agitated.

"Paul, you should have stayed here. I know your father isn't well but this cookout is only one day. You can see him anytime. I don't think I'm being unreasonable here" she said in a low tone so not to be heard if anyone was nearby. Actually, the real reason she wanted Paul to remain at the cookout was so that there was no possibility that he would have happened to see Brent and her together.

"Look, some of these guys from the plant don't like me and that's fine at work but I'll be damned if I'm going to put with that on my own time. I'm sorry but this is how I feel. I told you this before anyways. If you had been here then I would have stayed."

175

"I had to go and comfort my sister. She was very upset" Norma said raising her voice slightly.

"I know and that is perfectly understandable" Paul said softly.

"Well, you don't have to see Fletcher anymore today. He got pretty drunk and his girlfriend took him home" Norma said to Paul grinning slightly. "C'mon, let's get something to eat."

Paul noticed that George Baxter was still there so he grabbed a burger and a bottle of beer and joined him. They talked for a bit and about seven thirty, George left. Brent came over as soon as Paul was alone and sat down across from him.

"Tell Bill Pyle to be in my office Monday at ten in the morning" I want to get this straightened out once and for all."

"Ok. I will call him tomorrow."

"Next week, Wednesday or Thursday, one of the new presses will be arriving at the Allendale plant. You are going to unload it for the guys from the company that we bought it from. The other one is due to arrive shortly after that."

"You want me to unload it?" Paul asked a little surprised.

"Sure. There's a crane inside that you can use. When you get it off the truck, uncrate it and by that time the people from the press company should be there to assemble it."

Brent walked off and joined Edwin who was talking to Meredith. Paul thought to himself that he will worry about getting the press unloaded when the time comes. He walked to where Wanda is and stopped beside her.

"I have never had a cheeseburger that could even come close to the one that you made for me. It was great. Thank you."

Wanda is a short slim woman who looks like she has worked hard all of her life. That is because she has. She works full time as the Clay's housekeeper and on her time off, she does the book keeping for her husbands plumbing business. She is always pleasant and cheerful.

'Well Paul, for a nice compliment like that, *I* will make you another one. How about a little pepper and onion with it too?" she said giving Paul a gentle pat on his shoulder.

"Ya sold me" Paul said. "Pepper and onion it is."

Paul took a bottle of Coca Cola and some potato chips and had it with his burger. He has had enough beer for the time being when he ate with Jenny. He still can not stop thinking about her. She has made a strong impression on him. He sat down on one the benches in the yard and thought about how this day has unfolded; how he never would have guessed that it would have been like it was.

The humidity has not lessened very much as the evening moves on. It is dark now and the back yard lights have come on. There is a small breeze but it really hasn't helped very much. The stickiness is still very present. As Paul finished eating, he saw Norma coming over to him.

"Grab you swim trunks and let's go for a swim. I'm roasting" she said. "Change in the pool house."

Paul came out after changing into his swimming trunks and dove into the pool. The water is really refreshing as he swam the length and stopped by the steps at the shallow part. Norma came out of her house wearing a two piece bathing suit and flowered cap. She came down the steps into the water where Paul is, dunked herself, and began swimming towards the deeper end. Paul swam after her and joined her at the other end. They both hung onto the edge because the water is over their heads at this point.

"I think that in a couple of weeks, you can get me a diamond ring, that is of course that is if you want to marry me still" Norma said smiling at Paul and moving in close to him.

"Ah, yes, sure I do" Paul said a little surprised.

"We can tell mom and dad then. I know they will be happy."

At the other end of the pool, Brent slid in and swam towards them. When he got closer, he went underwater and came up and grabbed the back of Norma's thigh just beneath her bottom causing her to flinch. She looked at Paul who looked rather shocked. Brent grabbed onto the side of the pool beside Norma.

"Boy, this feels good doesn't it" he said with a wide grin.

"I'll be back" Paul said. "I've got to use the toilet."

As he swam off towards the shallow end of the pool, Norma glared at Brent who has his hand on her hip under the water.

"What the hell is the matter with you grabbing me like that?"

"I thought you liked it when I touch you" Brent said still grinning.

"I love it when you touch me but not with him right next us. We're too close to having this work for us to screw it up doing something like that. If he thinks we are fooling around, he'll be gone in a flash, believe me."

"Ok. Ok. I see what you mean" Brent said moving away from her slightly. "I think Meredith is ready to leave anyway."

"I love you and I really enjoyed our little session today" Norma said as she gave Brent a quick wink.

"Same here. It was great as it always is."

Brent turned and swam back towards the pool steps. As he began to climb from the pool, he can see Paul heading back to the pool. He has changed back into his clothes.

"Remember. Monday morning in my office at ten with Pyle" Brent said as he reached for a towel.

Paul nodded at him and said nothing. He walked around the pool apron to the deep end where Norma is still as she was when he left.

"How come you changed?" Norma asked him as she wiped the water from her face with her hand.

"I'm tired. I think I'll go to my apartment and crash."

"Oh stay here for a while longer. I didn't see you all afternoon."

"How come Brent goosed you? What was that all about?"

"What?" Norma said laughing slightly. "He accidently bumped me when he came up, that's all."

"I probably shouldn't say this but I don't care for his attitude" Paul said. "He has this superiority way about him when he talks to me and it looked to me like he meant to do that to you."

Norma boosted herself up onto the walkway beside the pool where Paul was and stood up. She pulled off her bathing cap and shook her hair with her hand.

"You'll get used to him. After all, you're going to be brothers in law before long."

"You are my guy darling, not anyone else. Just remember what I said about the diamond ring" she whispered as she leaned up and kissed his mouth. "I really love you."

Paul thanked Rita and Meredith for the cookout and made it a point to see Wanda too before he left. Edwin and Brent are inside of the house so Paul did not see them. Paul drove up Temple Street and headed for his apartment. He still can not stop thinking about Jenny and what a nice time he had with her and how he felt when she kissed him. He also keeps thinking about Brent and what had happened. It had looked to him like he had grabbed Norma under the water but he has to trust her and believe her or their relationship can not survive.

Jenny shut the water off in her shower and stepped out onto her bathmat. She dried herself off with a clean crisp towel and put on a large tee shirt that she sleeps in during the hot summer months. She went to her small kitchen and put three ice cubes into a glass and filled it with ginger ale. She is still feeling relaxed from the wine she had earlier. She went into her bedroom and turned the small oscillating fan on the dresser on and then stretched out on her bed. The room is hot and the little breeze from her fan feels nice. She propped the pillows up so her head will be elevated. As she sips her ginger ale, she begins to let her mind wander.

She thinks about Ben whom she had dated for a while. Their relationship appeared to be getting serious but then his former girlfriend that he had been briefly engaged to came to see him. She had dumped Ben for another man and wanted nothing to do with him. That was when he met Jenny and they began seeing one another. Three months later, the former girl friend showed up at Ben's apartment and told him that her new beau had taken off with a young eighteen year old girl and eloped. Ben immediately went back to her and left Jenny by the wayside. Apparently, things after a while soured between Ben and the girl and he tried to once again court Jenny but she told him politely to keep on going. She has dated a little after that but nothing at all serious. She has never felt about any man the way she feels about Paul.

Jenny's concentration is broken by the ringing of her telephone. She put down her glass and picked up the receiver.

"Hello" she said softly.

"Hey girl, how was the cookout? Did you get drunk?"

It is her best friend Sandy whom she shares everything with. They are like sisters.

"Hey girl yourself" Jenny said.

"I had a great afternoon but not at the cookout."

"Yeah, well what happened. What'd you do?"

"Well you know Paul. You know, that nice cute guy at work I told you about. Well, he offered to give me a ride home because I don't have my car. Well, his dad is a patient over at the Longworth Hospital so we stopped in there to see him. I went in with him to try to make it easier and then he took me to the Pine Acres Inn for lunch afterwards."

"Isn't he the guy that's going around with that little bitch Norma?"

"That's him" Jenny said.

"So .... he was nice you say?"

Sandy asked knowing that Jenny will say yes.

"Oh Sandy. I've done what I didn't want to do. I've fallen in love with him. Oh God. I think about him all time and I know it is hopeless, I mean . . . he's going marry Norma but I can't help it. I am completely gone over him."

"Jen, what the hell is the matter with you? You went out with that dipshit Ben and he put you through the ringer and this will go nowhere with Paul."

"I know. I know. I'm just going to have to make up my mind that nothing is going to happen. I guess in the back of my mind, I've been hoping that something will happen between them."

"Look Jen, Paul's a guy and guys want girls like her. She's really good looking, sexy and loaded with money and you told me that he's going to be managing his own plant? He's not going to give up on that. It's too bad but that's the way things go."

Jenny and Sandy talked for a short while longer and then made plans to see each other the next day and have lunch. Jenny hung the telephone up and lay back on her bed. She starts thinking about what Sandy has said about Norma and how she is the kind of girl that guys are looking for. She is right Jenny thought to herself. How can I even think about competing with Norma. I remember seeing her walk across the parking lot with spike heels and her spaghetti strapdress swishing; her hair done up just right and her tits jiggling around with the guys in the shop standing in the overhead doorway looking hypnotized at her like they have been stranded on a desert island and haven't seen a woman for twenty years. How can I ever compete with that?

She suddenly feels very sleepy so she pulled the bed sheet over her and snapped off the lamp beside her bed. She will just have to get her mind on other things besides Paul Wilker but her last thought before drifting off is that there is always the slim chance that something might happen and Paul and Norma will not marry. The unexpected can happen but it's doubtful. The little fan turning back and forth is making a low steady hum that helps Jenny sleep peacefully.

It is almost three o'clock and Paul finally fell asleep. His mind had been racing with different thoughts. He was thinking about Bill Pyle and how he was going to handle his meeting on Monday. He was also thinking about the proposal that Brent had not talked about since he gave it to him. Norma's statement about getting married soon was popping up too but mostly, he was thinking about Jenny. He had a most enjoyable time with her and he couldn't get her kiss out of his head. He felt so different when she did it. The way she looked at him as she was getting out of the car haunted him too. "Am I beginning to have feelings for Jenny" he asked himself. This is crazy. Norma is gorgeous and has got me into a position where I am going to get promoted to a high paying level as the manager of a publishing plant. I've only been with Jenny today for any length of time but I still feel this funny way about her, like an attraction. Her kindness and sincerity are overwhelming. "I'm so confused right now" he thought.

Paul figured that tomorrow when he sees Norma again, he will get back on track. He cannot hurt Norma at this point after all that has happened. He decided that he will start to really concentrate on his position at Allendale. When he slept, he had the dream again about the highway and the pre-war cars traveling along it but just as before, he can not get over to the other side where the gasoline station is with the endless emptiness behind it.

Paul awoke at eight fifteen in the morning and to his surprise, he feels pretty good despite the short amount of rest he has had. He got up and poured a glass of tomato juice and filled a bowl with Wheaties. He made a piece of white toast with strawberry jam and decided to cook a few strips of bacon. His landlady, Mrs. Bradford, tapped quietly on his door. Paul opened it and asked her to come in.

"You had a telephone call last night from a Ray Webber. He asked if you could call him when you have a chance. He said he wanted to know how things were going. He said that you have his number."

Mrs. Bradford is a nice kindly woman in her early seventies. She is very thin and short, just five feet tall. She is widowed and has two sons who maintain her apartments for her.

"Thank you Mrs. Bradford. I'll call him shortly. Would you like some bacon?"

"Oh thank you no, Paul dear. One of my boys took me out for breakfast" she said slowly backing out of the door.

Paul finished his breakfast and went to call Ray. He uses Mrs. Bradford's telephone and pays her at the end of each month for any toll calls that he makes which are only to Ike when he does call him. Ray had called to find out how Paul had made out with his proposal and with the Bill Pyle situation. Paul filled him in on what was going on and how he planned on doing it. Actually, it was good that Ray did call him because he gave Paul some excellent advice on how to handle Pyle's case. He also told Paul that his company has reached a tentative agreement. Paul feels much more confident now with the upcoming meeting with Brent. He also is still thinking about Jenny and he realizes too that he does not want to stop.

He called Bill Pyle's house and informed him about the scheduled meeting regarding his job. Bill was his usual complaining self but did agree to be there at ten in the morning.

Sunday went by quickly. He went to Norma's house for lunch and played some tennis with her. Later, they went out for ice cream and played some miniature golf. It seemed that before he knew it, Monday morning has arrived and he is pulling into the company parking lot. He went in and took the job sheets into Jenny. She is her usual outgoing, pleasant self. Her new hair style is most flattering to her appearance and her eyes look stunning the way she has them made up. She thanked Paul again for treating her to lunch and he thanked her again for accompanying him to go in and see his father. Paul definitely has developed some feelings for Jenny and feels strange. After he left her office, he began working with George and Owen. Gus Tanner has begun to set up a job and needs Paul's help.

About nine forty five, Bill Pyle wandered into the shop and went directly down to where Fletcher's gang is working. Paul can see Bill waving his arms around as the men are listening to him intently. Just before ten, Paul walked down to where Bill is and informed him that they should go to Brent's office.

"What are you gonna say when you get in there. You're gonna have to speak up ya know!" Art barked at Paul.

"When we get in there, I'm going to handle it" Paul replied looking directly at Art and speaking back at him.

Fletcher started to chime in but Paul walked away and began speaking to Bill in a low tone.

"When we get in there, let me do the talking. If he asks you something, answer him by all means but go along with me ok?"

"I need my job back. We got bills comin in ya know."

"Just do what I tell you Bill. They seem pretty bent on letting you go but I am going to do my best to get you back, but like I told you that day at your house, you can't have anything to drink during working hours and that means lunch too."

"Hey, some of those other guys go out for a beer at lunch and nothin's said" Bill said pointing down toward Fletcher's bunch.

Paul is beginning to get frustrated with Bill's lack of understanding about the whole situation.

"Look, those guys are not the issue here. You just do what I told you!" Paul said abruptly.

They entered Jenny's office and approached her desk.

"We have a ten o'clock appointment with Brent" Paul said quietly.

"OK, I'll tell him you're here. Hi Bill" she said.

"Hi". Bill said gruffly.

As Jenny got up from her desk and walked out to Brent's office, Paul noticed her dress. It is a very pale yellow with short sleeves and a white collar. It has a matching cloth belt and her high heel shoes are black. She looks very nice.

She returned momentarily and told them that they can go right in.

"Pretty dress" Paul said as he walked her.

Jenny gave him a wide smile and returned to her desk and resumed her typewriting. She is trying her best to concentrate on her job instead of Paul.

Brent is standing at his file cabinet and has removed a folder from the top drawer. He is wearing dark blue suit pants with a white dress shirt and a gray necktie. His matching suit jacket is hung on the back of his office chair. He sat down in his chair and pointed to the two chairs in front of his desk. He flipped through the papers in the folder quickly and then leaned back in his chair.

"Bill, we have a business here and safety is a top priority. Not only did you act in an unsafe manner, but you also caused damage to our fork lift. It could have been much worse and because of your negligence, this happened."

"Yeah, I drove behind the truck and the driver started backing up and hit me" Bill said sharply. This really wasn't true because the truck was already slowly backing up and Bill tried to beat it around behind rather than go way around in front.

"You had been drinking at lunch. You admitted that and the blood tests proved it to be true. We simply won't tolerate this so because of the evidence, we want to terminate you."

"Hey, there's other guys here that . . . ."

"Brent listen" Paul interrupted. "Bill made a mistake. He has admitted this as you stated but if you look at his record, he shows up every day on time and until now he has had no problems.

Now he has pledged that he will no longer drink any beer or any alcohol at lunch any more."

"Pyle, go outside and wait in Jenny's office" Brent said waving his hand toward the door.

Bill looked at Paul with a confused stare.

"Go ahead Bill. It's ok" Paul said almost feeling a little sorry for him.

Bill stood up and shuffled out the door closing it behind him.

"Look, we don't need this guy here after this. We can easily replace him" Brent said coldly.

"I understand what you are saying but he really needs this job. His poor wife is crippled and does the best she can. If you get rid of him he may not be able to get something right away and they could lose their house."

"Well, he should have thought of this before" Brent said.

Paul could see that he wasn't getting very far here so it was time for another approach. This is where Ray Webber's advice would come into play.

"Pyle works with machinery and it was just fortunate that he didn't injure someone" Brent said sharply.

"You're absolutely right Brent but truthfully there are other people here that work on machinery that have alcohol problems and you are not trying to fire them."

"Just a minute here!" Brent snapped. "You are talking about Alvin Brown aren't you. He is way more valuable than Pyle ever was to us. You leave him out of this!"

"I will . . . . but you see, Mr. Pyle's lawyer won't and if we can't resolve this, you and I, he is prepared to get an attorney and besides that, Alvin Brown has missed much more time than he has. Now Mr. Pyle has agreed that he will not have any alcoholic beverages during working hours ever again. He needs a second chance."

Brent pressed the button on his intercom and called Jenny.

"Jenny, have you been able to get a hold of Edwin Clay yet?"

"No I haven't. Do you want me to keep trying?"

"Keep trying and pass his call to me when you get it."

"Look Wilker, I have the medical report right here and Pyle was drunk. It shows it here and besides, he admitted it."

Paul leaned forward and quickly read the doctor's statement. He sat back in his chair and looked directly at Brent.

"Brent, where are the blood test results on the truck driver? I don't see them here" Paul asked in a cool tone.

This was one of Ray Webber's tactics and he hit the nail on the head.

"What report? He wasn't drunk."

"That's good to hear but I'd like to see his test results."

"There's no report. He wasn't drunk!" Brent said getting angry.

"See, we won't ever know this now because there is no report. You see, these are the things the attorney will be using in Mr. Pyle's defense."

Brent tapped the eraser end of his pencil on his desk. He pressed his intercom button again.

"Yes Brent" Jenny's voice said from the intercom.

"Bring your pad and come in here."

Jenny came in and sat down in one of the chairs in front of Brent's desk. He dictated a statement to her stating that: *I, William Pyle agree with the following terms. I will be allowed to return to work under the following conditions. I will be subjected to periodic testing for alcohol in my system and the tests will be at random. If at any time I fail such a test, I will be terminated immediately.*

"Type up two copies and bring them right back to me" Brent said. "Send Pyle back in here too."

Bill Pyle came back into the office and sat down in the chair that Jenny had sat down in. Brent informed him that he will be permitted to return to work provided that he signs the agreement and does what he is supposed to do. He informed him too that there will be no more chances if he is caught drinking during working hours. Jenny returned shortly with the forms that Brent has requested. Bill signed both of them and Brent took one copy and put it into Bill's file.

"All right. Report back tomorrow morning for work" Brent said handing Bill his copy of the agreement.

Bill started towards the door and Paul followed him. Paul turned to Brent and thanked him.

"Wait a minute Wilker" Brent said.

Bill Pyle stopped but Brent waved him out of the office.

"You put the squeeze on us. Just don't push too hard. You stand to do all right here but don't push too hard."

Brent is obviously frustrated but Paul has represented Bill as his union steward which he feels he is supposed to do. Paul started to say something but Jenny's voice came on the intercom.

"Brent, I have Mr. Clay on the line two for you" she said.

"Go back to work now" Brent said holding his hand over the mouthpiece of the telephone. As soon as Paul was out of the office, Brent spoke to Edwin who is at his home.

"What happened?" Edwin asked Brent.

"Wilker pulled a squeeze play. He said that Pyle is going to hire an attorney if we can't settle this. He also pointed out that there was no blood test done on the truck driver to see if he'd been drinking. He said that the attorney will use this against us along with the fact that Alvin Brown has a drinking problem and doesn't get canned."

"How did it end up?" Edwin demanded.

"I made him sign a letter. If he tests positive for alcohol any time in the future, we can fire him; he signed it."

"You know if he gets hurt or hurts somebody, we'll have to pay out workman's compensation."

"I know. I know" Brent said.

'Ya know, if it wasn't for Rita, I'd get rid of Wilker but she thinks he's some special guy or something."

Brent thought to himself that this will be a real disaster if this happened. That would mess everything up that he and Norma are planning on.

"Well, Pyle will screw up again. He can't stay off the sauce for too long. We'll check him every now and then."

"Are you coming in today?" Brent asked.

"I'll be there in an hour" Edwin said and hung up.

Paul went out into Jenny's office.

"May I say that you are looking very nice this morning" Paul said to her.

"Yes you may" she said smiling. "Nice going with Bill" Jenny said practically whispering.

"I just hope he lives up to his agreement" Paul said.

When he returned to the pressroom, he saw that Bill is back down talking to Fletcher and Art.

'Hey" Bill yelled to Paul.

Paul walked down to where they are. Several other men from Fletcher's crew joined the group too.

"Hey, what about my pay? You didn't say anything to him about my pay?"

"What pay is that?" Paul asked confused.

"My pay while I was out. My brother in law says they should pay me for that time if they don't fire me. He got canned where he worked and when they took him back, he got paid for the time he was out" Bill said pointing his finger at Paul.

"I don't think you are going be paid for the time you were out but at least you have your job back" Paul said.

"Look, my brother in law says I should get paid. He did."

"Bill, what was your brother in law let go from his job for?" Paul asked him.

"They said he was stealin shit but after they canned him, they found out it was two other guys and not him."

"That's different. He didn't do anything wrong. You did. You're going to be working again tomorrow. That's good isn't it?" Paul asked.

"Hey, I'm calling Lester. He'll make 'em pay me" Bill said moving back to where Fletcher is standing.

"Good idea Bill. Have Lester handle it" Paul said realizing that it is hopeless attempting to get through his thick head.

"Hey, what about the proposal? What are you doing about?" Art asked in his usual surly tone.

"One thing at a time" Paul said. I got this business straightened out and that is next."

Mike Cole, the day foreman came walking up to where the men are standing. Paul has discovered that Mike is alright to work for when things are going smoothly but if problems come up, he becomes extremely short tempered and not easy to work with. He has worked for the company for a number of years and knows the publishing business fully.

"Come on and get to work" he shouted. "You guys aren't being paid to shoot the shit."

Paul started heading back to the other press where George and Owen are. He thought to himself that Bill Pyle is ungrateful and rather stupid. "Hey, I did what I could for him. If he isn't happy, then it's tough shit for him" Paul said to himself.

That night, Paul went out to eat with Norma and they had a pleasant time. She told him that she has a big photo shoot the next morning so Paul went back to his apartment at eight thirty. He showered and took a bottle of beer from his refrigerator, turned on his television set and sat down on his sofa. He is not concentrating on the program. His mind is on Jenny. He finds himself thinking about her constantly. He laid his head back and started thinking about everything that has been going on in his life lately.

Am I really happy at the publishing company? Not really.

Was I happier working at Ike's garage? Yes.

Am I looking forward to managing the new Allendale plant? Yes, I guess so.

Am I starting to fall for Jenny? I don't want to . . . . but I can't stop thinking about her.

Wait a minute. How could I not be still in love with Norma? She's a girl any guy would want for his wife. And besides, because of her, I am going to step into a high paying job and be very comfortable financially . . . . but I still can't stop thinking about Jenny. I get that funny feeling in my stomach when I see her. What the hell is happening to me?

Well, when I go to Allendale, I won't be seeing her all the time and it will be easier . . . . but will I miss seeing her? I am really confused.

The next morning when Paul arrived at the plant and began to work, Jenny came out onto the floor and told him that Brent wants to see him. He walked in with her and then entered Brent's office. He is wondering what is on Brent's mind.

"Hi Brent. What's going on?"

"The delivery of the first new press that we purchased for Allendale has been delayed. It was supposed to be coming in the middle of this week but I got a call last night and it's not coming in until the middle of next week. You will be here all week."

"Ok" Paul said. Is that all you wanted to tell me?"

"That's all."

Paul went out into Jenny's office and noticed that she is not at her desk. He feels a little disappointed that he won't be seeing her again. As he went out on the floor, he saw Bill Pyle driving past on the fork lift. He has a pallet load of printed flyers that are ready to be shipped. He drove down to where Fletcher's office is and set it down beside it. Fletcher and Art are inside and came out to talk to Bill.

"Hey Bill, you got the job back huh?" Fletcher asked him.

"Oh yeah. He wasn't gonna let me come back but when I told him I was gettin a lawyer, he backed right down. I would've got one too. Hey, I don't give a shit."

Both Fletcher and Art laughed and then headed toward the press when they saw Mike Cole coming. He approached Bill and told him what he wants him to do.

"Go up to Gus's press and get two rolls of newsprint and put them over by the gantry so they can load them on the press. They're setting up a big job and it's a rush so hurry up."

Mike continued over to talk to Fletcher as Bill drove up to the other end of the shop where Gus is. The large rolls of newsprint are stored up past the second press. Bill drove the fork lift over to one of the rolls and stopped. He climbed out of the fork and placed a lifting bar through the hole in the center of the roll. The bar sticks out enough on both sides so the fork lift blades can lift it. He moved the blades so they cleared the sides and as soon as he got back into the rig he noticed that Edwin is coming over to where he is.

"Hi Mr. Clay" Bill said

"Shut you motor off" Edwin said pointing to the fork lift.

Bill quickly turned off his engine. He figured that Edwin is going to tell him that the company will pay him for the time he missed. Bill had called Lester the night before at his house and told him what his brother in law had said about being paid. Lester had told him that he will see what he can do about it which of course is not going to happen. He is humoring Bill like he had done to Melvin Pine before.

"Mr. Pyle, I understand that you threatened to hire an attorney and go to court over the termination business, is that right?"

"Well . . . . uh . . . that Wilker guy told me to say that. He . . . he told me that. Yeah, he told me that" Bill stammered. No, I wouldn't do that."

"After we loaned you money and all, I was really surprised when I was told that you said this."

"Ah . . . no no. Wilker told me that."

"All right Mr. Pyle. You have your job back for now but you're walking on thin ice. I'll be watching you and if we have any more trouble with you, you're done. Remember, you signed that letter."

"Oh no. no more trouble. No more" Bill said as he wiped the perspiration from his face with his handkerchief.

Edwin stared at him for about five seconds and then said "All right, back to work."

The week has progressed well and Paul is pleased that he is with George and Owen along with Gus. On Thursday morning, he took the job sheets into Jenny and noticed that she is wearing new eyeglasses. They are much more complimenting that her previous pair.

"I like your new specks" Paul said

"Thank you sir" she replied with her warm friendly smile.

Paul thought to himself that Jenny looks better every time that sees her. He noticed her freshly painted fingernails as she reached for the job sheets.

"Is Brent in yet?" Paul asked.

"He is. Do you want to see him?"

"Yes, just for a minute."

Paul tapped on Brent's door that is partially open and Brent told him to come in.

"Brent, have you made a decision regarding the proposal that I submitted to you?"

"I'll let you know tomorrow. A lot of the stuff on there is out of the question, I can tell you that."

"These guys work hard here and do a really good job. They deserve it don't you think?"

"I said I'll let you know tomorrow!" Brent answered impatiently.

"Ok, tomorrow then."

"I got a call last night from the trucking company that is bringing the first press here and it will arrive on Monday morning. I want you to go there and unload it. There will be several people from the press manufacturer who will begin to assemble it. Stay there as late as you have to. I want you to stop by here on your way home and leave off the paper work, you know, the packing list and whatever other papers come with it. I want you to actually start working there instead of here."

"Beginning Monday?" Paul asked.

"Yes. Once those presses are set up, we're going to begin printing jobs there. We have tons of orders, tons. We are ordering rolls of paper and drums of ink along with another fork lift. You will be getting a crew too. Several people from here and I'm hiring some new people for there too."

"Will I get someone to help unload the press that is coming Monday?"

"See Mike Cole on the floor and he'll give you someone" Brent said picking up his telephone to make a call.

"Ok" Paul said and returned to the pressroom.

That evening he told Norma that he is going to be starting at Allendale on Monday. She is ecstatic because that means that she and Brent are getting closer to their goal. She brought up the marriage plans too and told Paul that she plans to tell her parents on Labor Day weekend which is the weekend after the coming one.

"You seem to be acting funny. What's wrong? You do want to get married don't you?" she asked in a very serious tone.

"Oh sure. Sure I do. I'm just a little nervous about going to Allendale."

Norma kissed him and assured him that he will do just fine.

When Paul got home, Mrs. Bradford called him into her downstairs apartment. She told him that Ike had called and wanted him to call as soon as he got home. Paul thanked her and called Ike's home telephone. After two rings, Edna answered.

"Oh Paul, Ike wants to talk to you. Larry Nicholson was badly injured this afternoon. He was riding his motorcycle and collided with a car. He is in the hospital but we don't know how bad off he is."

"Oh no. Was he going home from work?" Paul asked finding it difficult to comprehend this.

"No, he was on a week's vacation. Wait, Paul. Ike just came in. He was just at the hospital to find out how Larry is doing. Here's Ike."

Paul could hear muffled voices and then Ike's voice came on.

"Hi Paul. I was just over the hospital to see about Larry. His wife was there and I guess the doctors told her that he is going to loose his right arm, his back is badly injured and his vision has been messed up from his head injury. I think I heard her say that he has a couple of broken ribs too."

Paul could hardly speak. Larry is a really decent guy and does not deserve this. He has a 1948 Indian Chief motorcycle that is his pride and joy. It is full dressed and Larry was always tinkering with it to keep it in top condition. He was very careful when he rode the motorcycle and was never reckless.

"I should go to see him" Paul said. "I feel really bad for him."

"Aw he's really drugged up Paul. I would wait a day or so. The doctors seem to feel that he should pull through but I can't imagine him working on cars anymore. I was going to pretty much retire very shortly because between my heel and my back aching a good deal of the time, I am ready. Larry was going to take over the whole shooting match but that looks like it's out of the question now."

"Gee, Ike, this is terrible. I'm supposed to start working over in Allendale next week and manage that whole plant but after hearing this . . . ."

"No no", Ike said butting in. "I don't expect you to change you future plans Paul. I'm going to bring Benny in from the salvage yard and have him work with me in the shop. I'll hire another mechanic and we'll be ok but I'm sure going to miss Larry."

Ike and Paul talked for a bit longer and then hung up. Ike said he will get back to him within the next few days and update him on Larry's condition. Paul took a bottle of beer from his refrigerator and sat down on the couch. He popped on his television but did not pay attention to the program. Instead, he began thinking about Larry and this most unfortunate turn of events. He thought about the station and how different things would be now if he had not met Norma that Sunday but most of all, he thought about Jenny. He put his head back against the couch and closed his eyes. He finished his beer and after placing the empty bottle on the floor beside him, he admitted to himself that he loves Jenny. He feels about her like he should be feeling about Norma. He thought to himself that once he and Norma get married, he'll forget about Jenny but quickly realized that this is not how he wants the rest of his life to be.

"She is always so pleasant and I'll never forget the swell time that I had with her the other day" he thought to himself. The more that Paul thinks about everything, the more confused and uneasy he becomes. He decided to take a ride in his car. It is starting to get dark earlier now that the summer is fading away. He thought about going to see Barbara, Larry's wife, but he decided against that. He figured that she may still be at the hospital but if she is home, she probably will prefer to just be with the children tonight. He drove out into the country, out to Southbrook where Junior Hutchinson's salvage yard is. After Paul drove through the small town, he noted how desolate it is and how it would be a real pain in the ass if one was to break down here. There are no street lights and both sides of the road are dense woods. Paul continued to go another three miles and then turned around and headed back towards Saxon. He suddenly felt very sleepy and started yawning continuously. Paul rolled the window down and the cool night air perked him up a bit.

The ride helped him somewhat but Jenny keeps coming into his mind. His admitting to himself that he loves her is kind of like the feeling you would get when you did something wrong and finally confessed what you did. You know you have done wrong but you feel better now that it is out into the open. He fell asleep quickly once he got into his bed but awoke at quarter past five and could not return to sleep. He got up and made himself some breakfast. He remembered that Brent is supposed to give him a decision about the proposal today. He thought to himself; this should be interesting.

CHAPTER FIFTEEN

Paul got to work early on this bright Friday morning. As he is walking into the plant, he is confronted by Fletcher who wants to know about the proposal. Paul informed him that Brent is to give him his offer today and he will report this offer to the union as soon as he hears anything. Fletcher started to preach to Paul about how he should be handling the situation but he cut him short and went to pick up the job sheets from the night shift. Paul went into Jenny's office and noticed that she is not at her desk. He placed the sheets in the basket on her desk and started to leave when Jenny came in from Brent's office. She is wearing a white cotton blouse and a blue pleated skirt with blue high heeled shoes.

"Good morning" she said walking over to her desk.

"Yes, it is" He said back to her.

"Paul, I have a box in the supply closet and can barely reach it. Could you help me get it down?"

"I can't think of anything I'd rather do" Paul said.

Jenny smiled at him and went over to the closet and entered it. Paul went in behind her.

"It's this one up here" she said pointing up towards the carton.

Paul looked straight into her eyes and had a serious sincere look on his face.

"Jenny, I want you to know that I had a really great time with you that Saturday when we were together. It was one of the best days of my life. I am so confused about everything that's happening. I can't sleep sometimes . . . . and I just don't know . . . but I do know that that day was really special and you're really special."

Jenny looked into his eyes with a searching stare. She is trying to understand what he means, what he is really trying to say. Paul wants to kiss her; he wants to kiss her passionately like she had done to him that Saturday. He reached up and pulled the carton out to the edge of the shelf. Jenny reached up to help him but Paul told her that he will get it down. He took the carton out into the office and placed it on the table.

"Jenny, I just want you to know that no matter what happens, you . . ."

Paul is cut off by Norma's voice as she suddenly appears in the office door.

"Ok. I caught you; flirting with the secretary. I've got to watch him like a hawk" Norma said laughing and looking at Jenny.

"What's going on?" Paul asked surprised to see her.

"I stopped by to see the new catalog. I was in a lot of ads in this one."

"I'll get a copy for you" Jenny said heading into the main office.

"Jenny, can you let me know when Brent gets in?" Paul asked.

"Oh, he's not coming in today. I guess he's making it a long weekend" Norma said.

"Not coming in? He told me he was going to give me answer about the proposal today."

"Oh, why don't you forget about that. You're going to Allendale next week so let it drop."

"Hey, I am taking Lester's place while he is out and the guys here say that this is what they want so I am doing this."

"Ok. If that's what you think you should do then call him. Call him now before him and Meredith go off. I think they are going up to the Pine River house for the weekend" Norma said.

Paul went out onto the floor and headed to where George and Owen are. He went by them and out in back to where the rolls of paper are stored. There is a telephone there and Paul picked up the receiver and dialed Brent's home telephone number. After several rings, Meredith answered.

"Hello" she said

"Hi Meredith. It's Paul."

"Paul. How are you? Hey, I understand that you and my sister are going to tie the knot really soon. Is this right?"

"Pretty soon" Paul answered.

They spoke for a minute and then Paul asked to speak with Brent. Meredith left the phone and shortly afterwards, Brent answered.

"Yes Paul. What is it?"

"I called about the proposal. What have you decided?"

"At this time, we don't feel that we are in a position to offer any pay raises or benefit increases. We have a huge amount of orders and I say that we do the work now and then we'll see about more increases later."

"So this your final answer?"

"Yep . . . . for now" Brent replied curtly.

"I'll tell the union body then. Goodbye" Paul said and returned the receiver to the telephone.

The more he deals with Brent, the more he is disliking him. He really does not care for the way he just did not show up at the plant and tried to blow him off. He stopped where George and Owen are and told them that he was going to meet with the union men at lunch and discuss the results of the proposal. He then went down to where Fletcher is and told him the same thing. Fletcher and Art started to question Paul but he said that he has to get to work on the other press and that he will see them at lunch.

Brent's telephone rang and he picked up the receiver. It is Norma.

"Can you talk?" she asked.

"Yeah, Meredith's upstairs in the shower."

"Did you tell Paul about the proposal?" Norma asked.

"You have a perfect ass, you know that?" Brent said quietly.

"Brent, what about the proposal? What's he gonna do?"

"What can he do. I'll be so glad when he's in Allendale next week" Brent said raising his voice slightly.

"I'll be so glad when we can dump him and be together for good my love" Norma said in a sexy tone.

"Oh yeah. I can't wait for that."

"I love you so, so much. "Goodbye for now" Norma said softly.

Norma had called from Brent's private office telephone. She went back out through Jenny's office and walked over to her desk. Jenny is seated and typing and stopped when she sees Norma standing there.

"I've got some news for you Jenny" Norma said

"Oh boy. I hope it's not bad" Jenny said smiling.

"You are going to be at the new plant in Allendale in a week or two. Brent's cousin Donna is going to be working here for him and you will be Paul's secretary."

"Are you serious?" Jenny asked with a shocked look on her face.

"Yes. Donna will be better off here because she is not familiar with the system like you are; and furthermore, you can keep an eye on my new husband. You can make sure he behaves."

"They are sending me to Allendale?" Jenny asked still shocked.

"Yes they are. In two weeks, Paul and I are doing it. We can't wait any longer. I want him so much" Norma said.

Jenny felt like she had been hit by a truck. She realizes now that Paul and Norma will be married really soon and now she will have to be working for him at Allendale everyday. She can not do this. It is going to be hard realizing that she will never be able to be with Paul now but seeing him on a daily basis now that he is going be married will be too much for her to bear.

"I really don't want to transfer to Allendale Norma" Jenny said firmly. "I think I have this office running smoothly and I would really prefer to remain here."

"They won't stick Donna there because she is not at all familiar with the company procedures. You are and that is why you are being sent there. Oh, and they are going to want you to show Donna the ropes before you leave" Norma said brushing a piece of lint off of her skirt.

"We are having a very small wedding but you are definitely invited. Paul speaks very highly of you and I know that he will like to see you there. I've got to run Jenny. Bye bye."

Jenny quickly exited her office and went directly into the ladies room. She began to cry and tried to stop so she would not look all red and puffed up when she went back to her desk. She cannot figure Paul out. She is puzzled as to the way he was talking to her before Norma had come into the office. It is Friday and when she gets through work today, she will go to her apartment and try to figure out what to do next. She does know one thing for certain. There is no way in hell that she will be going to their wedding.

When the buzzer went off signaling the lunch break, Paul went over to the area where the men eat. He generally eats lunch out in his car but today he wants to meet with the men. Everyone in the union on the day shift came over and began eating.

"Well, what's goin on?" Fletcher asked.

"The proposal was turned down. I was told that at this time the company can't pay any higher wages. I was also told that there are a lot of jobs coming up and after they are completed, then maybe they will review the proposal again. It sounds like a stall to me."

"So what are you going to do now?" Art asked.

"It's not what I'm going to do. It's up to you guys to decide what you want to do."

Art began egging Paul on and making it look like he was really interested in the proposal.

"So you want us to vote on whether or not we want to go further on this or forget it, right?" Art asked.

"That's right, yes."

"You mean strike?" Fletcher asked.

"Look, they have a lot of work coming up. They aren't going want labor disputes at a time like this. I think if you stand you're ground and insist on more pay and benefits, they'll come up with some of the stuff we are asking for at least" Paul said looking around at the group.

"Some of us have money loans with the company. If we strike, they will demand it in full" one of the men said.

"I am sure that if you actually do strike, it won't last long. You guys know what you are doing and they are not going to be able to bring in people to take your place. Experienced press workers won't work for this money and as far as the loans go, how can you pay it up if you aren't working?"

"We gotta think about it" Fletcher said.

"Yes. I have to tell the men on the other shifts and give them time to decide. I figure that we should vote on it next Tuesday morning first thing. I will be in Allendale all day on Monday but I will stop here Tuesday morning and we can vote."

Mike Cole came over to the lunch area and walked over to Paul.

"You've got to go to the Allendale plant right now. They are delivering a fork lift and some drums of ink. Maybe some rolls of paper too. You can drive a fork lift, right?" Mike asked.

Paul noticed that Fletcher and his gang were listening intently.

"Sure, I can drive one" Paul said confidently.

He figured if Bill Pyle can operate one, it can't be that difficult.

"Now Monday when the press comes, you are going to send someone to help me aren't you?" Paul asked Mike.

"Yeah yeah. You'll get a helper. Now get going. I don't want the stuff to arrive and have the driver leave because nobodies there to receive it."

Paul arrived at Allendale and opened up the building. He wasn't there ten minutes when a truck pulled up with a trailer behind it carrying the second hand fork lift that has been purchased. The driver let down the ramp on the rear of the trailer and backed the fork lift down onto the ground. He is a really nice man and gave Paul a crash course on how to operate it. The fork lift runs on propane and the driver left two extra full tanks besides the one that is already on the rig. He showed Paul how to change them.

Paul drove the fork lift around outside the plant and then inside and practiced with the controls. About forty five minutes later another truck came with two skids containing four 55 gallon drums each of different colored ink. The driver told him that rolls of newsprint are coming too but not until Tuesday. Paul unloaded the two skids and put them inside the building. He is pleased with himself and feels confident that he can handle the deliveries now. He figures that he will worry about unloading the new press on Monday.

After the truck left and Paul put the forklift inside, he went across the street and bought a bottle of Coca Cola and some peanut butter crackers. He is very hungry because he has not had any lunch with the meeting and all. He went back to the plant and ate his crackers and thought about Jenny and what he had told her earlier. He is glad he did but he feels so mixed up. He really cares deeply for her now but knows that he can't hurt Norma. He figures that he will get back on track now that he is going to be in Allendale and not be seeing Jenny everyday. He thought about Norma and what it will be like to be married to her. He has to curb his feelings for Jenny. Deep down though, way deep down, he feels that he is kidding himself.

Paul checked to see if the telephones have been connected and discovered that they have. He decided to call Lester and let him know what is going on. The telephone rang and no one was answering but just as Paul was about to hang up, Lester answered.

"Yeah hello" Lester said sounding like he had just woken up.

"Hi. It's Paul Wilker. How are you doin?"

"I'm doing alright. I got an infection where they operated on my leg but that's getting better. I'm still using crutches but I get around."

Paul told Lester what is going on with union at the plant. Lester humored Paul and made it sound like he is in favor of what he is doing.

"So, you got Pyle back to work I hear."

"Yes. He's been doing well so far that I can see. He hasn't been going out at lunch and having beer like before" Paul answered.

"How come you told Brent Royce that Al Brown works drunk sometimes?" Lester asked.

Paul thought to himself "how did Lester know that?" He must have been talking to Brent.

"I didn't say that. Brent did. I merely said that other people besides Bill have been in here drunk. He was the one that brought up Al's name."

"I'm surprised he took Pyle back. He's a pain in the ass. Ya know, he keeps calling me up and asking me to have them pay him for the time he was out. He'll screw up again. He won't last."

"I hope not. He really needs the job" Paul said.

"I wouldn't push these people too much if I were you Paul. Like I told you before, you got a good thing here" Lester warned.

They talked for a few minutes more and then after they hung up, Paul saw that it is just about time to leave for the weekend. He locked up the plant and headed home. "Thank God it's Friday!" he said aloud to himself as he pulled out of the parking lot.

Jenny opened the door to her apartment and dropped her pocketbook on the kitchen table. She took off her shoes and her nylon stockings and walked into her kitchen barefooted. She heated a bowel of chicken noodle soup and poured herself a glass of milk. She had a cup of jello and washed up her dishes. She went into her bedroom and decided to call Sandy. She needs to talk to someone.

"Hello" Sandy said breathing heavily.

"Hi Sandy. What are you panting for?"

"I was just coming in when the phone started ringing and I ran for it. What's up with you?"

"It's going to happen. Norma and Paul are going to be married very shortly and that's not bad enough. They're sending me to the new Allendale plant and I will be working for Paul" Jenny said with a shaky voice.

"Are you serious?" Sandy asked.

"I don't know what I'm going to do but I can't do that. I really love him and I would be really uncomfortable working there with him being married to Norma."

"How did you find this out. Who told you?"

"Norma told me . . . . And ya know what else? she wants me to come to their wedding."

"Geez Jen. What are you going to do?"

"Well I'm certainly not going to the wedding. I guess when I go in Monday to work, I'll try to see if Brent will let me stay and send the new girl to Allendale as soon as I train her."

"What new girl?" Sandy asked raising her voice slightly.

"Brent's cousin. She's starting there on Monday."

"Cut the shit . . . and they want you to train her for your job?" Sandy said in an even louder voice.

"Yes they do. Ain't that just peachy?"

"Is this cousin experienced at secretary work?" Sandy asked.

"I don't know what she is. I haven't met her yet . . . . but here's what really has me baffled. Paul came in my office this morning and got me aside and told me what a great day it was when we went to see his father and went to lunch. He told me that I was special and he was beginning to tell me something else but Norma came in and he stopped."

"He said that . . . . that you were special?" Sandy asked.

"He did and he said that he was really confused and couldn't sleep. He really seemed troubled and unhappy. Sandy, when Norma told me that they are getting married really soon, my heart broke" Jenny said with her voice shaking again.

"All right Jen, I'm coming over and I'm bringing white wine. You stay put. I'm on my way" Sandy said and hung up.

Jenny hung up her phone and lay back across her bed with her hands behind her head. She stared at the ceiling and thought how fortunate she is to have a friend like Sandy. She is the only person that she can really confide in. Her mother is no help and her aunt in Perkinsville is sweet and kind but Jenny can't comfortably tell her the things that she has told Sandy. She will have some wine with Sandy and talk some more. Jenny enjoys drinking white wine but knows her limit. One time when she first dated Ben, she got quite drunk and paid dearly later on when she was sick all night and part of the next day. She realizes that whatever pleasure she feels while she is drinking, the awful headache and the vomiting that follow is just not worth it. Jenny got up from her bed when she heard Sandy knocking on her door.

Paul woke up at seven thirty and for a few seconds didn't realize what day it is. When he remembers that it is Saturday, he is pleased because he doesn't have to work. He decided to call Ike and see if he is home or has gone off for the weekend with Edna. Ike answered and told him that Edna has had a cold all week so they decided to stay home. Ike planned to work at the garage and get some of the work done. Paul said that he is going to drive over to Fairdale to see him. Norma is going to be busy a good part of the day with a photoshoot that had been canceled earlier because the sets had not been completed.

Paul got dressed and left his apartment. He stopped at a small diner on the way to Fairdale and had breakfast. He ordered two dropped eggs on wheat toast, homefries, orange juice and coffee. He has eaten there before and really enjoys their breakfast specials. Outside, the weather has warmed up considerably and the sunshine is brilliant so he started the Plymouth and lowered the top. He noticed that he is running low on fuel but he figures he'll wait and buy it at Ike's.

It is a pleasure driving along with the convertible; the breeze blowing and the smooth highway ahead. Paul entered Fairdale and turned onto Willow Street. He pulled into the service station and up to the gasoline pumps. Bobby Myres came out and walked up to Paul's car.

"Bobby. How have you been?" Paul said reaching out his hand.

"Doing good Paul. How about you? I hear you're going to be managing your own publishing business or something like that."

"Yeah it kinda looks that way" Paul said. "Hey Bobby, I didn't know you were back working here again."

"I asked Ike if he needed weekend help because Sally's going to have a baby and we need extra money; you know how it is Paul."

"A baby! Congratulations. Hey, how is Sally?"

"Aw she's great Paul. Things are really going well" Bobby said with a wide grin.

"Well you give her my best. She is a really nice person."

"I will Paul. Do you want to fill it?"

"Oh yeah" Paul said and removed the gas cap.

Bobby placed the fuel hose nozzle into the fuel fill opening and began filling the tank. Paul went inside the first bay and saw Ike and Benny. There is a Rambler station wagon up on the lift with the corroded exhaust pipe hanging down in sight. In the bay next to it there is a '54 Chevrolet two door sedan with the hood raised. The cylinder head has been removed and is on the workbench. The valves are removed from the head and have been placed in order in a wooden yardstick that has holes drilled into it for this purpose. The valve springs are lined up neatly beside the stick.

"Hey, does anybody in here have any idea what they are doing?" Paul asked loudly.

Both men walked over to Paul and greeted him. Paul noticed that Ike is moving very stiffly and appears to be in some pain. After talking a few minutes, Ike motioned to Paul to accompany him to the rear office. Benny resumed working on the Rambler that is on the lift. When they got inside the office, Ike gently sat on the edge of the desk.

"Ike, are you ok?" Paul asked looking very concerned.

"Between my heel and my stiff, aching back . . . . well, I can't put in the time that I did before. I can do four or five hours and I have to stop and rest. I just don't know how much longer I can keep this up."

"How's Benny doing?" Paul asked.

"Benny's good. He does the best he can but he doesn't know the half of what Larry does."

"How is Larry doing?"

"Not so good. I told you that they had to remove his arm just below his shoulder and he completely lost the sight in his left eye. A bunch of his teeth were knocked out and they are not sure how long it will be before he can walk again . . . all because some idiot ran through a stoplight."

"Jesus, that's terrible. He is such a great guy" Paul said shaking his head.

"I haven't been able to find anybody yet but we've put an ad in the paper and I've got a sign in the window".

"Ike, do you want me to come back and help you at least until you can find someone? "I'll explain to them at the plant and see . . . ."

"No no. nothing doin" Ike said firmly. "You have what sounds like a great opportunity and you will be marrying Norma . . . . no I don't want you to do that."

"Yes but . . . ."

"We'll be ok. You stay where you are" Ike said standing up and placing his hand on Paul's shoulder.

Paul and Ike went back out into the bay and talked with Benny for a short while. Bobby joined them between them between gas customers. Paul went outside and moved the Plymouth away from the pumps and over beside the station. Edna spotted him and came out of the house and walked over to Paul.

"I'm not going to hug you dear because I don't want you to get my cold. How have you been doing?" Edna said smiling at her nephew.

"I'm doing fine" Paul said.

"Now you're staying for lunch aren't you?" Edna asked.

"You just try and stop me" Paul said laughing slightly.

Paul stayed until three o'clock and decided it was time to head back to Saxon. He feels very depressed because of what has happened to Larry and because Ike seems to be struggling so hard. As he drove along the road back to Saxon he has everything that is going on racing through his head. He really wishes that he could help Ike in some way but he can only hope that things will improve shortly for both Ike and Larry.

John Reddie

Earlier in the day Brent and Meredith sat at the breakfast table at the Pine River house. Meredith has made them a nice breakfast with waffles and has fresh maple syrup along with oatmeal and coffee. Alice is running all around the house. Up the stairs and down again she is going.

"Gee honey, don't you wish you had a third of her energy?" Meredith asked Brent amused by Alice's friskiness.

"Yes, that would be nice" Brent answered.

Brent is thinking of Norma and how he would like to be with her right now in bed. He can't stop thinking about her and how sexy she is. He knows that she is tied up with her photo shoot for most of the day and tonight she will most likely be going out with Paul.

Meredith suggested that they take a nice hike through the woods. There is a beautiful trail that begins behind the house and leads to a fire road that goes deep into the forest. It is a beautiful morning for a hike. The weather is warm but not oppressive with humidity as it had been earlier in the month. Brent agreed so Meredith packed some sandwiches with some snacks and water.

"Maybe this hike will use up some of Alice's energy so she'll sleep tonight" Meredith said reaching out and squeezing Brent's hand.

"If I can get her into bed fairly early, maybe we can have some overdue sex. I brought a new little night gown to wear. What do you think?"

"Sounds good to me" Brent said trying his best to act enthusiastic.

Meredith stood on her tip toes and kissed Brent passionately with her arms around his neck.

"It's a date" she said quietly and beamed at him.

Meredith loves to walk in the forest behind the Pine River house. When she was a young girl in her teens, she would walk up the fire road as often as she could. She would stop by one of the big rock formations and sit on the rocks and smoke and open up her mind to many different thoughts. The fire road had been built back in the thirties during the depression by the Civilian Conservation Corp. They also constructed some of the roads that now exist thus making this beautiful area more accessible. People now live here year round. The park department maintains the fire roads now. Meredith was not a popular girl with her school classmates like Norma had been. Norma participated in many school activities and was constantly being sought after by most of the boys. Meredith was more of a loner and was often overshadowed be her sister. Although she had several girlfriends from school, she enjoyed being alone too, especially if she could get away into the forest. She loved to go there in the fall when the foliage turned colors.

In 1944, a girl in her late teens who had been reported missing, was found murdered in the forest not far from where Meredith went. She had been strangled and the killer was never caught. Meredith often thought about this but was still drawn to the peace and solitude that the forest provided her. Back then, the area was far less populated than later on when Meredith hiked there. From 1950 to 1955, the Pine River area grew in homes and residents tremendously although the part of the fire road where she went was and still is vast and unpopulated.

It was actually in the forest where she first met Brent. He was working for the park department during the summer then and one of their tasks was to keep the fire roads through the wooded areas clear. He was a handsome young man with an athletic build and Meredith was immediately attracted to him. Brent liked her some but became really interested when he learned that she came from a well to do family. His family has gotten by over the years but can not come close to the wealth that the Clay's possess. Brent is now doing very well financially. He and Meredith have a beautiful home with a large secluded yard and the neighborhood where they live has equally nice homes owned almost exclusively by professional people. Most men would be more than content with Brent's situation but his obsession with Norma and her plot to take over the business is what he wants. His material wealth and Meredith's devotion to him is not enough.

Meredith feels that things are not quite right with Brent and her from time to time but she shuts those feelings out of her mind when they happen. She loves him so much and is willing to put up with almost anything to keep him. She has no idea what her sister and husband are concocting. They have done a good job of concealing their intentions for the future . . . . so far.

As Paul is entering his apartment, the telephone is ringing. It is Norma calling him to see what they are doing tonight.

"How are you my sweet guy?" Norma said. "I really missed you today."

"Hi. I really missed you too. How did your session go?"

"It went alright but I have to go back on Monday because we couldn't finish. More trouble with the sets."

"Those sets have been a real pain huh" Paul said.

"So, how about we get a bite to eat and then hit the drive-in. You girl friend is playing there."

"My girl friend?" Paul asked.

"Yes. Natalie Wood. They're showing "Sex And The Single Girl" and maybe I'll let you watch a little of it" Norma said laughing a little.

Paul had two movie starlet heartthrobs growing up. The first was Terry Moore whom he had first seen in a movie called "The Return Of October" when he was eight. She was so pretty and perky that he developed an instant crush on her. When he saw Natalie in "Rebel Without A Cause", she joined Terry in his dream girl interests.

Paul told Norma that he will pick her up at her house in an hour. After they had some supper, they went to the open air theater and parked. They did some hugging and kissing and afterwards Norma talked about their engagement. She also surprised Paul by telling him that she thinks that he is doing a great job filling in for Lester. He is a little baffled because earlier she had more or less told him to back off about the proposal. Norma is of course saying this to keep Paul from becoming frustrated. Things are going smoothly and she doesn't want to mess anything up at this stage of the game.

What is really bothering Norma is that she hasn't been able to sneak off with Brent even though they had gotten together during the recent cook out. This weekend is out because he and Meredith have gone to the Pine River house. "Patience, I must be patient" she keeps telling herself.

Sunday was a quiet day for Paul. He had lunch at the Clay's house and in the afternoon, he played several games of tennis with Norma. At one point Paul excused himself and went into the house to use the bathroom. As he was heading back out to the tennis court, he met Rita in the kitchen. Rita pushed herself up close to Paul and looked him straight in his eyes.

"Are you nervous about starting in the new plant?" she asked in a husky voice.

"Well, maybe a little" Paul said.

"Don't be" You're going to be just fine" Rita said pushing herself even closer to him.

Paul is sure that Rita is a little buzzed as she seems to be most of the afternoons when he is over at the Clay residence. She is not slurring her words or walking unsteadily; she just seems to be a little drunk. Paul likes Rita and is concerned about her. She smokes constantly and seems to have an air of sadness about her at times. Paul figures that this explains the drinking and excessive tobacco use. Rita looks older but is still attractive and has a radiant smile when she seems happy.

"Well, if you are happy about me going to Allendale, then that what's most important" Paul said smiling at her.

Rita put her arms around Paul and gave him a good squeeze. "I'm happy" she said looking up at him and smiling. "I'm very happy."

Paul joined Norma outside and told her that he is going to go to his apartment. He wants to get ready to go to Allendale the next day. Norma gave him a lingering kiss and put her hand on his face.

"I'll call you tomorrow after work" she said to Paul as he got into his car. Paul started the car. Norma kissed two of her fingers and reached in and touched them on Paul's lips.

"See you tomorrow" she said softly.

Paul backed his car down the driveway and out onto Temple Street. As he headed towards his apartment, he began thinking about Jenny and how he is going to miss seeing her now that he will be at the new plant. Neither he nor Norma knows that tomorrow will bring big changes in both of their future plans. No one knows what the future holds, but in this case they will find out theirs in less than twenty four hours.

CHAPTER SIXTEEN

Paul did not sleep right away and when he finally did, he had another of his recurring dreams. This one was not the one with the filling station and the total darkness behind it. In this dream, he is driving into an area that he is completely unfamiliar with. As he goes along further, the road becomes more and more surrounded with water on both sides until finally it covers the entire road in front of him. Deep water is all that is ahead of him. He turns his car around just before it enters the badly flooded area of the road and he begins to hurriedly head back in the direction that he has just come from. As he continues to drive, he goes further and further into areas that he has never seen and begins to realize that he cannot find a way back to where he recognizes. The further he drives, the more unfamiliar the surroundings become. At this point he awakens and feels uneasy and then is relieved that this is not real.

He got up and showered and decided to stop and get a cup of coffee and an apple turnover on his way out to Allendale. He arrived at the new plant at quarter of seven. He opened up the small door that led into what will be the office. He sat down on one the new chairs that have been delivered the previous week along with two desks and several filing cabinets. He removed the lid from his cup and sipped the fresh, hot coffee. He mulled over in his mind how he will handle the upcoming events that are scheduled to take place on this first day here.

As Paul is finishing his coffee and turn over, the telephone rings. It is one of the representatives from the company that is coming to set up the new printing press. Paul said that the first press is due to arrive sometime in this morning and that he will unload it inside of the building and uncrate the pieces. He is also assigned to check off the parts that are received per the packing invoice and drop the paperwork off with Brent at the end of the day. The representative said that he and another man are coming from New Jersey and will arrive tomorrow morning. That will give Paul time to get things in order for them. The man seems very pleasant and courteous and gave Paul his number in case he has any questions.

As he hung up the telephone, he looked outside and notices George Baxter getting out of his '52 Pontiac. Paul walked over to the doorway and looked at George as he walked up towards the building.

"Hey George. What are you doing here?" Paul asked.

"They told me to come out and help you. I guess you've got stuff coming here today they said."

"Who told you that?"

"Mike Cole" George said.

Paul sees now what is happening here. George is a great guy and a pleasure to work with but he is almost eighty years old. Those guys at the Saxon plant know that Paul won't let him do any heavy work so by sending George, Paul will have to do all of the heavy stuff himself. Paul at this point is very happy that he has been sent to Allendale.

"Well right now George, we're kind of at a standstill until the truck arrives. When that happens, we can get the pieces unloaded and open up the crates. You can check off the items on the packing lists as I remove them. Sound good?"

"Hey, whatever you say. You're the boss man ya know" George said smiling at Paul.

Jenny arrived at the Saxon plant just before eight o'clock. She looks tired. She, like Paul, had not slept well either. She entered her office and put her pocketbook down on the floor beside her desk. Brent came to the door and asked her to come with him into his office. They entered and a young girl about her age is sitting in one of the chairs in front of Brent's desk. The girl stood up when they appeared. She is short, just five feet tall. She has a cute face and her hair is parted in the middle and comes down just above her shoulders and flips up slightly. It is a strawberry blond color. She is wearing a black pleated skirt with a ruffled white long sleeved blouse. She has on flesh colored nylon stockings and black high heeled shoes. She looks more like a sophomore in high school than the twenty two year old woman that she is.

"Jenny, this is my cousin Donna. I want you to show her what you do in your office because I am sending out to Allendale next week. You will be working for Paul Wilker as his secretary."

"Hi Donna" Jenny said forcing herself to smile. 'It's nice to meet you."

"Hi Jenny" Donna said in a squeaky voice and smiling back at her.

"I want you to show her everything" Brent said to Jenny.

Jenny and Donna started toward the door leading to her office. As they got inside, Jenny stopped.

"Have a seat Donna, I'll be back in a minute or so."

Jenny went back into Brent's office and closed the door behind her. Brent looked up from his desk and appeared surprised to see her again.

"Brent, I don't want to go to Allendale. I'm very happy here and I'm sure that when I show Donna the office procedure, she will be able to function there just fine."

"No chance. I need you're experience there. I'm not subjecting her to all of that responsibility so soon. You are going there next Monday . . . . oh wait. Next Tuesday. Next Monday is Labor Day."

Jenny's heart sank. She really isn't happy with all of this. She entered her office and sat down behind her desk. She began talking to Donna about some of the duties connected with her job. It is not Donna's fault that this is happening. She is in need of a job just like anybody else but after a few minutes of talking to her, Jenny realizes that Donna has next to no secretarial training or knowledge.

At twenty minutes past nine, a White Freightliner tractor trailer truck pulled up in front of the Allendale plant. It has a flatbed trailer with the crates containing the press sections and parts covered over with heavy canvas tarpaulins tightly tied to the trailer bed. On the doors of the tractor, there is lettering that reads:CROSS COUNTRY MOTOR FREIGHT and beneath that: COLTONVILLE, OKLAHOMA. The driver climbed down from the cab and noticed Paul and George standing in the office doorway. He walked over toward them and they met him halfway.

The driver is tall and thin as a rail. His face is long, thin, bony, and red in color. He is wearing a thin moustache and his hair is brown what can be seen of it. He has on a black Stetson hat along with a black tee shirt, blue jeans, and pointed toed cowboy boots.

"Mornin" he said to Paul and George.

"How are you today?" Paul asked looking straight into the driver's gray eyes.

"I'm doin ok but I'll be a hell of a lot better after I get some breakfast. I drove all night."

"Where did you pick this load up. In Indiana wasn't it?" Paul asked.

"Yup. Just outside of Indianapolis. Where are you goin to unload this?"

"I guess we are going to do it inside with the crane" Paul said pointing to the building.

"Have you got lift cables to sling these crates?" the driver asked.

"Lift cables?" Paul asked.

"Yeah. A couple of these crates are pretty big and heavy. You gotta have cables or lift wires to pick them up with your crane. The crates are setting on four by four oak planks so you can get under to lift them."

"We don't have any of the wires. You don't by chance have any do you?" Paul asked him.

"No sir I don't."

"Hang on. I gotta make a call" Paul said

"While you're doing that, I'm gonna run over to that diner and grab a quick bite" the driver said.

"Yeah, sure" Paul said.

Paul went into the office and picked up the telephone. He called the Saxon plant to see if they have or know where he can get the wires he needs. The phone rang twice and Jenny answered.

"Rollins Publishing, Jenny Morris speaking."

"Jenny. This is Paul. How are you this morning?" Paul asked.

"I'm ok. How is it going out there so far?"

Jenny's heart sped up when she heard Paul's voice.

"Well, not as good as I'd like. I need to talk to Mike Cole. Can you connect me to him?"

"Sure. I hope things get better for you Paul."

"Jenny . . . . I already miss seeing you in the office and it's only been a couple days . . . . You know."

There was a pause and then Jenny said "I'll page Mike for you now".

The intercom that went out into the shop had been fixed over the weekend so Jenny no longer has to go out onto the floor. She can call Mike from her desk which makes things easier.

Mike is down talking to Fletcher and Art along with Denny when he hears the call. He took it in Fletcher's office.

"Hello" Mike said abruptly.

"Mike, this is Paul. I've got a problem out here. The press is here but I need lift cables to get it off of the truck. Do you have anything like that that I can use?"

"Nope. You'll have to figure something out."

"Like what?" Paul asked rather agitated.

"Hey, you're a big manager now. You gotta work out your own problems. Did your helper show up?"

Paul could hear Fletcher and Art chuckling in the background.

"He's here and believe me, he's the only guy from there that I would want to help me."

Mike began to say something but then realizes that Paul has hung up his phone.

"Seventeen years I been working here and it took me ten to get a foreman job. This asshole's planking the boss's daughter and he gets his own plant in a couple a months" Mike said aggravated.

Fletcher laughed and put his arm around Mike and shook him lightly.

"C'mon you guys! Get busy and get this job set up. It's gotta be done today."

"Yeah sure, sure Mike. We'll get it done for ya" Fletcher said still laughing slightly.

Paul went back outside to where the truck is and walked over beside George.

"Well, they were no help as usual" Paul said.

"'You know, I been thinking. Maybe that lumber yard down there has something we could use. They handle big loads all the time and they must have something."

"George, you deserve a pay raise" Paul said patting him on the shoulder.

The truck driver came back and looks refreshed after his meal. Paul asked him to uncover the load while he walked down to the lumber yard. At the end of the long row of buildings where one of them is the new plant, there is a lumber yard. Allendale Lumber Company is displayed on the sign by the highway that runs past the yard. Stacks of lumber are piled beside an enormous shed that is open on one side. More lumber is stored inside the shed also.

As Paul approaches the yard, he can see two men stacking boards onto a skid. He walked over to them and when he got close, they stopped what they are doing.

"Hi. I'm sorry to interrupt you but I'm hoping you may be able to help me."

The larger of the two men wiped the perspiration from his face with his red checkered handkerchief. He is wearing green pants and a matching short sleeved work shirt with the company name over one pocket and his name "Tex" over the other. The other man appears to be younger and has the same style uniform. His name "Lew" is displayed on his shirt. Both men have plastic yellow safety hard hats.

"What's that that you need?" Tex asked still drying his face.

"Well, We're working in that building over there and we have some large crates that arrived. We have a crane inside but no wire slings to lift them off. I was hoping that you may have a couple that we could borrow. I'm Paul by the way" he said reaching his hand out to them.

"Glad to know ya" Tex said with a broad smile and shaking Paul's hand.

"We do have cables for lifting loads but maybe I can get that stuff for ya with our big fork lift. We use it to pick up big stacks of lumber all the time."

"Gee, could you." Paul said. "That would be really great."

"We can do anything" Lew said. "The impossible just takes a little longer."

All three men laughed.

"You guys won't get into trouble with your boss will you? "I wouldn't want that" Paul said seriously.

"Na. We're getting ready to take a break anyway" Tex said. "I'll get the rig and be right up."

Paul walked back to where the truck was. The driver had the tarps removed and was starting to take off the fastening straps.

"Those guys are going to help us. They think that we can get this stuff off with their big fork lift" Paul said to George.

"That's how these were loaded; with a fork lift. That'll work" the driver said.

"Hey, do you go all over the country?" Paul asked the driver.

"Yes sir. When I leave here, I'm going to Albany New York and taking a load from there to Sacramento in California."

"Wow, that will be a good ride" George said.

"Before I leave here, I'm pulling this here truck down over the far end of this lot and sack out for a spell. I'm beat" the driver said grinning and exposing his tobacco stained teeth.

Tex and Lew pulled up beside the truck with their fork lift. There is lettering on the mast of the fork lift that reads 10 ton. It is a large rig and capable of lifting heavy loads. It is open with safety bars that protect the driver. Both Tex and Lew got down from the fork lift and surveyed the crates on the trailer. Two of the crates are quite long; almost the width of the overhead door opening. They contain the sections of the press frame.

"I'm gonna pull the fork inside the building and then you can back in and I'll unload this inside. We can place these crates so you can set them where you need to with the crane later" Tex said to Paul.

Tex drove the fork lift inside the building and pulled to one side. The truck driver backed the trailer into the building and stopped so Tex can get at the crates easily. Lew spread the lifting blades out as far as they would go. Tex lifted the crates from the trailer and placed them on the blocks that Paul has taken from the trailer and laid evenly on the floor. The truck driver drove back out into the parking lot. He handed Paul the paper work to be signed and then drove to the far end of the lot like he said he was going to do.

Paul walked over to where Tex and Lew are. They are talking to George.

"If you need the lift cables later, let me know" Tex said with a friendly smile.

"What do I owe you fine gentlemen?" Paul asked. "We couldn't have done it without you."

"How about coffee?" Tex said again with a wide grin.

Paul walked up to the fork lift and reached into his pocket.

"How about dinner?" Paul said handing Tex a ten dollar bill.

Jenny and Donna are in the secretary's office and Jenny has been going over the different phases of her job. She is very depressed because of what is happening. She cannot stop thinking about Paul and how much she cares for him and how crushed she is because he is marrying Norma. Donna is asking her questions about various things related to the job but Jenny is hardly hearing her.

After about an hour, Brent entered the office. He asked how it is coming with the training.

"Jenny, I want you to show Donna as much as you can today and tomorrow, you'll go out to Allendale and start working there" Brent said

"But you said next week" Jenny said standing up and looking directly at him.

"I've changed my mind. I need you there tomorrow. I'll bring Phyllis in for a few days to work with Donna."

Jenny stood still for a moment and then walked past Brent.

"I'm sorry. I can't do this. I'm leaving. I can't go . . . ." she said tearfully and waving her right arm.

As she got to the door, she realizes that she has left her pocketbook on the floor next to the desk. She went back and picked it up and headed for the door again.

"What do you mean you can't? You're quitting?" Brent asked in a raised voice.

"I'm quitting" Jenny said wiping her eyes with a tissue and walking around Brent.

"Wait a minute. You can't just leave like this!" Brent said even louder.

"I'm sorry. It has nothing to do with you Donna. Nothing" Jenny said and walked hurriedly out into the parking lot. She got into her blue Ford Falcon sedan and drove away.

"Well, this is just great" Brent said and stalked off into his office.

On the way to her apartment, Jenny has decided that she will go and stay with her aunt in Perkinsville for a while. She just wants to get away from Saxon and everything to do with what has happened. She has saved some money and still has the rest of her inheritance that her father left to her so financially, she is alright for a while. She got to her apartment and packed some of the things that she will need like clothing and canned food. She went down stairs and told her landlady that she will by away for a while and not to worry. She also told her that she will give ample notice if she decides to give up the apartment. The landlady is extremely fond of Jenny and realizes what a good tenant she is. She even offered to lower the rent a little if she will not move.

"We'll see" Jenny said.

Her landlady is concerned because Jenny does not seem herself. She seems despondent and troubled but she figures that if Jenny wants to talk about it, she will. At this point, Jenny just wants to get away from Saxon and the publishing company and try to focus on other things. She gets along really well with her aunt in Perkinsville who is her father's sister. Jenny had lived with her when she went to secretarial school. The only reason that she moved to Greengrove was to be nearer the plant but now she wants to be away from it.

Paul has brought some tools from Saxon to open the wooden crates. He brought a hammer, crowbar, a cat's paw nail puller, and several screwdrivers. He has one of the crates that contained a frame section opened and has George checking off the items on the packing list. As he began to open the next crate, Edwin came in and walked over to the frame section and inspected it.

"The representatives from the press company will be here tomorrow to begin assembling this" Edwin said to Paul.

He has a cool air about him and Paul figures that he is still a little peeved about the Bill Pyle incident. Paul has noticed a change in Edwin's demeanor since then.

"Yes, one of them called here this morning. When do you expect the other press to be delivered?"

"Sometime later this week I believe" Edwin said looking closer at the press section.

"How are you doing George?" Edwin asked.

"I'm still kickin", George answered

Paul went back to the crate that he had been opening while Edwin walked around the floor checking things out. He came back to where Paul and George are working.

"How did you get these pieces off of the truck?" he asked Paul.

"Well, we didn't have any lifting cables so we asked the guys over in the lumber yard if we could use their cables. They were kind enough to unload these pieces with their fork lift for us. That's something we might want to do maybe."

"What's that?" Edwin asked.

"Well, shouldn't we get some lifting cables so we can take the crates off when the next truck arrives?" Paul suggested.

"Just use theirs. You said that they had cables didn't you?" Edwin asked sharply.

"Yes. They do have cables."

"Well, use their cables then."

"Ok" Paul said and went back to opening the second large crate.

"Paul, on your way home, stop by the Saxon plant and give Brent the paperwork that came with this shipment. I'm leaving early this afternoon so give them to him."

"I'll do that" Paul said.

"All right then. I'll see you men later" Edwin said and went outside to his car.

Paul and George opened the rest of the crates and piled the wood neatly by the overhead door. Paul looked at his wristwatch and sees that it is twenty minutes to one. This explains why his stomach is growling. He has not eaten since early this morning.

"George. What do ya say we stop and have some lunch? You must be hungry and I know I am."

"Ok by me" George said.

Paul left George at the plant and walked across the road to the diner. He ordered two hamburgers, two orders of French fries and two cups of coffee to go. Paul brought back some small packets of mustard and ketchup and some sugar and cream for the coffee. He walked back to the plant and he and George sat down and began eating.

"Hey George, that diner is pretty good. It looks like they have a nice breakfast menu."

"Yeah?" George said as he chewed his hamburger.

"I'll have to try it some morning" Paul said. "Not tomorrow though. I'm going to stop by the Saxon plant on my way here for the vote . . . you know . . . the one about the pay raises and all."

"Paul" George said and then hesitated and took a sip of his coffee

Paul looked at him and wanted to hear what he had to say. George stood up and took his cigarette pack from his pants pocket, withdrew a cigarette, and lit it. He returned the pack to his pocket and sat down again.

"Paul, I'm telling you this because I like you and I think you should know what is going on. Those guys are stringing you along. They're all going to vote against the proposal that you submitted. Lester got Fletcher and Art and a few of the others to spread the word around the shop to vote it down. They're making it look to you that they want it but nobody's going to vote yes on it."

"Hey, I'm not the least bit surprised" Paul said pushing a French fried potato into his mouth.

"If I were you Paul, I'd just come here tomorrow and forget the voting thing" George said.

"I mean, you're going be here from now on so the hell with them. Why waste your time?"

"Oh no". They put me on the line and demanded that I do something for them. It would be too easy for me to just blow the whole thing off. This way, I'll have a little fun with 'em" Paul said.

"Well, you do what you want. Ya see, me, I don't care. I'm just working there to keep busy and save some money. I'll be eighty a year from this coming November and I'm going to retire then and take my daughter on a nice car trip out west. All this money I'm making at the plant goes into a savings account for this trip we are planning. I have a nice pension from the town that I collect every month and it's more than enough to get by on. I was the tax collector in Wellton for many years."

"Geez George, that sounds great. Are you taking your old '52 Pontiac out west?"

"No no. I'm buying a brand new Pontiac and when we get home, I'll give it to her and keep mine."

"That's nice George. Really nice" Paul said smiling.

"I bought my '52 brand new and the next morning, my wife and I left and went out west to California, Oregon and then through the Grand Canyon. My daughter couldn't go with us so I'm taking her next year. The only thing I really feel bad about is that my wife died and won't be with us. She passed away eleven years ago."

"I'm sorry to hear that George. I'm sure that you and your daughter will really enjoy this trip" Paul said.

"Paul, my daughter had a stroke a while back and went through a lot. She was engaged to be married at the time and her future husband bailed out on her after she had it, the son of a bitch. It's taken a long time but she's pretty close to fully recovered now and pretty soon she'll be able to drive a car again."

"I can't believe that those guys are always giving you flack about getting out and retiring. That is your business. Do they know what you've been through with your daughter and loosing your wife and everything?"

"Yeah some of em do but I don't give a damn what they say. A good percentage of the guys there are ok but some just seem to enjoy giving other people shit. Paul, you're lucky because you got your whole life ahead of you. You are going to be married and this will be really nice. I wouldn't trade one second of the years that I had with my wife for anything. She was always healthy but when she did get sick, she went right downhill and died in three weeks. I've had all kinds of stuff wrong; gall bladder, burst appendix and teeth trouble. When you have the right person with you, there is nothing better."

Jenny quickly popped into Paul's head when George said this but his train of thought is interrupted by the telephone ringing. Paul picked up the receiver and answered it.

"Paul, this is Brent. How are you guys doing with the shipment?"

"We're doing good. We should have all of the crates opened and most if not all of it checked in today" Paul answered.

"All right. Drop off the paperwork to me here on your way home tonight."

"Ok. I'll see you later" Paul said and hung up the receiver.

Paul and George went back to their task of opening the crates and checking the contents against the packing lists. Everything seemed to be in order and by three thirty in the afternoon, they had everything opened, checked and ready for the men that are scheduled to arrive the tomorrow to begin the assembly.

"In the morning when I get here, I'll ask the guys in the lumber yard if we can borrow their cables so these pieces can be placed where they belong. Are you coming back here tomorrow George?"

"Unless I hear different, I'll be here with ya."

"Good. I hope so" Paul said as he gathered the packing papers together.

"So you say you're going to go to Saxon first tomorrow before coming here?" George asked as they begin to leave.

"That I am. Hey, I've got to represent my fellow workers. They're counting on me" Paul said laughing slightly.

"Yeah right. Ok then. I'll see you tomorrow Paul" George said and walked towards his car.

Paul got into his car and started the engine. As he pulled out onto the road in front of the plant and began to drive away, he started remembering about what George had told him about the men at the Saxon plant. He thought about Lester having Fletcher and some the guys spread the word around to not vote for the proposal after leading Paul to believe that they are in favor of it. Paul thought how Junior sure has those guys pegged. He pulled up to the intersection and stopped for the red traffic light. The green light flashed on and he turned left onto the road heading to Saxon. Before long, he will find out more things that are going on that he has no idea have been happening.

Earlier in the day, Norma awoke and got out of bed. She has to go to have a photo shoot this morning. She is not feeling too well because she has started her period and has her usual cramps that accompany it along with a dull headache too. Fortunately for her, the session is going to take place in Wellton which is only about twelve miles from her home. Sometimes, she has to travel to Boston but recently, the studio opened a new branch in Wellton. She is really not up for a trip to the big city today.

After dressing, she had some orange juice and a piece of white toast with marmalade. Wanda is off today so she had to prepare her own breakfast. She decided to stop and get a cup of coffee rather that make a pot. As she is getting ready to leave, Rita comes into the kitchen and pours herself a glass of orange juice.

"What's the matter sweetie? You looked a little washed out" she said to Norma.

"Guess" Norma said looking rather sour.

"Oh no. Why don't you call the studio and see if they'll reschedule the shoot?"

"I can't. This is a make up and they're already behind now. I'll be ok once I get going" Norma said taking the last bite of her toast.

Rita went over to Norma and kissed her cheek. Norma smiled and nodded her head slightly.

"Where's dad?" she asked.

"He left early. I think he said something about going out to Allendale."

"I gotta go mom. I love you and I'll see you later."

"You be careful baby, and come home if you don't feel good" Rita said and gave her daughter a hug.

"I will."

"Wish me luck. I'm playing golf later with the girls. I'm doing a little better than I used to."

"Good luck mom. I'll see you later on."

Norma arrived at the studio in Wellton and went in the side entrance. She walked out back to find Abby who is the woman that manages the wardrobe that she is to be modeling. She found Abby talking to Andrew who will be doing Norma's hair and make up. Andrew has always had a thing for Norma ever since he first saw her. She told him about Paul but he still possesses a strong attraction to her.

"Here she is" Abby said walking over to Norma. Abby is in her middle forties, slim and attractive. She is a fashionable dresser and in her younger days she modeled clothes.

"Hi" Norma said forcing a smile.

"This session won't take as long as we had planned because the client pulled some of the clothing" Abby said.

Norma let out a slight sigh of relief. Her headache is increasing and she is wishing she was still home. Andrew came over and spoke with her for a few minutes about things unrelated to the session. They went over to Andrew's area and Norma sat down in front of the large mirror where he does his work. He made

Norma up and did her hair. She looks beautiful and any signs of her feeling poorly are not evident.

She modeled four different dresses and three different skirt and blouse combinations. The shoot has ended and it is twelve noon. Norma's head is pounding. She sometimes gets headaches like this at the onset of her period but not always. She feels nauseous and really tired. She has a pale color about her also.

As Norma starts to come out of the dressing room after changing back into her own clothes, Abby approaches her and placed her hand on Norma's forearm.

"Is anything wrong dear?" she asked sympathetically.

"I don't feel well, that time of the month . . . you know" Norma answered looking at Abby slowly.

Norma suddenly felt like she needed to vomit. She left Abby and quickly went into the washroom. She gagged several times and then does throw up. Her head is still aching and she is a little unsteady on her feet. She pulled several paper towels from the dispenser and ran them under cold water. The cool wet towels feel refreshing on her face and neck.

Abby tapped on the washroom door and asked quietly if she is alright. Norma opened the door and walked out. She is actually feeling slightly better.

"Here. Take these, they'll help" Abby whispered and handed Norma two Midol tablets.

"Thanks. I'll take them when I get home" Norma said and smiled.

"Do you want me to have Andrew drive you home? You can pick up your car later when you are feeling better. I would drive you myself but I have a dentist appointment" Abby said.

"Yes. Ok" Norma said. "Thank you."

As they walked to Andrew's car, Norma walked ahead of him. She is wearing fitted blue jeans, high heels and a pale blue tank top. Andrew checks her up and down from the back and then moves quickly up beside her to open the car door.

"I'll tell you Norma, you may not be feeling well but you'd never know it to look at you. You look fine . . . as always."

"Thanks. I just want to go home and collapse into my bed" she said as she rested her head on the seat backrest. She pulled her sunglasses from her purse and put them on. The outside air blowing in the open window as they move along feels good. Norma has closed her eyes and is pleased that she is starting to feel a little better. The weather is nice and not as humid as it had been. The sun is out in full force and the forecast stated that the week ahead looks good; there are no storms in sight.

Andrew pulled into Norma's driveway and stopped the car. He started to get out but Norma thanked him and went in the rear door of her house. It is just after one o'clock in the afternoon and no one is home. Edwin is at the plant and Rita has gone out to play golf with several of her lady friends and then out to lunch so Norma went upstairs to her room and closed the door. After taking one of the Midol pills that Abby had given her, she opened her two bedroom windows half way and closed the blinds. She turned her table fan on and took off her top and her jeans. She left her bra and underpants on and laid down on the bed and pulled just the bed sheet over herself. Within several minutes, Norma has dropped off into a deep, sound sleep. She is exhausted.

Just before three o'clock, Rita pulled into the driveway and parked her car in front of one of the garage doors. Norma's car is back at the photo studio where she had left it so Rita figures that no one is home. She entered the house and dropped her handbag on the kitchen table. She had a nice time playing golf and eating lunch with her friends. She went into the dining room and opened the liquor cabinet. After making herself a Manhattan, she went out to the sun porch and sat down in one of the wicker chairs. She lit a cigarette and sipped her drink. The outside air is cooling and a slight breeze is evident. Rita crossed her legs and relaxed into the chair. After twenty minutes passed, Rita made herself another drink and returned to the porch. She put her drink down and picked up the telephone receiver and called Meredith.

"Hello" Meredith answered cheerfully.

"Hi sweetie. What are you up to?" Rita asked.

"Oh we just got back from the store. Alice is all excited because she got her favorite breakfast cereal."

Rita and Meredith talked for several minutes and then Meredith put Alice on the telephone. She talked non stop to Rita telling about everything that she has been doing. Rita listened patiently and is delighted with her granddaughter. Meredith came back on the line and they continued talking.

Edwin pulled into the driveway and entered the rear door of the house. He can hear Rita talking out on the sun porch so he made himself a drink and joined her. After a minute, Rita handed him the receiver so he can talk to Meredith. Rita went into the kitchen and returned with some cheese and crackers. Edwin had hung up the phone and is seated across from her.

"How's everything at the plant? Did you go out to Allendale?"

"Everything's fine . . . fine and yes I did go to Allendale."

"How is Paul doing?"

"He's ok" He got the press unloaded and should have the parts checked in by the end of the day."

"He will do fine, I'm sure of that" Rita said lighting another cigarette.

"I'm not happy with him. He had no right defending Pyle and going against us. I'd get rid of him if it wasn't for you and this foolish fascination that you have for him."

Norma awoke and turned over on her back at stared at the ceiling. She feels groggy but much better than she did earlier. Her headache has vanished as they usually do after she sleeps. She is actually quite good and refreshed. She sat up on the edge of her bed and yawned several times. She stood up and put her jeans back on and took a white shirt from her closet. She put the shirt on without tucking it in and walked barefoot into the hall. She entered the bathroom and looked into the mirror. She took her hair brush and made her hair look presentable. She reached the top of the staircase and is about to go down when she can hear Edwin and Rita talking loudly. She sat down on the top step where she can not be seen and starts listening to their conversation.

"You'd get rid of Paul, I don't think so" Rita said in a slightly raised voice.

"Hey I don't like it when someone puts the squeeze on me."

"As soon as Norma and Paul get married, I'm signing the entire business over to Meredith and her. If you do anything stupid that makes Paul leave, then I will sell the business and some of the Pine River property and be done with it" Rita said slurring her words a little.

"You'll sell the business? What have you gone nuts?" Edwin shouted.

"I will sell it! Norma and Meredith and Alice will get a nice settlement. I'll keep the two houses and sell off some of the Pine River property. I'll be in good shape."

"What am I supposed to do?" Edwin asked looking a little shocked.

"I'll throw you some money Eddie, but you'll have to settle for the less expensive whores, no more high priced spread for you" Rita said smirking at him.

"Jesus Christ Rita! I make one mistake and you hold it over me. That was years ago, get over it."

Rita stood up and looked out the porch window at the back yard. She stood silent for a few seconds and then turned and faced Edwin.

"Ever heard of Earl Hallisey?" Rita asked him.

"Who?"

"Earl Hallisey" Rita said slowly.

"No. What about him?"

"He's a private detective. Look him up in the phone book. I have hired him on a few different occasions to check up on you on your supposed overnight business meetings and guess what, every time you were with a girl; one time with that little whore I caught you with at the Pine River house so don't try to tell me that that was a one time thing my stud. Earl has a nice file on you . . . and with pictures too" Rita said still smirking.

"You can stay or go, I really don't care. You have done really well with the business over the years as I knew you would. You are good at business matters because you don't care about people. You hurt me really, really deeply that day and that is why I don't care what you do."

"Rita, those other girls . . . . they're nothing. You're the one I love."

"Please my stud, spare me the bullshit" Rita said as she walked into the dining room for another drink. She is beginning to show the effects of the alcohol.

Norma is sitting at the top of the stairs in shock. She knew nothing of all this that has happened in the past. Rita came back into the sun porch and sat back down. Edwin sat across from her tapping his finger on the table.

"It's too bad that I didn't get you to sign half of that business over to me right after your father died. Hey, I broke my ass building up that business to what it is today. I did it. I'm the one . . . ."

"What's too bad is, that I didn't meet a man like Paul way back, a nice decent guy like him" Rita said interrupting Edwin. "Do you know what I mean my stud?"

"Stop calling me that!" Edwin said angrily.

Norma returned to her room and closed her door. She is still in shock over hearing what Rita and Edwin said. She has to call Brent away. All of a sudden, the bulb in her lamp on the nightstand went out. She sat for a minute and waited for it to come back on but it didn't. She looked at her electric clock and saw that it too is not working. She picked up her telephone and sighed with relief when she heard the dial tone. Norma has her own private line that is separate from the household one. She can make and receive her own calls. She needs to call Brent and inform him of the new details that she has just learned. She dialed the private number in Brent's office but no one answered. She hung up and dialed the number in Jenny's office. After four rings, Brent answered.

"Hello" he said.

Paul noticed that once he got into Saxon that none of the traffic lights are working. He thought that the power must have gone off. Everything was fine in Allendale so it either just occurred or the problem is restricted to the Saxon area. He just wants to give Brent the paperwork and go to his apartment.

When he reached the plant, he noticed that the parking lot is almost empty. As he turned in, Cal Beller, one of the second shift workers is heading out. Paul stopped his car and waved out the window for Cal to stop. Cal stopped beside Paul's car and leaned out the door window.

"What's going on Cal? Where is everyone?"

"They cancelled the night shift. No power" Cal yelled.

"What happened?"

"Not sure. Some big trunk line blew out somewhere I think. Whole towns out and they think it may take most of the night to fix it."

"Ok Cal" Paul yelled back.

The other few cars in the lot pulled up behind Cal and left. Paul noticed that Brent's car is still here and is the only one left. Paul drove up to the building and parked his car. He gathered up the papers and headed to the entrance of Jenny's office. As he entered and headed towards Brent's office, he heard what sounded like Norma's voice on the receiver on Jenny's desk.

Apparently, Brent had answered the call on Jenny's phone and then took the call in his office. Where everyone has left, he didn't bother to hang that receiver back up. This, both he and Norma will soon discover, is a major error, for them at least. Paul put the phone up to his ear and heard Norma say: *"I've got to go see Paul tonight and tell him that I want to marry him right away. If I don't and my mother decides to sell the business, that will ruin our plan, ruin our future together."*

"What happened again now?" Brent asked sounding confused.

"I guess mother caught my father fucking some girl up at the Pine River house."

"When, today?" Brent asked.

"No no, a long time ago. That's why she never signed over half of the business to him. I guess too that she's had a detective checking up on him and he's been screwing around on her other times too. She's pissed off and she said if things don't work out between me and Paul, she'll sell the business. We just can't let that happen. I've got to marry him now!"

"Yeah . . . . I see what you mean. How long will you have to stay married to him though?"

I told you before darling. Just long enough to get the business signed over to me and Meredith. "Then we will both get divorced and we'll be together and have the business and everything will be great."

"Hey, maybe Wilker and Meredith will get together. They're both pretty dense aren't they" Brent said chuckling.

"That they are. Ok I'm going to have Meredith take me over to get my car and then I'll go and tell Paul that I can't last any longer."

"Ok doll. I love you" Brent said.

"And I adore you" Norma said in a whispering, sexy voice.

Paul was about to say something into the phone but the little voice in his head told him to be quiet and think it out. As soon Brent and Norma hung up Paul laid the receiver back down where he found it and entered Brent's office.

"Here's those papers you wanted" Paul said.

"When did you come in?" Brent asked looking surprised to see him.

"I just got here" Paul said.

"You headed to your place?" Brent asked.

"Maybe. Why?"

"Oh, I just wondered" Brent said with an odd expression on his face.

"See you later" Paul said and walked out of the door.

Brent does not suspect anything. He has made huge error on his and Norma's behalf. They have gotten away with so much but this is the mistake that will throw a monkey wrench into their devious plans. Paul drove out of the parking lot but instead of heading to his apartment, he drove away from Saxon center. He decided he will get a motel for the night. He has no desire to see Norma until he thinks everything out. One thing is certain in his mind. He is through with the Rollins Publishing Company. He also decided that he will call Ike as soon as he can and see if he wants him to come and work at the garage. Suddenly he thought about Jenny. Here he was thinking all along that he can't hurt Norma and here she has been playing him for a real sap; and Brent, what a snake he is. He plans to dump Meredith, a girl who is the perfect wife and mother, and marry her sister. "Well, they deserve each other" Paul said aloud to himself. Paul realizes suddenly that with this new turn of events, that he can now tell Jenny how he feels about her; how he loves her. He will no longer have anything to do with the publishing company. He now knows that feeling that he has heard countless times in the past; the feeling that the whole world had been lifted off of his shoulders.

Paul drove out of Saxon and into the next town, Whitney. He is glad to see that the power failure has not affected this area because the traffic lights are functioning as they should be. There is a motel there that he had stayed in when he first came to Saxon before he found his apartment. It is an old style place with the small individual cabins. It had been started in the early thirties and had done very well until the new highway branch diverted some of the traffic away from it. It is reasonable, clean and suitable for what Paul needs for the night. Up ahead, a neon sign reads: REST EASY MOTOR COURT and beneath it:VACANCY.

He turned in and stopped in front of the office. He entered and walked up to the counter. There is a small copper colored bell on the counter with a small sign beside it that reads: RING FOR SERVICE. Paul rang the bell and a woman's voice sounded from the other room.

"Be right there" she called out.

A stout woman in her sixties appeared from the other room and walked up behind the counter. She has a friendly, pleasant smile with a voice to match.

"How are you tonight?" she asked Paul.

"Very well and you?"

"Very well. Would you like a cabin?"

"Yes. Would it be possible to get the end one furthest down?" Paul asked.

"Sure. You can have any one you like. They're all empty at the moment."

Paul paid the lady for the cabin and took the key from her. He asked her if there was an ice machine and she pointed to the other room off of the office. He went outside and got back into his car and drove down to his cabin. As he was pulling away, a Dodge station wagon with Illinois license plates pulled up to the office. Paul can see a man and a woman with several children in the car. He selected the end cabin because he will be able to park his car around to the side of it and this way, it will not be visible from the highway or inside the court. He does not want to take a chance that Norma might catch up with him. He will deal with her tomorrow after he mulls things over in his mind.

He unlocked the cabin and entered. It is small but clean and well lit. There is a radio, a television set, a single bed with a nightstand and a bureau. In the corner by the window, there is an armchair. Off to the side is a small bathroom. He looked at his watch and saw that it is just after six o'clock. He is hungry and decides to take a chance and drive down the road to the small plaza shop that he went to when he stayed here before. There is a pizza shop there and also a package store.

Paul pulled into the plaza and went into the pizza shop. He ordered a small pepper and onion with sausage pizza to go and went out side to the pay telephone beside the building. He placed his coins in the slot and dialed the operator. When she came on, he placed a collect call to Ike. After several rings, Edna answered and accepted the call.

"Hi Edna. It's me, Paul. I'm sorry to call collect but I'm at a pay phone and I really need to speak to Ike. Is he there?"

"Paul. Is there anything wrong?. Are you alright?" Edna asked sounding worried.

"I'm ok. No need to be concerned. I just need to talk to him."

"Ok dear. You hold on and I'll get him."

"Hello Paul. What's goin on with you. Where are you?"

"I'm over in Whitney. Are you still looking for someone to work at the garage for you because I want to come back there."

"Well, yeah I am but ain't you going to work out at that new plant in Allendale?"

"Nope. That's all changed now. Look Ike, I've got a few things to do tomorrow morning and then I'm coming there and I'll tell you everything that's going on, ok?"

"You really want to come back and work at the garage?" Ike asked.

"I sure do. You show me what to do and I'll do the work, how's that?"

"That sounds fine" Ike said cheerfully.

"Good, ok then. Oh Ike, if Norma should call there looking for me, please tell her that you haven't heard from me and you don't know where I am. I'll explain everything tomorrow."

"If that's what you want Paul . . . then ok."

Paul went in and picked up his pizza and put it in his car. He went into the package store and bought a six pack of Shlitz beer in cans. He returned to the motor court and went inside the cabin with his food. He took the ice container and went to the office and filled it with ice cubes and put three cans of beer in the bathroom sink. He dumped the ice in to keep them cold. After taking one of the beer cans from the sink, Paul sat down in the armchair with the pizza box on his lap and began to eat. "Boy, nothing like pizza and cold beer; really good" he thought to himself.

Jenny sat at her aunt's kitchen table and sipped the iced tea that her aunt had made for her. Her aunt Maggie sat across from her and listened intently as Jenny told her what has happened. Jenny looks tired and a little depressed but she is starting to feel better as she talks to her aunt. She told her about Paul and how she feels about him and how she can not go to Allendale and be with him.

"He's just the nicest guy and he hasn't had a very easy time of it" Jenny said.

She told her about Paul's father and how he was is a patient at the sanitarium and how his mother was killed in a tragic automobile accident. She told her about Norma and how beautiful and wealthy she is.

"He's going to be in charge of the entire Allendale plant. He'll be making a great deal of money and very soon a member of the Clay family."

"Well dear, sometimes things don't go the way we would like them to but we go on just the same even though it can be hard" aunt Maggie said sympathetically.

"I will just get a new job and forget about the publishing company and everything else that has to do with it. But you can see why I don't want to go to the new plant, can't you auntie?" Jenny asked hoping that her aunt would agree with her.

"I can dear. Yes I can. You'll be alright in time. Yes you will."

Jenny loves her aunt Maggie. She possesses the same kindness and thoughtfulness that her brother, Jenny's father, had when he was alive. Maggie has been more of a mother to her than her real mother has ever been. After she had the trouble with her stepfather, she moved in with her aunt and stayed with her while she attended secretarial school. She figures that after she settles into a new job, she will get her own apartment. For now though, she will move out of the existing place in Saxon and stay with her aunt. She wants to be away from everything in Saxon. She needs a fresh start.

Paul finished his pizza and popped open another can of beer. He turned on the television but left the volume turned down low so he can think. He decided that he will go into the plant in Saxon the first thing in the morning and deliver the Allendale keys to Brent and tell him that he is done. He will catch up with Norma later. He is sure that Brent will contact her just as soon as he hears what is going on. Let her sweat a little. While he is there, he will tell Jenny that he needs to talk to her and would like to see her after she leaves work. He will tell her how he feels about her and . . . . Suddenly, he began to worry that Jenny will probably think that he is only interested in her now because Norma doesn't want him other than for her selfish greed. He figures that he will just have to face that when the time comes.

Paul finished his second beer and decided to take a shower and then look at some television before turning in. As he entered the bathroom, he noticed that most of the ice in the sink had melted and he wanted to drink the other can of beer in there after his shower. He picked up the ice container and went outside and started to go to the motor court office. There is a faded, green and white '55 Chrysler two door hardtop parked in front of the cabin next to his. It is dark now but Paul recognized it as the same car driven by Carol Collier who works in the paste up department at the Saxon plant. He noticed that two people are in the front seat and passionately making out.

As Paul got a little closer, the passenger side door opened and to his huge surprise, *Brent* got out and started for the office. Paul quickly turned and went back and stood beside his cabin where he was out of sight. Shortly afterwards, Brent came out of the office and walked to the cabin that he has rented. Carol got out and joined him. They have rented the cabin next to Paul's and as Brent is unlocking the door, Carol is all over him. When he got the door unlocked he turned and embraced her. They kissed and quickly went inside and closed the door.

Carol is not homely but she is not gorgeous either, not in her face anyway. She is however quite shapely and very well blessed in

253

her chest region. In fact, when most of the men at the plant talk about her, they say "Carol . . . . from paste up . . . . ya know.. with the big tits" and they hold their hands up in front of their chest.

Paul decided to forego the ice and slipped back into his cabin. His car is parked out of sight beside his cabin but he is certain that Brent will not want to run into him here. Paul took his shower and dried off. He sat down in the armchair and opened his can of beer and began to drink it slowly. The television is on but Paul is not paying attention to the program. Instead, he is thinking about Brent. "What a jerk" Paul thought to himself. He's not only screwing around with Norma but with Carol Collier and lord knows who else; unbelievable.

Brent and Carol spent several hours in their rented cabin. This is not the first time that they have had sexual encounters. A few times when Norma has gone off on a photo shoot, Brent and Carol have gotten together. She basically goes with Brent because he has given her a nice pay increase. She likes him very much and finds him sexually attractive but really has no romantic feelings towards him. Brent has no feelings for her romantically; he just takes her out because he, like Edwin, is a sex fiend. He would prefer to be there with Norma but she said that she is going to see Paul.

On this particular evening, Brent has told Meredith that he wants to meet with the representatives from the printing press manufacturers to discuss the Allendale plant set up. She is trusting and does not have any notion that he is betraying her.

They used Carol's car so that if someone should see it there, they will believe that she is just there with some guy. She is not seeing anybody in particular so her presence at a roadside motel won't raise any real questions. At twenty minutes to eleven, they slipped out to Carol's car and drove away. Paul looked out his window shortly afterwards and saw that they had left. He watched the local news at eleven and went to bed. He lay still for a short while and thought over everything that has happened. Despite all of this, he actually feels somewhat relieved.

At five fifteen, Paul was awakened by a huge clap of thunder and pounding rain on the cabin roof. He had been sound asleep and it took him a minute or so to remember everything that has happening. He got out of bed at ten minutes of six and got dressed. He went into the bathroom and dabbed some cold water on his face and combed his hair. He looked at himself in the mirror for a few seconds and then turned off the bathroom light. He took the remaining three cans of beer and his empty pizza box and went to his car and put all of it in the trunk. The rain has stopped and the morning sun is starting to come up.

He returned the cabin key to the office and headed out onto the road leading back to Saxon. Right when he reached the Whitney and Saxon town line, he turned into a small diner and parked. It is one of the older type diners that is shaped like a street car. Once inside, he noticed that there are quite a few people, who like himself, have stopped for breakfast. Paul took a stool at the counter and ordered two dropped eggs on wheat toast, hash, tomato juice and coffee. It is a typical diner breakfast, excellent. He ordered a second cup of coffee and drank it slowly because he has time to kill before going to the plant.

When he got back in his car, he waited there for about fifteen minutes and then headed out to the Saxon plant. The first shift will be starting up in about fifteen minutes so Paul has timed it right. He walked across the parking lot and entered the door leading to the press area. As soon as he got inside he heard Fletcher's voice.

"Hey Wilker" You here for the big vote?"

Paul looked over and saw all of the men on the first shift standing there with Fletcher. He notices that Lester has graced everyone with his presence as well.

"I've got to go into the office for a minute. I will be right back" Paul answered.

Lester began to say something to Paul but he walked away towards the office. He opened the door expecting to see Jenny but saw Donna there instead.

"Good morning" Donna said with a friendly smile. I'm Donna and you're ... ?"

"Hello. I'm Paul Wilker" Paul said back to her.

Paul does not know about Donna's appointment to the office or that Jenny had been slated to go to Allendale either for that matter.

"Is Jenny here?" Paul asked.

"No she's not. She left yesterday."

Left?"

"She quit" They were sending her to Allendale and she quit" Donna said.

"She quit?" Paul asked her to be sure that he heard her correctly.

"Yes, that's right" Donna answered

Just then Phyllis returned from the ladies room and walked over to Paul. She has heard part of the conversation.

"Paul, poor Jenny. She got all upset and just quit. I wasn't here but Donna was."

Paul looked over at Donna and she nodded her head.

"Is Brent in his office?" Paul asked.

"Yes, do want me to tell him that you want to see him?" Donna asked.

"No that's ok" Paul said and walked around the corner and directly into his office.

He entered and saw Brent seated in his chair and Mike Cole standing by one of the file cabinets.

"What's going on? Why aren't you out in Allendale? Those reps from the press company are probably waiting there for you. What the hell are you doing here?" Brent said in an angry tone.

"These are for you sir. I'm done" Paul said dropping the Allendale keys on Brent's desk and turning around towards the door.

Brent picked up the keys from his desk.

'What am I supposed to do with these?" Brent asked holding them out towards Paul.

"You can put them in your ass if you want to. I don't care" Paul said stopping and turning back around.

"What the hell do you mean you're done" Brent said getting up and walking around the desk.

Paul stopped and turned back to look at him.

"Done, through, quit!"

"Mike, I'll get back to you on that" Brent said excusing Mike Cole from the office.

Mike walked around Paul and gave him a disgusted look.

"Come in here. What the hell are you doing? You can't quit. You're going to be running the whole Allendale facility."

"I overheard your little conversion with Norma last night here. You left the outer office phone off of the hook and I heard it all. I'm supposed to marry her so she can get control of the business. After that she will dump me and you'll dump Meredith and you two will have each other and the business. That pretty much says it all in a nutshell, doesn't it Mr. Royce?"

Brent looked a little horrified. He appeared to be in shock.

"You aren't going to tell Meredith are you?" Brent asked walking up close to Paul and practically whispering.

"Not me. I'm not going to break her heart for the world. You'll have to do that yourself. She's a damn nice girl and she sure deserves a better guy than you; and what about your little daughter and her feelings?" Paul said looking directly at Brent.

Paul walked back out through the office and glanced at Donna who looks slightly confused.

"Nice to meet you Donna" he said and kept walking out into the press area.

All of the men are standing down by where Fletcher's press is. They have been waiting for this moment for a while; the moment that they can make Paul look like a fool. As Paul got close to them, Lester moved out slightly from the group. He has one crutch under his arm for support.

"So, are you ready to do the vote?" he asked Paul.

"Yup. Do it. You're the steward after all."

Lester gave Paul a weird look and turned to face the men.

"All those in favor of working here the way things stand now and maybe bargaining later for changes raise you hands."

With the exception of Paul, everyone raised their hand. Paul stood with his arms folded in front of him.

"All those in favor of striking now if the proposal isn't met, raise their hand."

No one raised their hand of course.

"Hey Wilker. How come you didn't vote?" Art said sharply

"Because I'm not eligible to vote Art" Paul answered looking directly at him

"Not eligible?"

"That's right. You see, I no longer work here. I just stopped to give the keys back to Mr. Royce.

Art started applauding and looked around and grinned at the crowd.

"Actually, I'm the one that should be applauding. You know there are people in this world that get shit on and can't do anything about it, and then there are other people who get shit on and don't have the nut to do anything about it . . . . like you people."

"Are you saying we don't have any balls?" Art said walking right up close to Paul.

Paul stood firm and didn't move an inch and looked at him with an "I hate your guts" expression. Art stopped rather short and looked almost as if no one had ever done this to him before.

"Hey Art, if the shoe fits . . . you know the old saying."

"Yeah?, I see you outside sometime . . . ."

"I know, I know, you can't do anything in here; this must be my luck day" Paul interrupted.

"Ha. You'll be back here trying to get your job and they ain't gonna take you back" Denny blurted out.

Paul walked up to Denny and looked at him and then at the group.

"My God! This is amazing! It speaks! Now you see Denny, I just lost two bucks. I bet that you were a mute and here all along you do talk. This is amazing!" Paul said as he put his hand on the side of his face and pretended to look shocked.

"Who bet you?" Denny asked seriously.

Paul smiled and shook his head and thought for a second about trying to explain to him that he was joking but stopped.

At this point, Paul doesn't care what happens. He is just so glad that he is no longer going to be affiliated with this business and these people that seem to thrive on negativity.

Bill Pyle had walked away from the crowd and went over to where the fork lift is parked. As he is about to climb into it, Paul came by heading outside through the overhead door. Instead of ignoring Paul, Bill started stammering at him.

"Hey, I can't talk. I gotta start working. I . . . . I had to vote with the union. I . . . I gotta stick by Lester. He went to bat for me and got me back. He . . . he got me back" Bill said nervously.

Paul burst out laughing in Bill's face.

"Lester went to bat for you? Oh yes now, let's see. When you first got canned, I recall him saying to Mr. Clay and Mr. Royce that you are a hopeless drunk and that they should fire your ass. Oh, hey now, this is union representation at its best" Paul said laughing even harder.

"You're fulla shit. Lester didn't say that."

"You can go to work now" Paul said looking past Bill and pointing outside.

"Huh?" Bill grunted.

"Truck" Paul said still pointing at the semi truck that was backing toward the platform.

Paul went outside into the parking lot and headed for his car. As he got closer, he noticed that George Baxter has parked beside him and is getting out of his car. Paul walked over to meet him.

"George. I just want to say that you have been a pleasure to work with and that's more than I can say about the majority of the people working here" Paul said reaching out to shake George's hand.

George returned Paul's handshake but looks confused.

"What's going on? I figured I'd stop by here because I remember you said that you were coming here first" George said.

"George, I'm through. I found out some stuff last night that has made it impossible for me to remain here any longer."

"Jesus. Really?"

"George, I think you should get out of here too . . . . right away. Buy that car and you and your daughter take that trip and have the time of your lives. Why wait any longer."

"You're leaving now?" George asked still looking unsure of this sudden news.

"Right now. Remember what I said George. Do it. You deserve it."

Paul got into his car and proceeded to leave the parking lot when he spotted Norma's car pulling in. She saw Paul and drove over and stopped beside his car. She hurriedly got out and approached Paul's car.

"Paul, what do you think you're doing? Where are you going?" she said glaring at him. "Have you lost your mind completely?"

"Come on Norma. I'm sure that Brent filled you in when he called you."

"What are you talking about?"

"Last night when I stopped here to leave off the papers, Brent left the secretary's phone off the hook while you and him were talking on his office phone and I heard everything. I know what you and him are cooking up and it stinks so let's cut out the bullshit, ok?"

Norma came around to the passenger side of Paul's car and slid into the front seat next to him.

"Paul, listen to me. If you'll go through with this for me, I'll make it worth your while" she said as she put her arm around Paul's neck and moved even closer to him.

"I'll give you a nice settlement and you can even stay on and run the Allendale plant afterwards. You've got to help me. If my mother sells the business, I'll be screwed."

"Ok, let me get this straight. You want me to marry you so you can get control of the company from your mother. Then after that takes place, you will divorce me and marry Brent after he dumps Meredith. Is that how it supposed to work?"

"You won't regret it Paul. You will be set for life . . . . Alright! I love Brent! I have ever since I met him when I was sixteen! I can't help it!"

"Even if I wanted to be involved in your dirty little plan, I can't do it because I have fallen in love with someone else. I want to get married if she will have me so you can count me out of this deal. You must take me for the stooge of the century."

"You are in love with someone else, who?" Norma asked looking quite surprised as if he couldn't possibly love anyone but her.

"Jenny Morris; from the office."

"Jenny . . . . from the office . . . you're in love with her?"

"Very much" Paul said firmly. "Imagine, I was concerned that I would hurt you if I admitted this and all along you were screwing around with Brent, even though you told me you are saving yourself for when you get married. What a joke that is!"

"Jenny Morris. You have fallen for her. She's cockeyed for Christ's sakes! I don't believe this" Norma said in a cruel tone. "Oh boy, you must be really desperate!"

Paul bristled inside. He could not imagine at this point that he had had serious feelings for Norma earlier.

"Well, ya know Norma, I wasn't going to tell you this but since you said that about Jenny, I am going to tell you a little something about your lover boy Brent. Last night, I stayed at the Rest Easy Motor Court over in Whitney and guess who also stayed there . . . . for a short while anyway? None other than Brent and Carol Collier."

"What are you talking about. Brent and who?"

"Carol . . . . from paste up . . . . ya know . . . . with the big tits?"

"I don't believe that. You're lying."

"Ask your sister if he went out last night. She's the one I feel badly for" Paul said.

Norma got out of the car and slammed the door. She walked over to her car and stood motionless beside the driver's door. Paul drove past her and out onto the highway. He must locate Jenny and let her know how he feels.

Norma sped over to the plant and parked her car in front of the building. She entered the main entrance and walked into the outer office where Donna and Phyllis are. They both greeted her but Norma did not answer them. Instead, she walked directly into Brent's office and closed the door behind her. Brent is on the telephone and looked up at her.

"Hang up. I need to talk to you now!"

Brent held up his index finger to express to Norma to wait a few seconds. Norma walked up close to his desk and jammed her hand down on the telephone buttons cutting off Brent's call.

"Hang up the God Damn phone!"

"Sweetheart, what is the matter. What's wrong?" Brent asked standing up quickly.

"What went on last night? What did you do last night? Where did you go?"

"I had a meeting with the representatives from the press company. I was in Allendale . . . . meeting with them. Why?"

"I was just talking to Paul Wilker and he told me that you were over in Whitney at the Motor Court with Carol Collier!"

"What? That's crazy."

"He spent the night there and he said he saw you and her there" Norma said glaring at Brent across his desk.

"That's ridiculous. He's just pissed off because he found out that you don't want him."

"Boy, you really screwed up leaving the phone off the hook last night but I want to know about this business with Carol Collier!" Norma shouted.

Brent walked up to Norma and put his hands on her shoulders and attempted to pull her close to him. She raised her hands up and pushed his arms away and backed away from him.

"Look, it's bad enough that we aren't going to be able to get the company like we planned but if you were with her last night, I'll see that you don't get shit. Meredith won't forgive you and I'll tell mother that you were screwing around on my sister and you will be out."

"I told you. Wilker just said that because he's pissed" Brent shouted back at her.

"He doesn't want me! He's fallen for Jenny Morris from the office! I offered to pay him off if he'd go through with it and I even told him that he could still manage the Allendale plant. He wants no part of it so why is he saying that about you if it's not true?"

"Jenny quit. She's gone" he said.

Norma lifted her arms up and then dropped them down at her sides in desperation.

"Look Brent. I'm going to ask Carol about this and if it's true then you are going to be really sorry" Norma said with a shaky voice.

She stalked out of the office. Brent started to go after her but just when he reached the door, Donna's voice came on his intercom.

"Brent, I have Mr. Clay on line one for you".

As soon as Lester learned that Paul has quit, he wasted no time calling Edwin at his house to break the news to him. Brent stopped and returned to his desk and picked up the receiver.

"Hello"

"What's going on? I heard that Paul Wilker quit. Why the hell would he do that?"

"I don't know . . . . I don't know. He's a nut like his father I think" Brent answered.

Edwin's heart sank a little when he heard this. He remembered what Rita had said yesterday about selling the business if things did not work out for Paul and Norma. He said no more and quickly hung up the telephone.

Norma walked briskly into the paste up area to confront Carol Collier. She saw Carol working with another girl and approached her.

"Carol, I want to see you for a minute" Norma said pointing towards the door.

They went out into the hallway and headed single file to the door leading out to the parking lot. Carol is curious what Norma is doing. When they got outside of the building, Norma stopped walking and turned around and faced Carol.

"What's the matter?" Carol asked.

"I was told that you and my brother in law were together last night at a motel over in Whitney."

"Who . . . . who told you that?" Carol asked nervously

"Were you there with him; and if I find out that you're lying to me, I'll see to it that you get fired."

Carol has worked for the printing company for a while and has a good position in the paste up area, especially since Brent has boosted her wages in appreciation for her sexual favors he has received.

"Tell me now! Were you there with him or not?"

"Al right. Yes, I was but please don't get me fired. My mother lives with me and doesn't have good health. I am supporting her and I really need this job" Carol said sobbing.

"Did you ever do that with him before?"

Carol paused and looked down at the pavement and then off to her right.

"Yes, a few times before" she answered softly. "Is his wife going to find about this?"

"Oh. Yes she is" Norma said turning around and walking toward her car.

"Yes she is!" she repeated in a loud voice.

Paul turned onto Elm Avenue where Jenny's apartment house is located. He remembered where he had taken her that recent Saturday when they had been together. As he pulled in front of the house, he noticed that Jenny's car is not there. After sitting and thinking for a minute, he decided to go to the downstairs door and ask if they know where Jenny is.

Just as he reached the door, it opened and the landlady came out.

"Good morning" she said with a friendly smile.

"Hello" Paul said. I am looking for Jenny. Do know where she went?"

"Yes. She has gone to stay with her aunt over in Perkinsville. Are you a friend of hers?"

"Yes. You don't expect her back right away?" Paul asked.

"No I don't and the way she was talking, I am afraid that she may be moving out soon. I hate to lose her. She is a wonderful person and an excellent tenant."

The landlady is in her late sixties with gray hair and a kind, warm face. She has glasses with fairly thick lenses which makes her eyes appear large. She was born and raised in Greengrove and has lived in the same house all of her life. She never married and has a younger brother that lives on the opposite side of town and he helps her with the upkeep of the house. She has been employed at the town library for the past thirty one years.

"You don't by chance know what street her aunt lives on in Perkinsville do you?" Paul asked hopefully.

"I'm sorry I don't and I do not know the telephone number either . . . . but I think I have her mother's phone number. Just a minute and I will look."

She unlocked the front door and went inside the house. It is a beautiful morning with a clear blue sky and brilliant sunshine. The humidity that had hung on for the past several weeks has left for the time being and the temperature is a dry eighty degrees. The landlady returned several minutes later with a slip of paper with the telephone number written on it. Paul looked at the paper and read it. Wayne Kemmer—LA 6-7736 was written neatly.

"I would let you use my telephone but I've just got time to get to the library where I work if I leave right now" the landlady said apologizing.

"Oh no, that's fine. You have been very helpful. Thank you very much.

Paul turned his car around and drove back down Elm Avenue. At the end of the street, he turned left and headed toward Greengrove center. Just past the center, there is a Shell service station and he drove up to the pumps and stopped. The attendant came out and Paul asked him to fill the tank. When he was finished, Paul accompanied him into the office and after paying for the gasoline, he asked for two dollars worth of change for the payphone outside.

Paul moved his car away from the pumps and then entered the telephone booth. He took out the paper with telephone number on it that the landlady had given him. Lakeview, where Jenny's mother lives, is a toll call so Paul dialed the operator and had her connect him. The phone rang three times and then a boy with an adolescent voice answered.

"Hello" he replied.

"Hi. My name is Paul Wilker and I am trying to reach Jenny Morris. I believe that she is staying with her aunt in Perkinsville. Would you or anybody there know what the address is there?"

"I think she lives right near the post office but I don't know the street name."

In the background, Paul can hear a man's voice.

"Who's on the phone?" he can hear the man saying to the boy.

"It's some guy looking for Jenny" the boy answered

"Gimme the phone" the man voice said gruffly.

"Who's this? What is it you want?"

"I'm Paul Wilker. I'm looking for Jenny" Paul said trying to remain patient.

"Jenny doesn't live here and she's not welcome here so do not call here looking for her anymore."

"I just wanted to find out her aunt's address over in Perkinsville and I think I am all set. Sorry to have troubled you."

"Just don't call here anymore looking for her because we want nothing to do with her."

"Are you her stepfather?" Paul asked sharply.

"Yeah I am but what concern is that of yours?"

"Well, Jenny happens to be a really close friend of mine and I plan on seeing a great deal of her hopefully from now on. She is a kind, caring person so back off!" Paul said firmly.

"Wait a minute. Who are you again?" Wayne asked in a raised voice.

"My name is Wilker, Paul Wilker and I don't appreciate you saying this stuff about her so if you do have anything unkind stuff to say, just keep your mouth shut."

"You think I give a good shit what you appreciate or don't?" Wayne said loudly.

"I'm sure you don't. I have to go no now. What a pleasure it has been speaking with you. Just remember what I told you" Paul said and let the payphone receiver hang loose without replacing it on the hook.

As he exited the booth, he can hear Wayne yelling something but he is not interested. His only interest now is finding Jenny and telling her how he feels. He wants to see her in person rather than telephoning. He got into the Plymouth and headed out onto the road; he is on his way to Perkinsville. He is beginning to feel anxious. "How do I know that she isn't involved with someone? She has always been genuinely friendly to me but maybe that's just the way she is with people. Well. I won't know until I talk to her. If she is involved with another person, that will be hard for me but . . . . she did kiss me . . . boy, did she" Paul is thinking to himself as he drives.

Edwin walked into Brent's office and closed the door behind him. Brent is on the telephone but hangs up quickly when he sees Edwin.

"What's going on?" Brent asked.

"You tell me! I know that Wilker is kind of weird but I don't get it. Why would he quit here and give up the opportunity to run Allendale" Edwin asked and began pacing around the office.

"He doesn't even want to marry Norma now. Apparently he's fallen for Jenny Morris from the office. He's quit but don't worry Edwin, we'll get someone to run the Allendale plant."

Of course Edwin is not aware of the real reason that Paul has left. He has no idea that Brent and Norma have cooked up this elaborate scheme to get the business and get married afterwards and that Paul has stumbled onto it. Brent is acting as calm as he can but inside he is really stressed. He knows that once Rita learns what has happened, he will be on thin ice. He figures that as soon as he can, he will talk to Carol if it isn't too late. He excused himself and went over to the paste up area.

He went in and asked Carol to come outside with him. When they get outside, Brent stopped and faced her. As he started to speak, Carol burst into tears.

"Norma Clay was here and she knows about us. She said if I didn't tell her the truth, she'd have me fired. If I lose this job, I'll probably lose my apartment and the new furniture that I just charged . . . and my mother, what will happen to her?" Carol said wiping her eyes with her hand.

"What did you say to Norma?"

"She said that she was going to tell your wife too" Carol sobbed.

"What did you tell her" Brent demanded.

"I told her that I was with you. I'm sorry . . . I'm sorry" Carol said wiping her eyes again.

Brent turned and walked back into the plant without saying any more. Carol went back inside and directly into the ladies room.

After Brent left to see Carol, Edwin returned to his own office. Lester is in the receptionist's area and is heading to see Edwin but has stopped and is flirting with Donna. She is very polite but wishes that he would go on about his business. He has asked her a lot of questions regarding her personal life and told that she is really cute and must have a boyfriend which is making her uncomfortable. Donna breathed a sigh of relief when the telephone rang.

Lester went on into Edwin's office and began talking to him.

"So that's a shock huh. Wilker just up and quit. What a dope. What's with him anyways?" Lester asked.

"I don't know what the hell happened but I'm going to find out!" Edwin said slapping his hand on his desktop.

"Ya know, some of those guys in the pressroom would've voted for that proposal that Wilker made up if it hadn't been for me squashing it. I saved you some serious money ya know."

"Lester, I know you did" Edwin said quietly.

"Well, I think I should get a little compensation for that, don't you?"

"Look Lester, I've got a lot of things going on right now and besides, you're paid pretty damn good right now I think."

"Like I said, I saved you a lot of . . . .

"I can't talk about this now Lester" Edwin interrupted. "Haven't I paid you all along while you've been out with your leg; I mean Jesus, how much do you want?"

"I saved you a lot of money and I still think you should cut me some extra" Lester persisted more or less ignoring what Edwin has just said to him.

Edwin walked over and closed the office door. He sat down on his desk chair and leaned forward, resting his elbows on his desk.

"I'm going to level with you Lester and I don't want what I'm going to tell you to go any further than this office."

Lester leaned against one of Edwin's file cabinets and devoted his full attention to what Edwin is saying. Edwin's tone is serious.

"My wife, Rita, owns everything, the house, the property, and this business. I have run it all along but it's her's and her's alone. When my daughter and Wilker got married, she was planning to turn the entire publishing company over to Meredith and Norma."

"What, Wilker ain't marrying you daughter now?" Lester asked.

"No, it doesn't look that way now."

"So she never split the ownership of the business with you?" Lester asked with a slightly shocked look on his face.

"No she didn't. Now, Rita thinks the world of this Wilker and told me if anything happened that made him not marry Norma, she would sell the business. I understand that several publishing firms have been after her to buy the company. She will make a bundle if she sells out now and I think that's just what's going to happen."

Lester started to chuckle and changed his standing position.

"So. It looks like your wife has really got a hold of you where it counts" Lester said smugly and chuckling a little more.

"There's nothing funny about this; nothing funny in the least. If someone new takes this place over, you'll be working for new people and you will have to do a hell of a lot more than you've been doing, that is if they keep you on even. They may put a whole different crew in here so just remember that."

Lester's smugness and chuckling ceased immediately.

"Well why don't you try to talk her out of selling it?"

"She does what she wants to do and I think the drinking has messed up her head."

"So you think this is going to happen then?" Lester asked meekly.

"I will by very surprised if it doesn't" Edwin said staring out the window and looking depressed.

"How come she never split the ownership with you? That don't make any sense" Lester said.

Edwin is not going to tell Lester about that time Rita caught him with the girl up at the Pine River house. He figures that he probably has told Lester too much already. At this point though, Edwin doesn't really care if Lester blabs about what he has told him.

"I don't know. I really don't know" Edwin said slowly still gazing out the window.

Paul drove into Perkinsville center and started to look for the post office that the boy, one of Jenny's half brothers, had mentioned on the telephone. As he got about in the middle of the town, he notices a sign that reads: PERKINSVILLE FORD SALES AND SERVICE with an arrow pointing to a side street. Paul remembers that Jenny had told him that she bought her car from them. He figures that someone there will know where her aunt's house is; at least it is worth a shot. He turned right onto the street and right up ahead, he can see the dealership.

Paul pulled into the lot and parked. Shiny new Fords are lined up in front of the showroom and a large sign in the window reads: SEE THE NEW 1965 FORD MODELS HERE SOON!

He opened the showroom door and entered. A middle aged salesman in a brown suit stood up from his desk and greeted Paul.

"Good morning sir. How are you this fine day?"

"I am well thanks. I am afraid that I am not here to buy a new car but hopefully you may be able to help me out. I am trying to locate Jenny Morris and I believe that she has her Ford Falcon serviced here. Would you be able to tell me where she, or actually her aunt lives? I know it is near the Post Office."

The salesman rubbed his chin with his thumb and index finger for a few seconds.

"Let me check inside. Wait here for a minute."

He walked inside the office and while he waited, Paul looked at a nice new '64 Ford galaxy two door hardtop that is parked in the showroom. It is a deep maroon color with a white vinyl roof. The interior is a deep red color. Paul started to read the window sticker but stopped when the salesman returned from the office with a woman. They walked over to Paul and the women spoke.

"Hi. Are you looking for Jenny Morris?"

"Yes. Do you know where she lives?" Paul asked hopefully.

"If you turn left out of the lot here and go all the way down to the end of the street, her aunt lives in the last house on the left. It's a white house with yellow shutters. I live in the third house before hers" the woman said with a friendly smile. "It's number 90 Gale Street" she called to Paul as he is almost to the showroom door.

He turned and thanked her again and headed for his car. He turned left onto Gale Street and drove to the end. He slowed down and spotted the white house with the yellow shutters and the black number 90 on the front of the house. As he got directly in front of the house, he can see Jenny's blue Ford Falcon parked in the driveway.

The house has a long sloping front roof that extends past the front door and windows and ends over the front porch. There is a three window dormer that allows light into the upstairs rooms. The house was probably built during the 1920's and appears to be well kept. The paint looks to be fairly new and the shrubbery in front of the porch has been neatly trimmed. The house has a raised foundation and five wooden steps lead up from the front walk to the porch and the front door. There is a three foot high white picket fence that runs across the entire front yard with a gate at the front walk.

The yard also is nicely cared for with the lawn cut and raked. On one side there is a tall hedge that runs the length of the side yard providing privacy for both this house and the neighbors. At the end of the driveway just beyond where Jenny's car is parked, there is a small one car garage which is painted the same color as the house. The other side of the yard is vacant with three large maple trees and some lilac bushes. A street runs parallel to the house and just around the corner is the Perkinsville Post Office.

Paul pulled past the driveway and parked off of the street. He got out and walked back along the sidewalk. Jenny is in the living room dusting and spots Paul as he is entering through the gate. She turned and quickly ran into the kitchen where her aunt is seated at the table.

"Maggie, get the door, please. Paul is here from the plant. He's here to try to get me to work for him in Allendale. Tell him I went off . . . . off with Sandy or something and you don't know when I'm coming back. Please Maggie do this for me, please!"

Maggie stood up from the table and looked into the living room at the front door. As doorbell is ringing, she can see Paul's figure through the translucent curtain that hangs on the inside front door. Jenny backed into the hallway so she can not be seen. Paul's heart is beating faster and he has that feeling in his stomach that he has sometimes when he has seen Jenny in her office. Jenny is standing motionless but begins to realize that she will probably have to face Paul sooner or later. As Maggie got close to the door, the bell rings again.

"Wait Maggie. I'll get it" Jenny said walking past Maggie and up to the door. "I'll get it. It's ok."

As she opens the door, Paul is standing there with a nervous look on his face. Maggie left the room and went out to the kitchen. Jenny has on light blue shorts and a white blouse with the ends tied up around her midriff. Her sleeves are rolled up to her elbows and she has a bandana tied around her head. She is barefoot.

"Hi". Paul said "You're a hard person to find, ya know that?" he said smiling slightly.

"Hello Paul" Jenny said stepping out onto the porch and closing the door behind her.

"Jenny, I came here to see you because I have some things that I want to tell you. First off . . . ."

"Paul," she cut in. "I cannot come out to Allendale to work there. I'm going to work somewhere else. I'm sorry but that is what I'm going to do" she said nervously.

"You can't come to Allendale, I don't understand" Paul said looking confused.

"I'm supposed to go to the Allendale plant and be your secretary. That's why Donna is working in Saxon now" Jenny said looking surprised that Paul doesn't understand her.

"Jenny, this is the first I've heard of this but that can't happen because I just quit. I'm no longer working for Rollins Publishing Company."

Now *Jenny* looks confused.

"Wait now, you quit? Why?"

"It's a long story. Here, let's sit down" Paul said pointing to the porch swing in the corner.

They sat down beside each other on the swing. Paul is looking directly into Jenny's eyes and paused for several seconds before speaking.

"I found out that Norma and Brent were plotting to get control of the business. She was actually going to marry me so her mother would sign the business over to her and Meredith."

"Norma and Brent?"

"Yes. They have been carrying on an affair for years. As soon as she got the business, she was going to divorce me and Brent would do the same to Meredith and then they would marry and have the business all to themselves; can you believe it?"

Jenny looked absolutely shocked. Paul went on to tell her about how Norma had offered to pay him a settlement and allow him to manage the Allendale Plant if he will go through with her plan.

"What are you going to do now Paul?" Jenny asked.

"I'm going back to Fairdale and work for my uncle Ike at his garage. He wants to semi retire and his head mechanic was badly hurt in a crash. I want to help him out."

Paul stood up and walked to the porch railing. He turned and sat on the railing and faced Jenny who is still seated on the swing. He is nervous and hesitating because he is about to tell her how he feels.

"That's nice Paul. I'm sure you will be happy there but I cannot believe all this went on."

"You want to hear something really funny Jenny? I fell in love with another girl before I found out that all this stuff was going on but I couldn't bring myself to tell Norma. I was actually afraid of hurting her and made up my mind not to."

Jenny listened intently to Paul's every word.

"Where did you meet the other girl?"

"At the Saxon plant."

"Who is she? I must know her" Jenny said tilting her head slightly to her right.

Paul paused for a few seconds. He looked over at the side yard and then back at her again.

"It's you Jenny. I love you and I almost told you several times in your office. I think about you all the time and . . . . well . . . there, I told you. Do . . . . you have anyone that you are going out with?"

Jenny was almost convinced that this is a dream and that she will be waking up at any moment. She stood up and walked close to Paul. She has taken her glasses off and placed them on the small table that is beside the swing.

"I don't want you to think that I'm doing this because I discovered that Norma was using me for a sucker. I liked you right away but that Saturday we spent together was the day I really knew that it is love that I feel for you. The way that you treated my father and that kiss you gave me clinched it. Oh yeah, that kiss. I've been hooked ever since then."

"Paul, why do you think that I didn't want to go Allendale? It's because I couldn't bear to be there with you being married to Norma and feeling the way I do for you. I love you too and I have even before that Saturday; from the first day we met I think."

They stood and stared into each others eyes, both of them amused because neither one of them knew that they both feel the same way. Jenny reached out and took both of Paul's hands in hers.

"I afraid that I did something that maybe I shouldn't have" Paul said.

"What was that?" she asked smiling.

"Well . . . . I called your mother's house to try to find out your aunt's address here and one of your brothers answered. He was very polite and helpful but then your stepfather took the phone and informed me that you don't live there anymore and not to call again."

"What did you say to him?" Jenny asked squeezing Paul's hands slightly.

"Well, he started saying that you are not welcome there and I told him that you are a kind, caring person and if he is going to say anything unkind about you to keep his mouth shut."

"What happened then?" Jenny asked smiling slightly.

"I told him I had to go and just let the phone receiver drop. He was yelling something at me but I was through listening to his crap. You are right about him being a jerk" Paul said with his face flushing slightly.

Jenny let go of Paul's hands and quickly placed her left hand on Paul's cheek and the other behind his head. She pressed her lips on his and gave him a strong, passionate kiss. When she stopped, she looked at him with tear filled eyes.

"Paul, I love you so much. You're wonderful."

Paul leaned forward and kissed her with his arms around her tightly.

"Well now, this is nice, very nice indeed" a voice said coming from the front steps. It is Mr. Osbourn, the mailman. He stepped onto the porch and slipped the mail in the letter box that hung beside the front door.

Paul and Jenny stopped kissing and faced him with their arms around each other.

"Hi Mr. Osbourn. This is Paul" Jenny said breathing a little heavily.

"Hello Paul" he said with a wide smile as he walked to the edge of the porch and down the steps.

Paul turned back and faced Jenny again. He thinks that she is so pretty and is ecstatic at how things are working out.

"You know Jenny, seeing how you are not working right now, I think I know where you might be able to get a job. My aunt Edna runs the office at the garage but she is going to retire with my uncle. We will need someone to take over and I'm thinking that you would be an excellent candidate for the position. Let's see, we'll need someone that has business management and secretarial skills. You have that. The person must also be really pretty and . . . . you sure are that. You will however have to spend a great deal of time with me; every day . . . . and every night. So what do you say. Are you interested?"

"Why Paul, are you proposing? Is this what you are doing?"

"I am proposing. Yes I am."

Jenny looked away, paused for a moment, and then looked back at Paul.

"Well let me think about it. Yes!"

She opened her mouth slightly and kissed Paul passionately again.

"C'mon in the house; I want you to meet my aunt Maggie."

Paul looked out towards the street and at the horizon. He is thinking how the future is looking very promising. As Jenny reached for the door, Paul put his hand on her shoulder and stopped her.

"You know sweetheart, you are probably the only girl in history that has ever won a guy's heart because she ate sardines and applesauce."

THE END